Moon Song

Moon Song

Elen Sentier

Winchester, UK
Washington, USA

First published by Cosmic Egg Books, 2015
Cosmic Egg Books is an imprint of John Hunt Publishing Ltd., Laurel House, Station Approach,
Alresford, Hants, SO24 9JH, UK
office1@jhpbooks.net
www.johnhuntpublishing.com

For distributor details and how to order please visit the 'Ordering' section on our website.

Text copyright: Elen Sentier 2014

ISBN: 978 1 78279 807 1
Library of Congress Control Number: 2014944848

A CIP catalogue record for this book is available from the British Library.

Design: Stuart Davies

Printed in the USA by Edwards Brothers Malloy

We operate a distinctive and ethical publishing philosophy in all
areas of our business, from our global network of authors to
production and worldwide distribution.

For the Woodfolk of Nectan's Kieve

1. Beginnings & Endings

Tristan

O dark dark dark. They all go into the dark
TS Eliot: East Coker

Tristan left Caergollo at dead of night. He parked the car by the bridge at the bottom of the village and continued on foot to the harbour. The way was slippery. Jagged rocks and old ropes caught at his feet but, somehow, all his old strength had returned to him. He felt young again, as before the disease. Rounding the final corner into the harbour itself, the wind caught him, hurling him backwards. He got up, laughing, and pushed his way forward to the edge of the stone quay behind which the calmer waters of the harbour hid from the wild sea.

There was a hint of brightness ahead of him now, lighting the edge of the sea with silver. He stopped a moment, watching the powerful swell running into the bay. Moonlight grew, showing the half-hidden path. Cut away by wind and water, it led him upwards, towering two hundred feet above the waves. In crevices, he caught the scent of tufts of sea-pink, flourishing on the barest smidgeon of soil. The ocean beat deafeningly against the sheer, black walls and the sea-cave howled below, laughing at him as he followed the slippery path around the edges of the chasm.

He laboured up the long, narrow spur, while the west wind beat him back, disputing his passage.

'I am coming,' he told it.

Wind and waves laughed. He felt the excitement thrill across his skin. Tonight would be the last and the first day of his life.

Reaching the top, the headland stretched out into the water. The moon had risen further behind his back and would soon bring the foot of the pathway to the cliff edge before him. He waited, watching the light slither over the sea to stop right at his feet where he stood poised at the top of the three rough stone steps that led out into nowhere. Now, as the moonlight joined with the stone, he stood at the end of the silver pathway. Looking up he watched the horizon unfold. The lost land lay straight ahead of him at the end of the moonpath, floating on the horizon at the edge of vision. Beyond it only a bright darkness and the end of the world.

Below, the sea boiled. Waves thundered, shaking the rocks. The way was clear now out to the Isle of the Dead. Tristan stood a moment, balanced against the wind then stepped out onto the shining moonpath.

Isoldé

In my beginning is my end
TS Eliot: East Coker

Coffee mug in hand, Isoldé went to the door of the flat to collect the newspaper. She took it to the balcony and stood looking out over the gardens that stretched between her and the east side of the British Museum. The sun shone, the fresh smell of wet earth was interestingly mixed with last night's curry leavings. It reached her, along with the racket of ubiquitous dust carts, rumbling along four stories down on the other side of the building, collecting the hotel and restaurant garbage. Life in the twenty-first century; she put the coffee down on the little iron table and curled up in the basket chair to read. Furtling through the magazines, the headline in the Arts section stopped her.

Celtic folk-singer idol, Tristan Talorc, dead!

The body of the internationally famous gifted Celtic and mediaeval singer, Tristan Talorc, was found on Saturday night at the bottom of the fateful Lady's Window on the wild Cornish cliffs above his home at Caer Bottreaux. The Celtic singer and scholar had been ill for many years since contracting HIV from a dirty needle on a mercy mission to save a child's life while hunting songs in North Africa thirty years ago. He was last seen by his housekeeper, Mrs Protheroe, on the evening of Wednesday 31 st July when she left him after getting his dinner. When she returned before breakfast the following morning he was still out, and had not been to bed. She was not worried at first, 'He was often out all night,' she told our West Country arts reporter. 'But when he hadn't come home that night I was concerned. I phoned the police and coastguard and got a search started for him'. So far, there is no conclusive evidence for suicide, although the recent complications of his disease does

3

suggest that to be the case. No note was found but Tristan had been getting progressively worse over the past year. It is nearly two years now since his last live concert. It seems, sadly, very likely that he took his own life.

The paper slid off her lap as pictures formed in her mind's eye. There was the sound of singing inside her head.

That is the Road to fair Elfland,
Where thou and I this night maun gae

The song, True Thomas, was one Tristan had made very much his own early on in his career, he was always asked for it as an encore after a performance. The lines were from the fairy queen as she tells Thomas where she is taking him.

Fragments of last night's dream returned; she saw Tristan walk out across the sea on a bridge of moonshine to that impossible shadow-land on the horizon. Isoldé's breath caught in her throat, walking on water?

Tristan had been her hero and musical inspiration since Uncle Brian first took her to hear him in the smoky Belfast club when she was all of fourteen years old. That gig had begun Tristan's recording career, the right people happening to be in the audience, one of those luck-moments. Isoldé had lost her heart then, twenty-plus years ago, as she heard him for the first time. Groupie, she told herself, shaking her head.

A massive honking combined with an explosive shouting match from the street brought her back to the present. She went to the kitchen window just in time to see one of the dustmen trip and tip a mass of garbage over a silver BMW whose soft top was fortuitously down. The car driver, silk-suited, had his back to the disaster and was yelling at two other dustmen to get out of the way and stop blocking the road. He turned just in time to see a multi-coloured mess from the curry house opposite land all over the inside of his car. The shrieks he made would have done justice to a steam train. Isoldé had to grin as she took herself into the shower.

She got herself out of the flat only ten minutes past her usual time and headed for The Guardian's offices in Farringdon Street. She turned into the usual sandwich shop for her BLT and coffee and stood in the queue watching policemen in flak jackets patrolling Theobalds Road, truncheons in hand.

'Stupid Yanks! Why do we get involved in their messes?' Isoldé thought to herself. Coming from Belfast, after growing up in The Troubles, she had no patience with what she called American hysteria. 'No guns, yet,' she thought. Not quite Belfast, but far closer than she ever wanted to be again.

Arriving at the Guardian building she climbed three floors and pushed open the door to the main office. As usual, she remembered too late to turn her hearing down.

'Zoldé! Zoldé!' a voice called over the noise. 'They want us in Whitehall.'

'What is it this time?' Isoldé collapsed opposite her partner. 'Osama visiting Number 10?'

'No such luck,' Jeremy rolled his eyes. 'Another bomb scare, but stuff your face first,' he pointed to her sandwich and coffee which were rapidly cooling. 'Mickey's already there.' He thrust the mobile into her hand. Isoldé rolled her eyes at pictures of workmen, police and military shutting off Whitehall and the side streets around Downing Street.

'The terrorists have got us all running round like headless chickens,' she said. 'They don't need to actually do anything, we do it all for them.'

'Ha!' Jeremy snorted agreement.

Later, in the Cock Tavern by Smithfield, Isoldé cradled her beer morosely. Mickey squeezed in beside her.

'What's up?'

Isoldé's face, screwed up, she shut her eyes, took a deep

breath.

'I can't hack it,' she said baldly.

Mickey peered at her over the top of his specs, raised an eyebrow. ''Tis too much like home, so it is,' he said, perceptively.

Isoldé put down her glass and buried her face in his shoulder.

'Didn't think I'd ever see this over here,' Mickey said as he stroked her hair, his own Belfast twang getting more pronounced.

Isoldé sat back, fumbled in a pocket for an over-used tissue and wiped her nose.

'Sorry, Mick. I think I'd better go.'

'Email me the story,' he called after her.

Moon Hare Visions

Isoldé was dreaming. The hare sat in the path. Moonlight bleached the grass to silver so the last of the raindrops hung on the stems like glittering diamonds.

Hare and Moon regarded each other, staring up, staring down. A soft wisp of cloud veiled the moon for an instant casting a lacy shadow over the hare. When it passed, a girl sat in the path where the hare had been. Her lower limbs still ended in the long, leaping legs of the creature, her hands too were more paw than fingers and long ears stood up out of her soft silver-brown hair, but she was more girl than hare now. Unthinking, she scratched under her armpit with a hind leg.

Her ears flicked, she sat up straighter, long whiskers twitching around the human lips and then she stood and stretched. Something was here, something not herself, she sat back down, very still, waiting.

Over by the rock outcrop the earth moved, quivered, seemed to split open. Something like a new plant began to emerge, growing out of the crack in the ground. Its form was rounded, dumpy, folds of leaves surrounding it. The leaves looked like arms, opening out, showing the head rising out of them. The face was all folds like an old fashioned rose.

'Mother?' the hare-girl whispered.

'Aye, child. What d'ye do here?'

'The light is good,' the girl said after a moment of thinking. It was always hard to use words, they didn't come easily.

'Aye child and so it is.' The rose-faced woman-creature stood now and came rolling slowly forward on her short legs to sit beside the hare-girl. Long-fingered hands, like spidery roots, reached out to stroke the ears and hair. 'You can shift some now?'

Shift? The hare-girl told the word over in her mouth and then in her mind. It meant something. She looked down at her hands … paws. That was wrong. She looked at the root-hand that

7

caressed her. Taking hold of threads in her mind she tried to twist and twine them, watching as the paws became hands. The shapeshift steadied, held, the girl began to smile, then the fingers slipped again, the nails becoming claws and the hands paw-like once again. The girl sighed. It wasn't working, not properly. She didn't know what to do.

The rose-faced root-woman patted her shoulder, stroked the paws.

'Tis all right, my lover, tis all right. Tha's not got the full measure of it yet. When the song comes so tha'll have it all. Thee'll lead us all in the dance then, my darlin' girl.'

The hare-girl tried, every day she tried to shift and hold the form but it would never stay. She should know more of the moon too but always they just stared at each other and she never could understand the words the moon would tell her. But she could feel the pathways, the tingling lines that threaded through the land. Her paws knew the ways, her feet did too, even if she couldn't shift them. The ways were important but she knew not why. Root-mother told her it would come. She wished it could be soon.

Isoldé jerked out of the dream, half sat up and then fell back to sleep again. This time she found herself in the doorway of a beautiful old room lit by a wall full of French windows; they showed lawn and trees sloping away with a stream chuckling alongside. The walls were covered in books; there was a desk and a grand piano near the windows. In a big wing chair by the fire Tristan sat nodding, his fingers stroking the long black fur of the cat in his lap.

She let go the door handle and came over to him. She felt the attraction of him as she always had, but this was up a couple of orders of magnitude on anything she'd felt before at concerts or even at the master class she'd gone to. She felt his loneliness and, at the same time, his reaction to her. She stood beside him looking down into eyes that looked so hungrily up into her own.

Electricity sang through her blood, she reached out a hand to stroke his cheek and leaned into him to press her mouth on his. The effect was startling. Her hand felt nothing and she found herself kissing air.

She lurched back. 'You're dead ...' she whispered.

Tristan hadn't moved, he still lay back in the wing chair, watching her hungrily. Then tears started in his eyes. 'Why ... oh why ... why now? Why have you come now when I can no longer touch you?'

She felt his pain but there was nothing she could do except ache with him, she could not reach him across the worlds.

He turned his face away from her into a cushion, dry sobs hacking his throat, he was in the deepest pit of misery. The black cat reached up a soft paw to touch his ear offering comfort. 'Cat!' he whispered as he stroked the black fur. 'Oh cat. Why?'

Her body jerked again as the dream took another turn. Now she was somehow looking into the cat's golden eyes and feeling herself sucked down into them; it was like going down into a pool of darkness. She came out of the darkness to find herself in a strange grove of trees, there was an ancient stone standing at its centre that looked like a giant's head poking up through the earth. Suddenly Tristan was there. He took her in his arms, she could feel him now.

'Help me!' he whispered as their climax came.

'I will,' she told him, not knowing what it was she was promising.

The vision changed again suddenly, pulling her away from the ecstasy. It was as though she was rushing backwards down a telescope. She flew over a white pebbled beach, then over the sea on the moonpath, rushing backwards to find herself standing on a windswept cliff.

Her vision changed again. Now she was peering through a weird rock formation and seeing Tristan once more; he was alone in the strange grove without even the black cat for company.

'Help me!' he called across the worlds, reaching out both hands towards her. 'I need you. I cannot write her song without you!'

'Me ...?' she stuttered. 'What song? Where are you?'

'The moon's song ...' his voice was barely audible now.

Isoldé struggled to stay with him but the world was going to grey mush around her. The last thing she remembered was Tristan's voice.

'I want you!' he whispered. 'I want you so much ...'

At last Isoldé half woke up, wondering where on earth she was ... if indeed she was on earth at all. It felt as if she'd travelled the universe in her dreams. Tristan was still with her, she could sense him as though he was there in the bed beside her. She closed her eyes again.

This time it was different. The room was high ceilinged, coved and painted with flowers and leaves. The bed was much larger than hers, one of those old French beds that looked like a sleigh.

Shivers ran up and down her flesh, like fingers stroking her. Her body burned, on fire for the touch. If she opened her eyes it went away so she kept them closed. She could feel hands now, stroking the inside of her thigh, pinching the skin of her nipples into erectness, she mewed softly. The hands took her waist and pressed her back. She could feel the body now, the legs sliding between hers, and then the mouth, bitter-sweet, kissing her deeply. It left a metallic taste in her mouth and the scent of mothballs. Her body moved in rhythm with the one above her, fire rose in her belly and streamed down her legs and through the soles of her feet. Her mind exploded at the same moment as she felt the fiery stream shoot up inside her. She opened her eyes.

Nothing. Her hands groped wildly, feeling nothing, no-one. She was alone. She cried out, reached out, where had he gone? It couldn't end, not yet, not like that. She was back in her body, no longer in the dream. The sheets were wet, she dripped with perspiration, cold and slimy, shivering. Groggily, she sat up, her head pounding. She tried to get up and fell, sliding down the side of the bed onto the floor with a thump. Her legs wouldn't carry her. She crawled over to the chair and found the bath towel, pulled it round her, lay against the cold radiator, shivering.

There was light, the streetlamps shining through the curtains. She began to see things in the room, recognise them. For a while there, she had thought she was still in that other bedroom with the high coved and painted ceiling, in the big sleigh bed.

Isoldé shook herself. She was freezing cold, sat on the floor after the most incredible orgasm of her life with a man she couldn't see and she was going through an inventory of furniture like an antique dealer. She began to laugh. It got hysterical. She struggled over to the door and climbed up the door frame to reach the light. Seeing her own room, her own things, was strange. She had seen the other room so clearly, had felt so at home there. This one looked small and drab. It needed cleaning, there were cobwebs and the mirror was clouded with dust. She struggled to the shower. The dustcarts rolled into Montague Street and began their morning clamour.

'What ...?' she muttered through chattering teeth. 'What have I done? What have I promised?'

Mark

And we all go with them, into the silent funeral,
Nobody's funeral, for there is no one to bury.
TS Eliot: East Coker

Mark drove slowly down the track to Caergollo, pulled the handbrake on and switched off the engine. He didn't want to get out of the car. He didn't want to be here at all. He'd told the solicitors, everyone, to go away, leave him alone, let him go to the house on his own and now, here he was. With the car door open he could hear the stream singing and, further off, the faint sound of waves crashing against the cliffs. There was an empty feeling in the middle of him, like a stone, or rather like the place where a stone should be but wasn't. He kept expecting the door to open and Tristan's crotchety face to peer round the jamb and shout to him to come on in, get a bloody move on, they hadn't got all day. But it didn't.

Mark climbed out of the car and stood looking at the door. He felt in his pocket for the big, old key. It jangled against the iron ring as he pulled it out. The lock turned easily, well oiled. Mark pushed the door open and stood staring into the dim hallway. He was blinking like an owl after the bright sun outside when something soft touched his legs, wrapped itself around them and meowed. Mark bent to pick the cat up in his arms, burying his face in the black fur. At last, the tears came.

In the library, Embar on his lap and a tumbler full of Talisker in his hand, he sat staring. He could hear the voice inside his head.

'All yours now. Don't you go letting me down! Embar told me he wanted to stay with you so you make sure he does, right? Mrs Protheroe will do for you, and look after him while you're away. It's all yours, brother, all yours. Caergollo, the woods, the sea, the books,

everything. And my music, look after that too, but you'll have help. Embar knows.'

The voice faded. The words were the same as in the letter. It had arrived in Kyoto just after he got back from seeing the Ox Herding paintings. He touched his pocket; he carried his set of cards of the ten paintings always now. And the letter. He pulled it out.

'You were right, brother,' Tristan had begun. 'You'll never see me alive again. By the time you come back I'll be gone, but here is the key to the house. Don't lose it. I don't need it any more. Mrs Protheroe looks after me. And Embar. I go out in the woods when I can, up to the kieve, and the cottage. The woodfolk give me herbs for the pain. And the passing.

It's as easy as it can be, considering. Mrs P. lets me have anything I want, which isn't much. I'm not hungry but I keep drinking, just to maintain consciousness. I'm not like Dylan Thomas, I don't rage at the dying of the light, in fact I welcome it. I shall go to the sea at the end. It's full moon tomorrow night. Maybe one day you'll understand.

It's all sorted, the solicitor has confirmed everything. Jack Ellis is OK, if you get in a muddle just ask him. He doesn't cost the earth either. It's all yours now. All yours now. Don't you go letting me down ...'

Mark couldn't see to read any more, his eyes were full of tears.

Embar nuzzled his hand. Again he buried his face in the black fur, crying.

Moving to Exeter

Back at the flat, Isoldé pushed open her front door then turned back to triple lock it again once she was inside. This was a safe building. There were twenty-four-hour guards in the lobby and a computer-coded entrance system on the street door, plus entry phones to each flat. Isoldé still rattled the locks to make sure. It was thieving louts using terrorism as an excuse she feared, not terrorists.

She made more coffee, took it over to the computer. She lived on coffee. 'At least I still don't smoke,' she thought, 'but, at this rate, it won't be long. I have to go. I have to leave this place.'

Amongst the usual crud and work stuff in her email was a blast from the past. She hadn't spoken to Darshan for ages. He used to run Forbidden Planet, the sci-fi bookshop on New Oxford Street and they had met when she'd been looking for some out of print Roger Zelazny, he found the books for her, found they shared tastes, they had become friends. He'd been her holiday and weekend-job boss while she was at university; she'd had to work to make ends meet. Later he became her lover. He introduced her to classical music at the Wigmore Hall and the South Bank, jazz at the Hundred Club and, occasionally, Ronnie Scott's. She introduced him to The Troubadour, mediaeval music, folk and, of course, Tristan Talorc. He had left the Planet, and London, at the end of the nineties, after their affair was over. They had lost touch. Now, here he was again. And offering her a job.

'Look us up on the net,' the email gave the URL. *'We've got quite a reputation now, sci-fi shop of the west *g*, but I want to expand. Music, classical, folk, mediaeval, rare. That's where you come in. And there's more ...'* Darshan left the lures hanging, as always.

Isoldé remembered dragging him to The Troubadour coffee house in Earls Court to hear Tristan Talorc at the height of his fame. In return, he took her to original instrument and rare organ recitals. He'd even taken her to Lunenburg Heath, near Hanover, to hear some young bloke playing the Bach organ there. Isoldé remembered how impressed she was with the performance, and how totally under-whelmed she'd been by the B&B Darshan had found them.

'Why don't you jack in the paper and come and join me? ' the email went on. 'You gotta be fed up with London and all this terrorist rubbish. Was in Town last week – Sheesh! It's terrible. I don't know how you stick it. Come and breathe fresh air. Post me. Call me. I need you, Zoldé.'

She leaned back in her chair. Of all the coincidences … She pulled a road map off the shelf, where was Exeter? She found it, traced the route, it looked easy, M4, M5. There was a town plan at the back; Darshan's shop was in Cathedral Close. Sounded posh, just the sort of thing he would love. She called the paper, the editor grudgingly let her have a long weekend. She began to pack.

It was mid-afternoon when Isoldé stopped outside the shop. *Close Encounters* it said in gold letters on a deep blue ground over the door. The words were repeated in gold on each of the big windows, a half-circle of words over a bulge of golden sun setting, or rising, on a dark horizon. Isoldé chuckled at the sign, it was typical of Darshan, straight out of film-land. She got out of the car and stuck her head round the shop door, he saw her at once.

'Hi.' she smiled across to him. 'Can I park here?'

'Hey, Zoldé!' He came over, arms outstretched, hugged her. 'No, the wardens'll do you straight away. Go up to the top.' He pointed to a wider bit of road in front of a café in the direction she was pointing. 'Turn round and come down the bottom, past the turning you came in by.' Darshan waved towards the west side of the Close. 'I'll go down and clear the space I bagged for you.' He grinned and jogged off down the road.

Isoldé watched him lope away, admiring. Darshan was gorgeous, she'd forgotten just how much. With a sigh, she turned the car and drove carefully down behind him. There was a row of private parking spaces at the bottom and he was pulling a book-trolley out of one. It was decorated with a huge cardboard bill-board painted with, '*Really sorry folks, it's for my best girl !!!*'

'Oh ye gods, Darshan! How d'you get away with that?' Isoldé pointed at the edifice.

'I sweet-talk the wardens.' He had on his butter-wouldn't-melt look.

'I'll bet you do!' Isoldé told him.

He took her back to the shop, introduced her to the staff, showed her round.

Later, when the shop closed and everyone was gone home, Darshan made coffee and put his feet up on the desk. 'What d'you think?'

Isoldé carried on walking round the shelves, looking at the books, then she turned to the collection of CDs and slowly rifled through. It was a small but good quality, eclectic mix of classical, mediaeval, jazz and folk.

'What's your turnover?'

'Pretty good. We're in our third year now. Do you want the detailed figures?'

'Later, yes, if you really want me to chuck everything up in London and come in with you. I want to know what my risk is.'

Darshan tapped a filing cabinet. 'We can go through that lot after dinner.'

He took her to an excellent Thai restaurant in the Close. They went early and came back early so she could browse his accounts. He sat cross-legged on the floor, reading, while she went through the books. It was obvious he trusted her, he'd just unlocked the file-cabinet and told her to rootle to her heart's content.

'No secrets from a partner,' he'd said.

She'd been impressed, felt confident, or reasonably so, for the huge step of jumping out of her safe, known, hi-flying job at the paper into this venture. After an hour she closed the books and looked up at him, a half-smile on her mouth.

'Well …?' Darshan asked.

'I think so,' she told him. 'Ask me again on Sunday.'

'Good. Now, how would you like to meet some interesting locals?'

He took her a few doors up the Close and into what looked like a good wine bar.

'Ale bar!' Darshan corrected her, laughing at her nonplussed expression.

It was well but softly lit, white plaster walls panelled up to a dado rail in a golden coloured wood, solid oak floor underfoot. He led her to a table in the corner where two men sat with the remains of a meal in front of them.

'Jamie, Paul. This is Isoldé Labeale, my high-powered London journalist friend,' Darshan announced, eyes alight with mischief.

Isoldé coloured up, smiled, held out a hand.

Jamie stood up and took it in a powerful grip.

'Good to meet you,' he said, looking straight into her eyes.

Paul's grip was strong too, but his eyes had a softer expression, echoing the mischief in Darshan's. Isoldé pulled herself together.

'Good to meet you too.' She included them both in her smile.

'I can tell I've been set up here.' She rolled her eyes and glared at Darshan.

They all laughed.

'What're you on?' Darshan asked.

'Riggwelter,' Paul said.

'I'll get a jug.' Darshan disappeared to the bar.

Paul pulled out a chair for Isoldé and they all sat down.

'I gather Darshan's not told you who we are.' Jamie smiled. 'I run Exon Radio, the local station. That's why he introduced you with fanfares.'

'I've heard of you, even listened a bit. Sort of Classic and Jazz FM without the continuous adverts. You've had some interesting interviews too.'

'Thank you. Yes.' Jamie said. 'You hit the spot with that description. We both liked Classic FM when it started out,' he said, giving a sidelong glance to Paul. 'But it's impossible now it gets all its revenue from advertising. We're trying another way.'

Isoldé looked the question.

'Later. Maybe.' Jamie grinned, watching the journalist at work on extracting the story. 'What about you? Darshan said he was trying to get a friend of his down, and that you might be interested in some radio work.'

'Asshole!' Isoldé glared up at Darshan who had just arrived with a large jug of beer in one hand and two half-pint mugs in the other.

'Isoldé!' Darshan's large brown eyes looked limpidly into hers, his mouth drooped. He set down the mugs and filled them, then refilled Jamie's and Paul's.

'The only thing that's saving you is that jug of beer. Put the damn thing down so I can kick you properly. And,' she glared, 'don't you dare flirt with me!'

'But you love it ...' Darshan finally put the jug down.

A lot later, stretched out, alone, under the duvet on Darshan's sofa-bed, she watched the stars through the dormer window and sighed contentedly. Darshan had a loft conversion flat in Northernhay Street. There was a bit of traffic noise, an occasional group of loud students, but it was so different from London. Now, lying in bed, Isoldé felt contented. It was a huge jump to leave the safety of the London she'd known for the last sixteen years, since she'd left home and Belfast, but the job Darshan was proposing, and the move, pulled her strongly. She was doing OK at the paper but London horrified her since the clampdown after nine-eleven. That wasn't how she wanted to live. Exeter felt good. She'd see what the rest of the weekend brought.

Next morning, Darshan gave her the keys to the flat over the shop in Cathedral Close, telling her to go and look around for herself. She climbed the stairs to the top of the building and unlocked the door to what had been the attics. 'He must be doing well,' she thought, standing by the closed door, the keys in her hand. 'He's leased the whole place.'

She turned the key and pushed open the door of the flat. The main room faced south, over the Close, getting all the light through three big Georgian windows. The walls were simple cream-coloured plaster, the wooden floor had been sanded and oiled so it glowed. The window frames were oiled wood as well. The whole effect was of light and warmth. She went into the kitchen, simple again but enough worktop space and cupboards, one big window over the sink to give light.

The wooden, open-tread staircase curled up into the roof-space. Up there it was all peaks and points, lined with more of the gold-coloured wood, one huge room taking up most of the space. Dormer windows showed the cathedral roof and tower, giving light. A door to her left led to the bathroom. Half tiled, with a big mirror over the bath as well as the wash-basin, it gave a sense of space as well as light. She came back into the bedroom. It felt good, she could be happy here. She realised she'd made up her mind already and gave a wry grin to the Bluetit clinging to the window frame; he was peering at her from each eye in turn. Something else clicked. She didn't have birds in town, not close like this. 'I could have a feeder on the window,' she thought.
It was a new thing for her. There'd been no birds at the windows

of the various London flats she'd lived in. Nor the house off the Falls Road where she'd grown up.

Darshan's cats were a new thing for her too. There'd been no cats to share their life in London. He'd told her last night he had grown up with cats and that moving to Exeter had made it possible to have them again. These were ginger, half-Maine Coons; one was a huge long-haired tom who really looked the part. His sister was inexplicably tiny and delicate with short fur but exactly the same markings and a whole load of attitude. They were beautiful, soft. They'd nuzzled her, purred her to sleep last night. 'I'm not ready for cats yet,' she told the room. 'One day ...'

She remembered the soft, warm pressure of their bodies against her back, it had been comforting. The country, Isoldé thought of Exeter as the country, meant animals. She liked animals but had very little experience of them. She had watched as Darshan talked to his cats as he got them their breakfast, while coffee brewed for Isoldé and himself. It had definitely been in that order of preference, cats first, she laughed to herself now. She'd been fascinated how they came to him, watching their intelligent expressions, how they seemed to know exactly what he was saying. She still had no real idea of how they thought, indeed they felt a bit foreign, alien. Or perhaps, she wondered, it was her who was the alien. But she felt she would like to live with a cat. Later, when she was settled in.

She sat in the window seat reflecting. Running a business would be a new thing for her, but that was OK, she enjoyed a challenge. It was part of what had pulled her away from the Falls Road, the possibility of change, going somewhere new, somewhere where there wasn't the continual fear of bombs and knee-capping's.

She had arrived in London, aged eighteen, to do a degree in journalism and media studies at the City University. Working holidays and weekends at Forbidden Planet meant she could afford a life and that had been a challenge too, everything was so very different from Belfast. Growing up at all during The Troubles had been hard. Her mother had been killed when she was just three months old, Isoldé never knew her, shot by the IRA, suspected of fraternising, so Aunt Branwen had told her. Aunt Branwen had adopted her then, there'd been no-one else. Dad had gone off to America, fund-raising with NORAID, she had never known him either. Effectively orphaned, her aunt and uncle had brought her up. It had taught her to hate the sectarian politics, and to keep her head down.

'A plague on both your houses,' she muttered, glad it was behind her.

Leaving Belfast had been running away from all that. Having the degree, the prospects which London offered had been running towards something, something new. Now, was she running away again? Running from the government-contrived paranoia after nine-eleven? That was how she saw it. It could bring her out of London, here, to Exeter and Darshan, and a whole new set of challenges.

'I was running *to* something then, when I came to London, to university,' she told herself. 'And now, I'm not just running away. That's no good, you're still on the same road if you run away. But running towards is different,' she paused, thinking about herself, her life. 'Running *to* something means you've got a new end in view. It's not just fear, it's hope too.'

Another bird landed on the window-ledge, chirped, got her attention and then stared at her, cocking his head first to one side then the other. It felt like encouragement.

And what about her and Darshan now? Their relationship had been good but she'd drifted away from him as she got more and more into journalism. They had begun to lose the art of conversation with each other. Isoldé had seen it and pulled up sticks before they lost the friendship as well as the relationship. Even though they had lost touch it seemed to have worked.

Meeting again, now, they were still good friends. He obviously respected her if he wanted her as a business partner. There had been no sign of making passes since she'd arrived, almost a brother/sister thing, yet not. That was good; there was no place within her for a relationship at the moment.

She had joined the Guardian Newspaper after getting her degree and, when the chance of an exchange with the New York Times came up, she'd applied for it but her friend Evelyn had got the job. She had taken on Evelyn's flat, and her job at the paper, getting herself a good reputation as an investigative journalist, even been overseas a bit. There was a lot there to look forward to but ... she didn't like London now. It had changed. Security was so tight. Bomb squad sirens went off all the time and, every time, her skin crawled. She was terrified that, one day, Mickey or Jeremy or one of the others would turn up at a hot news scene and the bomb would go off, or the terrorist's gun would find its target and she would lose a friend. Another friend. It had happened too often before. Even her best friend at school had been the target for a Republican bullet, accidental or so it was said. Whatever, she was just as dead either way. It was how her mother had gone, another vengeance killing. The Belfast memories gave her no feeling of security about the way the British government was handling this situation now.

'Fools!' she muttered. 'Ass-licking to Bush!'

And now? Here was an offer to get her away from all that, into the other side of her life, the music part of herself. She would be running towards something. She chuckled, Darshan's offer seemed to include both her skills, music and journalism. It was obvious he wanted her to work with Jamie at the radio station as well as himself. She thought about that, it was Darshan, he was an excellent businessman and not at all dog-in-the-manger-ish. He wanted everyone to do well. His philosophy was one of osmosis, if everyone did well then he would do well too. It seemed to work, for him anyway; maybe it would rub off onto her.

She would be running towards something. It brought an unusual sense of freedom welling up from her belly. Yes, it would be good to do what you liked, what made your heart sing.

'Do what makes your heart sing,' Aunt Branwen had told her. 'That's what your mother always said and I should know, she said it to me often enough. "Don't worry about anything else, Branwen," she'd say, "just do what makes your heart sing, it'll work out." And then she'd be off again on one of her dancing gigs and nobody would see her for months. The only thing stopped her from dancing, eventually, was you, when you were coming. She did stop then, once she couldn't fit into the costumes.' Aunt Branwen's smile would go all misty then and Isoldé would put her arms around her.

A lump caught in her throat. Mother had followed her maxim herself but it hadn't stopped the terrorist bullet. She had loved life and been happy, right up to the end, so Aunt Branwen said. Isoldé wanted that, to do what made her heart sing. It seemed Darshan was offering her the opportunity to do just that.

She shook her head, shoving the memories back into the archives of her mind where they belonged. Re-locking the door of the flat, she went back down the stairs to the book shop.

'Well ...?' Darshan quizzed.

'Well ...' she answered back, smiling. 'Good. Pretty. I like it. Especially the golden wood.'

'OK.' He got up. She saw the desk was tidy.

'I'm off, now,' he called to the middle-aged woman arranging titles in the window.

'Right you are,' she said over her shoulder. 'I'll lock up, as usual.'

'Thanks, Hilary. See you Monday.'

He took Isoldé's arm and led her out into the Close, took her round the cathedral, showed her the great organ and introduced her to the precentor who happened across the Close just as they were coming out.

Heading her back towards his car, 'You want to see the sea?' he asked.

Her eyebrows went up.

'Exmouth.' He grimaced. 'Bit of an old folk's home sort of place, but the beach is beautiful.'

And so it was. The day was bright but a chill wind blew. A couple of people were walking dogs. Isoldé looked out to sea and saw the horizon, the curve of the Earth, the edge of the world. It had been a long, long time since she'd seen it. It took her breath away.

They stood at the edge of the water.

'I don't have things like this in London,' she told him. 'Got to drive for a couple of hours to do this and, even then, it's not the same.' She was thinking of Brighton, Hastings or Winchelsea.

Darshan looked down at her. 'No,' he said, 'it isn't.'

They walked the length of the beach, then went back to the car. He drove back up the river to Topsham, Exeter's ancient, historic estuary town. She loved the narrow, twisting streets that followed the old medieval tumbled shapes of the buildings in Fore Street.

Darshan stopped beside a large hotel. 'It's an old pub, dates back to the 1700's' he told her as he led her into The Globe. 'The place used to be an inn, does a wonderful selection of home cooked, local food.'

Isoldé looked about her. There were some tourists along with the locals in the small bar by the entrance.

'I recommend the Doom Bar,' Darshan said, grinning at her astonished stare. 'It's a rare good beer from Sharps Brewery down in Cornwall, you'll like it.'

'You lose me on all these beer names.' Isoldé laughed.

The landlord set a half in front of her.

'Try that,' he said. 'Are you eating tonight, Darshan? We've got some fresh sea bass or the Topsham Smokies?'

Darshan looked at Isoldé.

'What,' she asked, 'is a Topsham Smokie?'

'It's *the* special local dish.' Darshan was enjoying her confusion.

'OK. Why not?' she said. 'I'm hungry after all that walking and sea air so I'd better eat the local speciality. I've got the appetite for it.' She laughed.

'Topsham Smokies twice then, please,' Darshan said demurely.

'Right you are.' The landlord smiled encouragingly to her as he took the order.

'You know this reprobate then?' Isoldé turned to him.

'Aye, he's here of an evening, now and again. Murders the locals at dominos!'

'You do?' Isoldé's eyebrows scaled her hairline. The weekend was revealing facets of Darshan she'd never even suspected when they were together in Town.

He rolled his eyes and picked up their glasses.

'Enjoy the beer. I'll show you to a table.' The landlord led them through the sitting bar into a large, oak-panelled dining room.

'The folk club starts up in about an hour, you want to be here for that?'

'Of course,' Darshan told him. 'It's why we've come.'

Isoldé nodded but her expression was abstracted. 'You really play dominos ...?' she was dubious.

'I do. I've found bits of myself here that had no place when I lived in Town. There's lots of culture and not just the snotty-nosed kind you mostly get in London. You wait 'til you hear the singers and musicians tonight.'

After the folk club was over they walked down to the old harbour quay.

'It's good here,' Darshan told her. 'I've settled in. Interesting, good people and loads of history. For instance, did you know Ted

Hughes lived here for a while,' he pointed to a tumble-roofed cottage at the back of the quay. He knew Hughes was one of her favourite poets. Her eyes widened.

'And he lived on a farm up on Dartmoor, too,' he added. 'They've put up a stone to him on his favourite bit of the moor.'

'Can you walk up there?'

'Bit of a hike but you'll soon be fit enough.' There was a wicked expression in Darshan's eyes.

'You're assuming I'm coming …'

'Well, you are, aren't you?'

Isoldé's mouth twisted into a grin, 'Yes,' she said. 'I am.'

Driving back to London was strange, as though she was leaving home on leaving Exeter rather than returning to it in London. What would Mickey say? He knew her very well, likely he would understand. Mick was from a farming hamlet up by the Giant's Causeway, not a Belfast man by birth, although he'd lived there for ten years before coming to London. He would understand her needs. And how long would it be before she could move? Would the paper try to hang on to her? She'd have to find someone to take over her lease on Evelyn's flat, probably Mickey; he'd been in love with the place since she moved in. Yes, the move was good. For once in her life all the ends had come together at the right time. She took hold of them.

2. Concert

Invitation

The dark before dawn pulled Mark awake. The night had been full of dreams and memories of Exeter, the choir, the organ, his room at school. The darkness of the bedroom here at home was warm, comfortable, but there was a tingling, sizzling feel to the air. He got up.

Embar coiled around his legs purring, near tripping him on the stairs, then reaching his long, black length up the leg of the kitchen table as Mark made coffee. Mark opened a tin of cat food, deposited the plate under Embar's nose then took his coffee to sit in the hollow of the ash tree by the bridge.

Dawn came late here. The valley faced west, the next stop after the end of the cliffs was America, but from the house you could hear only a whisper of the sea. Light crept up over the trees, a mile away, eastward, at the head of the valley. The rowan trees at the top of the waterfall would be lit already. He waited. The light grew, dripping westward down the valley, bringing colour into the garden. The birds began their morning song. Suddenly the place was full of light and sound and colour.

Black, white and red wings flashed past him. Two swallows dived and swooped over the grass. He squinted at them, it seemed they were chasing a golden thread. The dance continued above the lawn in front of him, the birds coming closer and closer. With a shriek they let fall the thread right into his hands. He was holding a long, fine red-gold hair. His fingers tingled, holding it close to his face he could smell the perfume, flowery, elusive, distinctive. He could see its owner in his mind's eye, a small, slender, laughing woman, surrounded by green grass and backed by ancient grey stone. A wind blew up the valley, he grasped at the hair but it blew away and the vision was gone.

Later, at breakfast, Mrs Protheroe brought in the post as he lingered over toast and marmalade. There was a letter from Exeter, he slid a buttery knife under the flap and opened it. The Cathedral School headed paper stared back at him.

'Dear Mark,' the letter began. 'It's been such a long time since you've visited your old alma mater. We follow your progress through the news and the music programmes but it has been some years since we saw you in person. It would be good to meet again and catch up.

I wonder if we can tempt you to give us a Candlemass concert next year? We'd like the concert to be on Saturday 31st January, old Imbolc Eve, as I'm sure you remember, so we can do the thing on the day. If you can spare the time, there are several excellent organ students who would love to meet you as well. Perhaps you could even give a master-class?

Margaret and I would be delighted to put you up. I expect you remember the house from your time here at school. Looking forward to hearing from you. Do say you'll come.

Warmly yours,

Cedric Appleforth, Precentor, Exeter Cathedral.

Mark sat holding the letter after he had read it, memories of tea and musical evenings with the Appleforths crowding his mind from his years at the cathedral school. He shook his head, blinked and smiled. Candlemass was six months away, he pulled the diary to him, turned up the date. He planned to return from Italy in time for Christmas and had promised himself January at home after that. Yes, that would be good, he would like to go, give them a concert and catch up with old friends. And it was only a couple of hours up to Exeter at the most. He picked up the post and headed for his study, he would write to accept straight away. The precentor was right, it was a long time since he had been back to his old school.

Suddenly, a picture of the Cathedral Close formed in his mind, green grass and the ancient grey stone walls of the cathedral. And the shining, golden-haired woman standing there, laughing.

Sparrow

The cathedral clock struck one. Isoldé looked out across the Close, the rain had lifted, there was blue sky and the pigeons were strutting about on the grass. It was warm for the end of January.

'I'm off to lunch then,' she called.

'I'll keep an eye on things.' The girl on the till smiled.

Isoldé went to the brasserie in the alley, got her sandwich. Turning back into the close, she sat down on a bench and opened the ham and brie in ciabatta. The pigeons crowded round her feet, cooing and bonking, no idea of season. A sparrow stood at the edge of the flock. Carefully she aimed some crumbs to him and, quick as a flash, he dived in ahead of the pigeons, succeeding. She shook the last crumbs from the bag onto the grass and went into the cathedral.

'Hi, Zoldé, coming to the concert?' One of the vergers recognised her.

'Absolutely! Jamie's been on about it for weeks now.'

'You'd better get some of his CDs in the shop, there'll be a rush.'

'Done and dusted!' She told him as he went off up the side aisle.

For once, the cathedral was quite empty; Isoldé stood sensing into the quiet, the echoes of silence. At moments like this you really got a feel of the place. She stood at the west end. The wide floor of the nave was empty of chairs, the sun sent shadows of colour down through the great window behind her to paint the ancient flags. Huge arches reared up to either side as she walked slowly up the nave, it felt like being in a stone forest. She stopped under the organ, looking up.

A flutter of wings from the minstrel gallery interrupted her. Somehow a sparrow had got in. She looked around for someone to help but the place was empty. The sparrow flew up the nave and landed beside her on the golden gate in the pulpitum. Isoldé stood watching it as it watched her, wondering what to do.

'Here, little one,' a voice spoke beside her.

Isoldé turned. The man put a finger to his lips, eyes smiling, and held out a hand. He called the bird again. The sparrow chirruped, its head on one side, looking. Then it made up its mind and flew down to clutch the finger in tiny claws. The man stroked the grey poll. 'Come,' he said, catching the bird's eye. He turned to walk back down the nave and out the west door. Isoldé followed. In the close he held up his hand. 'Fly well, little one. In there's no place for you.' The bird chirped again and flew off.

'How did you do that?' Isoldé breathed.

He turned to her, 'Birds come to me.' The blue eyes were laughing. 'And animals.'

'I've never seen anything like it.' She smiled back, eyes questioning.

'It's cold.' He seemed embarrassed now. 'Shall we go back inside?'

'I can't,' she told him. 'Lunchtime's over. I must get back to the shop.'

He raised his brows.

She pointed to the bookshop on the other side of the green.

'Ah,' he said, seeing the shop. 'The bishop tells me you have a good selection of music and CDs.'

'That's good to know,' she said. 'But I must go. It was wonderful, what you did.'

'Mark King.' He held out his hand.

'Isoldé Labeale,' she managed in response, realising his CDs were all over the window of the shop and she still hadn't recognised his face. This was the man giving the concert tonight.

Something happened as they touched hands, both of them stopped still, looking at each other, then Isoldé let go and set off back to the shop. At the door she turned back. He was still there, watching her, smiling.

Concert

Isoldé went to the concert on her own. Jamie had fallen foul of a cold and Darshan was with the bishop's party.

'No way am I providing a cacophony,' Jamie told her over the phone, 'and don't you come round here either. Don't want you getting the blasted thing. Go and see what the bloke's like in real life. We like his disks and he's got excellent reviews.'

'Do you want me to do the interview with him as well?' Isoldé asked.

'Yes. It'll be good with a woman's voice and you've always wanted to meet him. Now's your chance to do a big name radio interview.' Jamie started to chuckle, it ended in a coughing spasm.

'OK!' Isoldé felt herself colouring, glad Jamie couldn't see her down the phone. It was true, Darshan had told him how entranced she'd been when she'd first heard Mark King, years ago at Lunenburg, and now he was using it. Not that she minded really but she didn't tell Jamie about the sparrow. That was something precious she would keep for herself. She wanted to know more of the man to whom birds would come and she didn't want the interview with him to ruin it.

The chairs were back in the nave for the concert. It had been good, earlier in the day, to see the old cathedral as it was originally intended. Isoldé laughed to herself, originality was an issue with all the early music crowd. There would studious, then gradually more drunken, pontifications in the Quart and Pint Pot later. She knew she would go and join the crowd after the concert and the ale bar would have a good supper for her, she never could eat before something important. It was quite a thing for Exeter, having the ale bar instead of a wine bar, although there were a few decent ones of those too. The Pot was next along from Robinson's antique shop, near the Clarence, on the north side of the close. Just along from herself too. Sometimes the noise irritated her late at night. But she wouldn't forgo the daily treat of waking up to the green and the cathedral and the bells.

She found her usual spot, a chair at the central edge of the nave at just the right spot to get the full effect of the magnificent organ, including the thirty-two foot contra-violone pipes in the south transept as well as the little jobs up in the minstrel's gallery. The programme said Mark King would be using the full works in the concert.

The Exeter Symphony Orchestra was taking its places in the space in front of the pulpitum. Isoldé dumped her cushion on the chair and snuck round behind them to the golden gate. No sparrow tonight but she touched the gate anyway, as a good-luck charm. 'Play well,' she whispered, looking up to the huge organ pipes massed above her.

Soft footsteps behind made her turn. Mark King was there.

'Hello,' he said.

'Break a leg!' She told him.

'Dancer, eh? Where d'you go afterwards to get over my playing? May I join you?'

'Isn't the bishop giving you supper?'

'He stood me lunch.' Mark's eyes twinkled. 'I managed to escape for tonight.'

'The crowd goes to the Quart and Pint Pot, if you can bear being lionised?'

Mark rolled his eyes.

'They do a good supper,' Isoldé added, 'and it won't be too bad. They'll shut up if you tell them to. But it won't cost you a penny as they'll all want to buy you drinks and get you to sign their beer mats.' She couldn't help chuckling at his horror-struck face.

'For you, anything!' He flung up his hands. 'See you later.' He went round to the stairs up into the organ loft.

Isoldé stayed a moment by the gate, looking up at the softly glowing organ pipes above her then turned back to her seat.

'Hi, Zoldé. Mind your feet, love.' Paul began to walk backwards down the nave on his rubber-soled shoes, stopping every few feet to clap his hands. He broke into a grin as he stopped to clap beside Isoldé's chair.

'Might have guessed you'd have picked the best spot, as usual.' He pointed to the boom-arm, hiding behind the pillar, from which the mike hung out in the nave several feet over her head. 'And you haven't got this bloody cold, have you?' He glared at her.

Isoldé laughed and shook her head. 'That's Jamie. You should know.'

Paul rolled his eyes. 'I'm sleeping in the spare room and he's going round with a medical face-mask on, won't let me near him!' He laughed. 'He won't risk me getting The Cold,' he capitalised the words. 'I had to promise the poor bastard he can sit in on the edits for Sunday's broadcast. It's rotten luck, he's been waiting for tonight for centuries.

'Mr King!' Paul called up to the organ loft, 'give me a middle A, please.' The note boomed out. 'Can you diddle a bit of the Dies Ires, please?'

Mark duly diddled the opening bars.

'And a bit from the middle of the Toccata, please,' Paul ordered, staring at his instruments.

To Isoldé, the organ sounded like the breathing of a wild beast, her spine shivered.

'Now I need something for the little jobs up in the minstrel's gallery,' Paul called, and the ethereal notes sounded down the nave. 'And could you just hit the big boys?'

That made the whole cathedral rock. It always blew Isoldé away, almost literally.

At last Paul was done with his sound checks. It was close to time now; people were coming in, the huge nave filling up.

'Better rescue your seat,' Paul said. 'See you in the Pot later?'

Isoldé nodded. She watched him scoot off out the south door

to the caravan where all the equipment was set up, imagined him tucking himself away behind his meters and loudspeakers, then went back to her chair.

The last notes of Poulenc's organ concerto died away into silence. The silence held a moment and then the audience rocked to its feet and roared. Isoldé couldn't manage it. She was still sitting, her hands flapping feebly in an attempt to clap, her throat dry and shut. She'd been hearing the old organ regularly for the past year and more since she'd moved to Exeter but never had anyone drawn out its magic as Mark King had just done. It was incredible. Isoldé pulled her legs in under the chair to sit in a small bundle while people climbed out around her. They seemed to understand, even if they were all shouting their heads off in admiration.

'You OK?' Paul crouched beside her.

Isoldé nodded, still speechless.

'Pretty stunning, eh? I'm keeping the master unadulterated,' he went on. 'King may want it for a recording. And I couldn't bring myself to desecrate it, cut it. I'll never chuck this one.'

Paul realised Isoldé still wasn't communicating, patted her shoulder and set off for the Pot.

The cathedral emptied. Mark King found her shortly after, still sitting there in the nave.

'That was good,' she managed to croak at him then coughed, trying to get her brain back in gear and her dry throat together.

'Thank you.' He offered his hand to help her up.

'Hungry?' she asked in a more normal voice, as she stood up.

'And thirsty.' He smiled down at her.

'Let's go then.' She took his arm.

The Pot was bursting at the seams but Jim saw who it was Isoldé had on her arm. He slid out from behind the bar and encouraged the three men in the corner to bunch up with the rest of Terpsichore, Exeter's early music group, on the next table. All eight of them were there tonight, including Munroe Watson, the leader. As soon as they saw who it was struggling through the crowd they gave in easily. Jim sat King down in the corner and put Isoldé between him and the excitable recorder players.

'What can I get you?' Jim asked.

'What's good tonight?' Isoldé asked.

'There's a stroganoff, or I've some excellent local steak.'

Mark looked at Isoldé.

'Steak?' she asked him.

'For two,' Mark said.

'How'd you like it?'

'Just frighten it with the match-box, please, Jim.' Isoldé told him.

'Bleu,' Mark told Jim. 'I guess that's the same?' he quizzed Isoldé.

She chuckled.

'Dark or light beer?' Jim wanted to know.

'You choose,' Mark told Isoldé.

'Riggwelter. Can you bring a jug?'

'Right you are,' Jim disappeared behind the bar.

'*What* did you order?' Mark looked at her.

'It's a Yorkshire brew, the strongest of the Black Sheep brews from Masham.' She laughed. 'Rigged means to be fallen down drunk, on your back and welter is a name for a male sheep. There's a picture of a pissed sheep on the pump, and on the bottles. It's got a distinctive dark hops flavour with a hint of after-taste, a bit like a very mild Guinness. Take it easy though. It's not a session beer, five-point-nine per cent, goes down smooth and foxes you before you realise. Gets you well rigged!'

'Ye gods! You'll have to lay on a wheelbarrow to get me back to the precentor's lodging.' Mark laughed back. 'Where did you learn about beer? You seem to be an expert.'

'I dare say these guys could arrange the barrow.' Isoldé nodded over to the early music group. 'My business partner, Darshan Buller, who owns the sci-fi bookshop and music store, is a real ale aficionado. I've learned all about beer from him. I hope he'll be along later, I know he came to the concert and I thought he might pop in but he's dining with the bishop so he might not. He wants you to come and do a CD signing in the shop tomorrow.'

'Arrrgh!' Mark groaned. 'I remember! The bishop did warn me and I've got the letter in my pocket. In fact, I know I've said yes!' His face was woebegone. 'As I suspect you already know if you work there.'

'Mmm ... yes. We've got you booked for tomorrow afternoon, circa three o'clock. And here is Darshan.'

'Hi.' Darshan smiled at Isoldé then turned to Mark. 'I'm stuck with the bishop, but I had to just pop in and congratulate you on a fantastic performance. I'm Darshan Buller. The music and book shop. You're doing a signing with us tomorrow.'

'We were just talking about that.' Isoldé rolled her eyes at him. 'Mark's very keen.'

Mark glared at her. 'Good to meet you.' He shook Darshan's hand. 'Sit down, join us?'

'Just briefly, the bishop's dinner is starting any minute, I told them I just had to come over and sort a couple of things. I see Zoldé's got you drinking some decent beer.' He accepted a glass.

'Yes.' Mark chuckled. 'Seems like I've got a very full day tomorrow. Exon Radio interview in the morning then you in the afternoon and tea with the organ scholars after that, I'll be wrecked. You'd better organise a good dinner for me after.' He turned to Isoldé.

Darshan watched the look passing between them. He didn't think they realised how struck they were with each other, not yet. But he could see it. Part of him coiled up in sadness, realising the missed opportunities. He'd forgotten, before she came down to Exeter, how much he felt for her.

'That can be arranged.' Darshan got his act together and began talking about organs and mentioning his trip to

Lunenburg. 'I heard you there,' he finished. He winked at Isoldé, not saying that she had been there too.

'That's way back,' Mark coloured slightly. 'Right at the beginning, but it was amazing to be actually playing a Bach organ.'

Darshan finished his beer, wished them goodnight and was off.

The whole of Terpsichore was leaning towards them, all ears pricked. Kathryn Handley, the viol player, poked Isoldé in the ribs. 'Come on, Zoldé! Don't leave us out in the cold,' she whispered loudly.

Isoldé looked at Mark, he seemed up for it. 'Mark, it's just about to get worse. These guys are dying to meet you. Can I introduce Terpsichore, Exeter's early music group?'

Mark held out a hand, leaning across Isoldé. 'Good to meet you,' he said. 'I've heard you on the radio, got your last CD.'

That was all the excuse they needed, names were exchanged, drinks offered, beer mats and pens pushed over for signing. The evening was hectic, convivial, fun.

Mark found himself enjoying the company, mostly musicians and artists, and a couple of ancient tabby-cats who Isoldé introduced as Ailsa Barque and Magdalene Hysse, the crime-writer duo. That did intrigue him. He'd forgotten they hailed from a little village just south of Exeter, Dunchideock, wasn't it? He remembered going to the pub there for folk evenings when he'd been at school. He usually travelled with one of their books in his pocket, as he did tonight. They signed it for him, he signed their beer mats. In fact, he laughed to himself, he thought he'd signed every sodding beer mat in Exeter tonight.

Terpsichore pulled out their instruments and did a turn then the musicians from the Exon Ferrets, the local Morris Side, set off with songs. Mark joined in. He had a goodish baritone, Isoldé noticed, but it was his fingers that held the magic in him not his throat.

Jim eventually got them all out into the street at ten to midnight. The whole crowd said goodnight to Mark, individually.

'My arms and shoulders are sore,' he complained unrepentantly to Isoldé. 'Every damn soul in that bar has patted my shoulder and wrung my hand. Shit! I'll never play again,' he wailed piteously, making Isoldé laugh.

'Well, you'll have to stop playing so well if you don't like it,' she returned.

'It was good,' he said ruefully. 'It's just I don't think I've ever experienced anything quite like that before, even at home.'

'Where's home?' Isoldé asked.

'Caergollo, by Caer Bottreaux,' Mark told her.

The cathedral bells began to chime midnight sparing Isoldé the need to reply. For the second time that day Mark King had struck her dumb.

Aftermath

Mark walked slowly around the close, thinking. The Clarence was still awake but he kept on past, considered turning up the passageway into the High Street. No, he thought, I need quiet. Not that Exeter High Street in the early hours of a Sunday morning was Leicester Square, but the students were still about, there was life. Down the east side of the close, towards his lodging with the precentor, all was quiet. He carried on. Despite it being the beginning of February, it was warm. Seasons all to pot, he muttered, but the warmth made him dawdle. The Candlemass concert had both elated and exhausted him. The organ was magnificent, and it had remembered him over all the years since he had been a student at the school. It was like riding a wild horse you had befriended. This one knew if you could play and, if it liked you, its paces were magic.

He remembered the first organ he had learned to play, in the tiny church out on the headland above Caer Bottreaux. That had been the same magical experience, orgasmic, he chuckled. Some boys went for sex with each other or with the girls in the city. He got off on organs. It was a whole-body experience. He would finish a performance drenched in sweat and glowing. The time it took to put the organ to bed, the rituals, gave him a chance to come back to earth.

The audience had been good tonight, he'd felt them with him on the thread, like he and they and the organ were all one being, led to ecstasy by the god in the machine. Like Pan. He laughed at himself but couldn't stop, the beer, the company and the woman carried his mood further. The organ was like the goat god, the piper at the gates of dawn who was, like himself, the friend of animals. He felt he was still riding the god's ecstasy now.

'I should have gone in with her,' he thought, but then, 'no, not yet. And she's not for riding this ecstasy with. This is my own.'

The god had brought the passion into the audience tonight, it was still with him now. Mark sat down on a bench, dreaming.

A scurrying at his feet brought him back to the world. A little mouse was hunting food. It stopped, sat up on its haunches and looked at him. Mark looked back. The mouse put a paw on his shoe, then ran up his trouser and sat on his knee. Gingerly, Mark put out a finger, the mouse allowed the stroking, sat up and polished its whiskers. Across by the houses a black cat sat, watching. Cat and mouse eyed each other then the mouse ran off his leg over the back of the bench and into the grass. The cathedral bell rang one o'clock. Mark shook himself and went on down the Close to the precentor's house. The cat watched him go.

A robin, singing on the bare wisteria branches outside his bedroom window, woke him. He stretched luxuriously. The clock said half seven. Out the window, he could see the moon's last quarter, pink-gold against the turquoise sky with the morning star hanging at its tail. He stretched again and his feet met a lump in the bed. The lump began to purr, then rose, stretched and stalked up his chest to lick his nose. He stroked its ears. They enjoyed each other for a few minutes.

'OK,' he told the cat, as the smell of eggs and bacon wafted up the stairs. 'I'm getting up.'

'Did you enjoy the Pot?' Margaret Appleforth, the precentor's wife, poured him more coffee.

'I did. I've not been in a place like that, oh, ever I suppose, although there were good pubs and bars at college. It was a bit like being at college again.' He laughed at himself.

'Yes.' She laughed too. 'It is a bit like that. The artsy students from the university go there, but it's really a meeting place for the working artists and musicians who live in and around Exeter rather than a students' bar. We go occasionally, usually lunch. And sometimes when Terpsichore do a session there. Munroe went to the cathedral school, you know, a bit after your time. Cedric has a sort of fatherly feeling for the group and we keep up with them. They do a concert a couple of times a year for us at the Deanery too, and that's always packed. We get out-of-towners for those,' she added proudly.

'They did a turn last night and, considering we were all three sheets to the wind, it was very good. None of the subtle recorder stuff though, lots of shawms, drums and cornettos, and good fast dance beats. Their percussionist is excellent and the fiddler.'

'Yes, Kathryn was at school here. Got a scholarship to the RCM, but came back home after.'

'How ever did that ale bar start?'

'Jim Carver had this idea,' she began. 'He's ex-navy, submarines I think, wanted to do something completely different when he got out and he likes beer. Oh, you can get wine there too, he keeps a few good clarets and burgundies, and some esoteric single malts, but nothing else. Just beer. He goes round the country looking for brews. In the trade, I understand, he's a bit of a showcase.'

'And he's found himself a superb chef.'

'That's Alice, his wife. She's got a couple of young chefs to help, sort of in training with her, but she's the business. Jim got the idea a while before he left the service, so Alice decided to get herself trained up to do that side of it. Put herself through catering college, then got into training with Hugh Fernley-Whittingstall at River Cottage.'

'Well, it works a treat.' Mark pushed his plate away.

'What're you going to do with yourself today?'

'I've got the interview with the radio station this morning, then a CD signing at the sci-fi book and music shop in the afternoon.'

'Why don't you try the brasserie for lunch? It's very good. Cedric and I have church this morning but he's bringing the students over for tea, we've got three organ scholars who are tripping over themselves to meet you. One's a very talented girl with a complete hero-worship of Marie-Claire Alain, so you have some competition.' She quirked her eyebrows at him.

'Excellent stuff! I'll do my best to be back on time but I don't know how long the signing'll go on for. What time is tea?'

'Four-thirty, all cake and buns but don't worry, you don't have to eat anything, the kids'll scoff the lot. Worse than gulls!' She laughed.

Mark's feet remembered. They took him out of the Close through the little archway to the High Street, crossed him to the passage that led into Gandy Street, over Queen Street and down into Northernhay Square where the headquarters of Exon Radio hid at the top of a three-story town-house. He rang the bell. Shortly, footsteps sounded, the door opened and Isoldé smiled up at him.

Mark's eyebrows went up.

'I'm sorry,' she said. 'I'm afraid it's me to do the interview. Jamie's got a bad cold and won't inflict it on you. Do you mind? Come on in.' She opened the door wide.

He followed her up the steep stairs into a big loft. All the attic rooms had been put together, knocking down walls and putting in steel beams to hold the roof up. The effect was a crazy mix of Swedish sixties and recording studio.

One end was hi-fi, antique stacked Quads and an incredible pair of huge horn speakers carefully placed in front of sound-curtains. The side wall was solid industrial shelving covered in amplifiers, tuners and tape machines, including an ancient high-speed Revox. The other end was all the radio gear including some very up-to-date digital and computer kit. Somewhere towards the middle of the room, a fifties glass coffee-table sat between a pair of comfortable leather armchairs.

'Coffee?' Isoldé pointed him towards the armchairs.

'Black please.' Mark sat down. He felt a bit thrown. He'd been with this girl the previous evening, liked her, perhaps more than liked, and now they had to do an interview for the radio. Then, this afternoon, she'd be at the bookshop signing. It seemed they were doomed to see a lot of each other. Mark didn't know whether to be glad or sorry. He wanted to get to know her, felt she wanted to know him too, but he didn't want all this official-work-stuff to spoil it. He wondered if he could handle it ... if she could.

Isoldé brought the coffee then went to sort out the recording gear. She came back and fixed up yet another piece of antique kit. He began to smile.

'I know!' She laughed back. 'It's Jamie. He's got a real thing about the old kit they used in the seventies, hence the Neuman.' She chuckled, tapping the microphone she'd just connected to the Nagra portable tape recorder. 'Fortunately, he shows me how to use the stuff.'

'You ... er ... work together?'

'Yup.' Isoldé watched him sideways. 'But that's all we do. Jamie's gay. His partner, Paul, is the recording engineer who did you last night,' she finished. She tested for levels and took up her notepad. 'He's given me a list of questions to set us off, but he doesn't mind if we divert a bit into interesting side roads, just as long as we get all the basic stuff about you and Exeter.'

She took a breath, raised her eyebrows, finger over the on-switch. Mark nodded.

'It's very good to have you back in Exeter at last, Mr King,' Isoldé opened the interview.

'Mark, please ...'

'Thank you, Mark. How long is it since you played here?'

'It must be seventeen years now. I came back while I was at the Royal College of Music, in London, and did an afternoon recital, but ...' he let the sentence trail off, eyebrows shooting up, an "oh help!" expression on his face.

'And how does it feel, now, after all that time?' Isoldé

prompted him, smiling encouragingly.

'Oh, good!' Mark paused. 'But strange too. Like coming here. My feet knew the way because one of my school-friends lived in this house and I used to hang out here in term time. Now it's the radio station.'

Isoldé's eyebrows went up, she flashed him a smile. 'That's a marvellous coincidence and hopefully makes you feel at home. But could we go back to the beginning? What drew you to music, to the organ?'

'The man who played in the little church on the cliff at Caer Bottreaux set me off.'

'Caer Bottreaux ...?'

'That's where I was born, grew up, North Cornish coast, just up the road from Tintagel. I'm a vurriner really.' Mark smiled as he pronounced the word Devon-fashion. 'From across the Tamar. And I forgot my passport!'

'As an old Exonian I think we'll count you as an honorary Devon man.' Isoldé laughed. 'How old were you then, in Caer Bottreaux? How did you meet the organist?'

'I had a good voice as a boy and they wanted me in the choir. The first time I went for practice and the organist started up with this incredible beast, it just rolled me up. I couldn't take my eyes off it and hit loads of wrong notes. Finally he got exasperated and said *"You just come over here, young Mark, so you can see her then. We've got to get that goggle-eyed look out your system or we'll never get a good note out of you!"* And he showed the organ to me. All those stops and pedals. And the pipes ... that's what did it, when I first heard them breathe. They do that you know, almost breathe of themselves. After a few more weeks, when I'd showed him I really could sing, he let me watch while he played after choir practice one evening. That was it. My hair stood on end. He took pity on me then and began to give me lessons.'

'Just like that? I understood organists were very protective about their organs.'

'Oh they are!' Mark laughed. 'But … yes … that's how it was, sort of. I already did piano lessons, so I knew my way round the keyboard, after a fashion, but the organ is very different and, of course, the pressure's the other way around. Piano's hard, percussive, whereas the organ's soft. I had to unlearn a whole load of things in order to play it.'

'But it stuck, you enjoyed it.'

'Ye-es … enjoy's not quite how it is. Organists are very passionate about their instrument, it's like a part of yourself, once you're bitten you're never free of it. Organs are my life.'

'So you learned with the organist in Caer Bottreaux?'

'Yes, but he soon realised that I could go much further than he could take me. He came down to our cottage by the harbour one evening and knocked up my parents, told them he'd help me get into the Cathedral School here and so he did. Wrote up a recommendation which got me an interview and then I had to play for them. They started me off on a little organ in the precentor's house but then they took me up to the cathedral. I was thrilled and terrified all at the same time, climbing up into the organ loft. It's huge up there, especially when you're only twelve. I could hardly reach the peddles but the organist helped me and I managed to play "Three Blind Mice" for them, and then a bit of some of the hymns we used at home. Then the organist sat beside me and began Bach's toccata and fugue in D minor. I knew it, of course, and he somehow got my hands to play the right notes while his feet fumbled the peddles and he pulled the stops I couldn't reach. In the end we were both laughing fit to bust. I followed him back down the stairs to where the precentor was waiting. The organist just nodded to him. "He'll do," he said. And that was it. I began at the Cathedral school the following week.'

'Did you mind being away from home, boarding school?'

'Yes and no. I missed the sea very much. Our cottage was right down by the harbour, you can always hear the sea there. When the gales are up the sea crashes on the rocks, the cliffs thunder and it's all you can do to stand upright outside the cottage door.'

'That sounds incredible!'

'So it is.' Mark chuckled. 'Not everyone's cup of tea, but if you're born there it's in your blood.'

'You missed the sea, here at school ...' Isoldé prompted him.

'I did. But the organ held me. I needed that more than the sea.'

'Did you sing in the choir too?'

'For a short while, until my voice broke. The good voice I had as a boy became quite undistinguished once it changed. I can sing along in a folk group now but that's about all.'

'You got a scholarship to the Royal College of Music, didn't you?' Isoldé took the interview forward into his early adult years.

'Yes. I worked really hard and did well there. It was great fun, being in London, not just the music but the life-style too. London's a great place to be a student, or it was when I was there. But on the music side, there's so many organs to hear, and to play as well if the organist will let you, so many different types. I always used to love playing in St-Mary-le-Strand, although there are better organs, I suppose, but the place is magical.'

'What are your most impressive memories of organs?'

'Oh, that has to be Liverpool! You can walk about inside the thing there. It makes me feel like being inside the engine room on the Starship Enterprise.'

Isoldé quirked her eyebrows.

'Star Trek.' Mark grinned. 'Beam me up, Scotty! The pipes and walkways between them are like being inside a starship. If ever you get the chance you should go and see it, it's quite incredible.'

'Your career took off soon after you left college, is that right?'

'I was lucky. The dean of the Royal College of Organists had a friend over from Germany and he heard me. I was invited to the church at Lunenburg Heath, to play the Bach organ. The senior recording engineer from Deutche Gramophone was there, heard me and steered me to a recording contract with them. I was just twenty-two. Things have sort of gone on from there,' Mark ended with a rueful grin.

Isoldé's eyes twinkled back. 'You spend quite a lot of your time abroad now, don't you?' she continued serenely, not telling him she'd been there, at Lunenburg Heath, heard him, fallen under the organ spell.

'Yes.' Mark rolled his eyes. 'Good for the bank balance, but I miss being at home.'

'Ah yes, home. You live in a very interesting house don't you?'

'No!' he put his hand over the mike and she obligingly hit pause. 'I won't talk about that on air. It's my home. Private.'

'Not even about Tristan Talorc?'

'Nope!'

'Not even to me, later?'

'That's different.' He smiled.

She carried the interview deeper into his career and the music he loved, finishing on a good upbeat note advertising his next recitals, the latest CD which was out now in the shop in Cathedral Close. Mark was surprised, it had actually been fun, she was very good, had got him to talk about himself far more than he usually would.

He watched as she packed up the recording equipment.

'Must be worth a few bob,' he said, fingers running over the steel casing of the old tape machine.

'Yup! It's Jamie's passion. He's been collecting since he was a kid.'

'I've never seen most of it before. You hear about it, from recording engineers, but the London studios don't use any of this now. Nor the European or American ones.'

'No, all digital, computerised, streaming. We do that too, for the radio output, and the computer radio, Exon's got a YouTube page. But Jamie loves using the stuff, even editing by hand with a razor blade sometimes. He's got the antique kit anyway and the radio station's almost a one-man-band. And Paul loves it too.'

'Exon Radio's got a hell of a reputation though.'

'He does get some good programmes, like the recording Paul got of you last night. That's a once-in-a-lifetime thing and I dare say the Beeb will be on to him to hire it for Radio 3. The interviews are special too but they can be a bit hi-brow sometimes, boffin-stuff for artists. You're relatively light relief.'

'Nothing wrong with that!'

She finished putting things away.

'Can I give you lunch?' he asked.

'Actually, Jamie's given me the order to take you out,' she said over her shoulder.

'Thank you ...' Mark blinked internally. This woman took charge in a very subtle way, you didn't notice until you were in up to your neck.

He waited while she locked up, then she led him back to the close and round to the Brasserie the precentor's wife had told him about that morning. They walked in silence; somehow there was no need to talk.

Isoldé helped him through the signing, making sure the queue was orderly, that he had water to drink and nobody overstayed their welcome. There seemed to be an inordinate number of people wanting his CDs, and wanting them signed. Exeter was a provincial town, he could hardly believe there were that many people who knew his music, and wanted it.

'Jamie's had a piece about you on the YouTube page since a few weeks back, advertising the concert and the signing, then a follow-up a few days ago. Radio 3 picked it up too, gave it a mention last week in up-coming events so there's a lot of out-of-towners here, people from all over I think, who've come for the day, maybe for last night too.'

Isoldé called a halt at four-thirty, giving him time to get back for his tea with the students. Every single member of the staff had bought a copy of his latest CD and one or two had brought previous ones for him to sign as well. Darshan had four copies, presents he told Mark, laughing.

Mark got back to the precentor's to be ogled and idolised and pelted with questions. He managed to arrive just after five, by which time all the food was gone, for which he was thankful, but he accepted a cup of tea from Margaret Appleforth. The students were fun, asking intelligent questions but also treating him like an elder brother even though he was twenty years older than most of them. He was giving a master class the next day and these young people would all be there.

They left about six-thirty, giving him time to shower and change before collecting Isoldé.

Mark arrived at the bookshop just after seven-thirty. Darshan was still there and invited him in, calling Isoldé on the house phone to say Mark had arrived. The two men chatted about the shop, music and sci-fi. Mark's reading included fantasy but most of what he liked was from way back in the eighties. Darshan steered him over to the shelf with the "Z's".

'We've got a complete collection of Roger Zelazny, some of it second hand, but I always try to have his work in the shop. It still sells regularly, and we're about the only place in the country where you can buy it direct. The internet's made such a difference to second hand book sales.'

Isoldé came down the stairs. She had dressed up for the evening in a short, clinging black silk frock and high heels. Darshan handed her into her cape.

Mark felt himself about to gasp and held it back, managed an ordinary-seeming smile.

'You look lovely,' he told her.

Darshan tactfully ducked out of dinner.

'Three's a crowd.' He winked at Isoldé as he gave her the

company credit card. 'Do yourselves proud,' he told her. 'Why not the Thai down in the Close?'

He could see there was a thing going between Isoldé and Mark, hustled them out the door then went back to his own flat where he stood making coffee and telling himself he was a fool. The cats purred agreement.

Isoldé steered Mark across the square to the little Thai place. They were given a quiet corner in the small, packed restaurant and allowed to amble their way through a long dinner.

'Did you mind horribly?' Isoldé broached the signing. She could tell it had been more difficult for Mark than he had said.

'No ... Not really.'

'Mmm?' She looked at him from under her brows. 'I'm not sure I believe that. It seemed a bit painful from where I stood.'

'I've done it before ...' Mark began.

'But not in Exeter?' Isoldé queried.

'No.' Mark paused, put another slice of mango into his mouth, chewed thoughtfully. 'You're right. It is being here that's different. Everyone seems to feel as if they know me.'

'Long lost brother?' Isoldé chuckled. 'And they all want a piece of you?

'Yes, that too.' He grimaced. 'Prodigal son more like than long lost brother, but let's not go there. I don't want to spoil tonight.' He looked at her.

There was something there, he could feel it. He told her about himself, and a little about Tristan. Thinking about it, he realised he'd never talked to anybody, except Tristan, like this before. And she listened. She was interesting, exciting, she knew lots of music, places, people. It had come out, by accident he was sure, about her going to Lunenburg and hearing him play there. They had both got red and embarrassed then but she had come out of it laughing, talking of small worlds and how funny things could be, connections.

'Would you come and stay, at Caergollo?' he suddenly found himself saying out of the blue. 'Visit me there?'

Her eyes lit. Carefully, he touched her finger-ends with his own. The magic was still there. The flush ran up her neck into her face, he saw the shock of his touch as it hit her. As it hit him. He could feel the heat in his own eyes.

'Wh–what …?' she said, not sure what they had been talking about.

'Err … I … err … would you like to come to Caergollo?' he stuttered.

Her fingers touched his back. This time the shock was gentle, didn't wipe out his brain.

'Yes,' she answered. 'I would love to visit you.'

Visitation

That night Isoldé dreamed.

She found herself in a shadowy room, it was familiar. Thick velvet drapes covered three of the French windows, the fourth was open. From the light she guessed it was late afternoon, the sunlight shone low through the windows but very bright, making the shadowy corners black. A fire crackled in the hearth, its light flickering over a dark Persian carpet. Slowly she turned on her heel. It was the same room that she had dreamed of when she dreamed of Tristan. There was the grand piano on one side, she took a step toward it, another, it all felt intensely real, not like a dream at all.

She walked slowly over to the piano, stroked the silky, dark, wood, touched the keys. They moved easily under her fingers. This piano was old, Darshan would be entranced, she thought, smiling She sat down and began to pick out Frère Jacques. The notes sang through the air, she stopped, worried that someone might hear.

Getting up, the French window called her. She went over and the smell of wet earth wafted up to her. The leaves dripped, light silvered the wet grass. She went out, crossing the lawn down to the noisy brook. There was a bridge and path going away from it along the edge of the wood. She looked up at the glimpses of moorland grass and heath beyond the confines of the garden. Another noise hid under the clamour of the stream, she listened hard. It was the sea.

Light came on in the room behind her. She turned quickly and stood still, hoping not to be seen. A tall man was there, his fine aquiline features still visible under the ravages of disease. He made for the piano and sat down. Then he noticed the lid was up, looked round and saw the French window ajar. He sat looking out into the garden.

'If that's you, my ghost?' he called to her, 'come back, come in ...'

She froze, not even breathing. Everything went misty in front of her eyes and she felt giddy, like she was fainting. Then it all went away into darkness.

Next thing Isoldé knew was she was sat up suddenly in her own bed. A glance at the clock said it was two in the morning, the middle of the night. Her head felt full of cotton wool and thumping. She staggered up, pulled on a robe and made it down to the kitchen. Later, on the second cup of tea, she began to think coherently.

Was it possible to re-enter a dream, carry on from where you left off, like playback on a video? She finished up the tea and closed her eyes.

To her amazement, she stood beside the stream again, just as she had before.

'Hello ...?' Tristan called to her from across the lawn. 'Hello? Is that you? Please come to me, please find me. I need you ...'

As Isoldé started back across the grass the French windows exploded silently in a ball of light.

3. Caergollo

Love is most nearly itself
When here and now cease to matter
TS Eliot: East Coker

Isoldé opened the letter. It was Mark. She had known it would be as soon as she touched the envelope. He was inviting her to stay with him at Caergollo in two weeks' time. He'd given her his private phone number and his personal mobile, even his personal email. He was allowing her right into his private world.

She sat down at her desk and tapped out an email to him straight away, giving him her private numbers in return. This was something she really wanted to happen.

Friday
Mark put warm honey-water into the vase of lilies and freesias, took them carefully up to the spare bedroom. He was fussing and he knew it. He really hoped the spare bedroom wouldn't be used but he wasn't making any premature assumptions. Anyway, it would be good to go slowly, take care. He wanted this to last, forever maybe, no more brief affairs. Something had turned over within him when he first saw her by the golden gate in the cathedral, looking as lost as the sparrow. He had gone to find her as well as to take the little bird out to safety, although he hadn't known that at the time. When they had touched hands the electricity had shot through him. He knew it now. He'd known in that instant that this was it, if he wanted it. And he did want it. He would go slowly, make sure she wanted it too.

He turned back on his way out of the door to look back into the room, getting the same impression he hoped she would when she arrived. It was the bedroom he'd slept in as a boy when he'd stayed with Tristan. After Mark's parents had died, Tristan had taken on the fathering role, although he was only about 15 years older than Mark himself, but at ten that had seemed ancient. Now, at thirty-seven and looking back to himself at twenty-five, he realised how young Tristan had been when he'd adopted him, only half-grown himself. What had Tristan really thought, felt, with this ten-year-old boy trotting at his heels? It must have been a drag at times yet Tristan had never shown it. They'd had twenty-five years together, a generation, and known each other so well. Tristan had never acted in a way the child-Mark had understood as fatherly although now, looking back, Mark could see that he had been. It had always seemed as if they were brothers, and that's what Tristan had always called him, brother.

It was odd, Tristan never seemed to have had any women in his life, never any that Mark had seen, although they flocked around him. 'Handsome bastard!' Mark was smiling. But never had Mark caught him with a woman, even when he'd turned up unexpectedly. And he wasn't gay. And he didn't act reclusive or celibate. 'Just never seemed to have any interest in all that …' Mark muttered again. Unlike himself. He had had many affairs, nearly got married once. 'Thank the gods that misfired!' he muttered, turning out of the room and shutting the door, but not on the past. That followed him back to the kitchen. He put on a CD, the Breton pipes and drums stirred his blood. He wondered if she would like it. Tristan had. It seemed Tristan's ghost was sharing his evening.

'Damn the man!' Mark told the onions as he got them out for making the casserole, but it wasn't any use. Tristan was here, prodding him, laughing out of corners just as he always had.

'Look.' Mark turned to the doorway back into the shadowy hall. 'What is this? What do you want? Are you jealous?'

Nothing answered him.

Mark got on with the casserole, still turning over old memories. The no-women thing was odd. He realised he had never really considered it before. He put the casserole in the oven, poured himself a glass of wine and went to the library where Embar climbed into his lap. He stroked the cat's ears, Embar purred, gently bit a finger.

A book lay on the table beside him, TS Eliot's Collected Poems. He picked it up, certain he hadn't had the book off the shelf for months.

'Not Mrs Protheroe,' he thought, 'definitely not her style!' The book fell open at East Coker.

'*In my beginning is my end*,' Mark read. One of Tristan's favourites. He looked up, a whiff of rose oil caught his nose, another of Tristan's favourites.

'What is it, old man? What do you want?'

Again nothing answered him but he could sense a presence in the room, a frisson in the air.

'If you want to tell me something you'll have to do better than that,' Mark told it. 'I never was up to snuff like you with all the faer folk, the Ellyon, walking between worlds. You know I'm as thick as a brick when it comes to that stuff, always was. I know you could, but I don't, not easily. It's got to be more solid if you want me to understand.'

Embar put up a paw and pulled his hand back to scratching his ear. The moment was gone. It had been a long day, driving down from London that morning, shopping, getting the house as he wanted it, making dinner. He was tired, he dozed, responding to the rhythm of the cat's purring.

It seemed he opened his eyes. The room had changed. It was like when Tristan was alive, the scent of him was in the room. Embar was alert, ears pricked, pointing. Mark could see nothing but he could sense the presence, he sat perfectly still, holding his breath.

There was a shadow sat on the piano stool. It turned towards the door just as the door opened. Another shadow came in. They seemed to talk, Mark could hear a rustling, like whispers, but could make out no words. It all faded. Then the French window was open, a scent of wet earth coming in. The shadow was beside the window now, speaking again. Suddenly, there was a bright flash and it was all gone. Mark woke suddenly, shaking his head at the soundless noise which still made his ears ring. Embar was asleep now, as though nothing had happened. But Mark knew it had.

He got up gently and put the cat back in the chair. A car was pulling up outside.

Isoldé drove down from Exeter in continuous rain. It poured down in bucket-loads over the car, splashed up like tidal waves from the big lorries on the A30. She needed all her concentration to stay driving safely. The traffic thinned out a bit after Okehampton and once she crossed the Tamar she truly felt herself to be entering another land. It had none of the feel of the Irish Celt of home, nor of the Gaelic of the trips to Scotland. This was very different. A bright darkness seemed to hang in the very air. The little people here would be very different from those at home in Ireland.

It was a long, dreary haul to Launceston and she breathed a sigh of relief when she crossed Davidstow moor and found the by-road which took her twisting down the steep cliffs to Caer Bottreaux. The clouds lifted as she slid down the hill, giving her a glimpse of the sea. And the sunset.

She found the little road to Tintagel and took it, skimming along the narrow, wet lanes high above the sea. Then the road dived down to a hairpin bend. This must be it, she thought, pulling up and peering round. The gate into Caergollo was all but invisible when she finally saw it. Rain dripped off the trees and down her neck as she opened it. She slid the car through then got out again to close it behind her. As she did so there was a rustle in the bushes by the stream. A pair of large brown eyes topped by two long ears looked up at her, Isoldé stood transfixed. The hare sat for a moment, then flicked off into the undergrowth. Isoldé remembered to let out the breath she'd been holding, she'd never seen a hare that close before. She got back into the car, let in the clutch and slid down the track to the house.

The car door opened and Mark watched the slight, fey figure climb out and fling a transparent, silk rain-cape over her head. It flew out like wings to either side as she fled across the wet gravel to the front porch. Instinctively, he put out his arms in greeting, she ran into them. In the joint hug the rain-cape fell off, Mark retreated with her into the big hall.

'Stay there.' He let go of her. 'I'll grab your bags. Is the boot unlocked?'

'Here.' She pushed the key into his hand.

Standing, watching, as he pulled bags out of the boot with the rain streaming off him, she wondered what was going to happen. The hug had been electric, knocking her off balance, him too she felt. She applauded as he locked the car and raced back to the door, dropping the suitcase onto the flags, putting her laptop carefully on the table then shaking himself like an otter. His black hair was plastered down on his skull, rain dripped off his nose. They both burst out laughing.

'Proper Cornish weather to greet you.' His voice was warm as he pushed the wet hair off his face and searched for a handkerchief. 'But it'll perk up tomorrow. Should be a good, bright day.'

'I don't mind.' She was grinning ridiculously as she looked him over.

'I know.' He grinned back, 'I look like a wet dog.'

'Or an otter,' she said softly.

'Nice one! C'mon, let's get you up to your room, you can shower, change, rest, while I clean up. Dinner won't be long. Shout when you're ready and I'll show you where the library is and all that. The house is very higgledy-piggledy, easy to get lost in.'

She followed him up the stairs and round the gallery to a large bedroom. A fire was going nicely in the grate, the wood scenting up the room. 'Oh!' She stopped in the doorway, staring. 'I've never had a fire in my bedroom before, never even been in a room like this, it's gorgeous.'

Mark found himself blushing, his efforts to make it nice rewarded. He put her bag on the oak chest at the end of the bed along with her laptop. 'The bathroom's through here.' He opened a door.

She followed him. The bathroom was cosy and warm with a window that looked out into the evening, big fluffy towels called invitingly to her. She came back into the bedroom. 'I think I do need to clean up. The drive was longer than I expected what with all the lorries and the rain. And you certainly do!' She was laughing.

'Too right! I'll see you in half an hour or so.' He backed out of the door.

Isoldé found herself blushing. It was a strange, slightly out of control feeling. He felt it too, she could see that, like in a car when you were learning to drive, being too heavy on both accelerator and brake. Slowly she walked round the room, touching the furniture, feeling her way into the place. For a moment, she sat down on the faded sofa, it was comfortable, not over-stuffed, wide enough to relax into and look out of one of the windows. Mark had put on the bedside lights so the room was softly lit, she could see out of the window rather than just mirror blackness. Raindrops snaked down the pane making twisty patterns, sometimes splitting and spreading. Eyes half shut, Isoldé found she was watching faces grow and dissolve in the raindrop shapes. A wizened face grew out of one big drop spreading sideways, the eyes sharp, shining, looking straight at her. Her own eyes opened wide. The face was really there, looking at her, she saw the mouth move and words formed in her head.

'Welcome!' The mouth smiled along with the eyes. 'Waited long for you, we has.'

The rain fell faster obliterating the face. Isoldé stared as it disappeared, the drops becoming just rain. A log popped in the fire jerking her awake. The room was warm, comfortable, she noticed the flowers, the curtains, the pictures. Slowly she brought herself fully conscious again. Time for a shower, she thought, pushing back the memory of the face.

Determinedly, she unpacked her bag, hanging things in the old tallboy and putting underwear on the shelves. She took her wash bag into the bathroom and turned the shower on. It was one of the enormous types you get in big hotels, nearly a foot across, pouring hot water down onto you in a flood. He'd left shower gel in there and a flannel as well. Everything provided. She stripped off and climbed under the flowing waters, allowing them to rinse away the travel tiredness as well as the visions. She turned her face up into the water stream and allowed it to pour over her, then turned her head down so it beat onto the back of her neck. Slowly, the water did its job. She felt the muscles loosen, the tension relax, the face and the hare and the visions got out of her head so she could feel herself again rather than this weird invasion by spirits not her own.

She turned off the water and stepped out of the shower, pulling a warm towel around her. 'Please, leave me alone!' she whispered looking back towards the bedroom. 'No more faces. I need my space. If you want to talk to me, tell me things, stand back now and give me some room. I'm not used to this and I don't know what's going on. Leave me alone tonight.'

It was odd but she could actually sense a withdrawing, as though some presence which had filled the room was shrinking back, becoming smaller, less obtrusive. There was also a sense of apology in the air. 'Thank you,' she said to nothing visible. There was an answering feeling, like a smile.

Later, dry, scented, hair shining, she pulled on a loose silk shirt and linen trousers, threw a long cardigan over her shoulders and went downstairs.

At the bottom Isoldé found herself again in the wide hall, big enough for a large room in its own right. She stood still, looking, then turned around on her heel. There were several doors leading off, which one was he behind? 'Mark! ' she called. 'I'm here.'

A door at the back opened and he appeared, dry and clean in jeans and a jumper, a cooking apron tied round his waist. 'Better?' he asked.

'Mmm,' she nodded. 'It's wonderful what a shower will do for you.' She was not going to tell him about the faces, not now anyway.

'C'mon through, we mostly eat in the kitchen.'

She followed him into a huge flag-stoned room, bright rugs on the floor. Steel and copper pans hung from racks on the walls around a Rayburn, a big beech table glowed in the soft light and good smells came from the pots on the stove.

'Suddenly, I know I'm hungry,' she told him.

'Wine?' He held a bottle over a glass. 'It's Margeaux, is that OK?'

'Oh! Yes, thank you.' She took the glass and sat down on the other side of the table from the stove, guessing he would want to be up and down serving. There was bread and oil on the table along with a paté and olives.

'Tuck in.'

She watched him watching her. He brought the casserole to the table and slid into the carver chair opposite her. For a few moments there was only the sound of satisfied munching as they dug into the olives. Mark was amused to see her dip her bread in the wine as well as the olive oil.

'French habit?' he asked her.

'Uhuh.' Isoldé's mouth was full, she nodded.

'It's good you're here in Caergollo.' Mark coughed, his voice had gone throaty. He concentrated on serving the casserole, then poured more wine. 'Sitting across the table from you …'

'It feels slightly incredible to me,' she replied, her own voice was a bit choked too. Stay on target she told herself, don't get into the real reason you came. 'It's somewhere I've always dreamed of, ever since I got into folk music, heard Tristan. There was always something about him, about his music. Still is.'

'He was, is, special,' Mark agreed, feeling a bit squashed that her first thoughts seemed to be for Tristan and not for himself. Maybe she felt as overwhelmed as he did. There was so much chemistry just being in the same room with her.

'You knew him all your life, didn't you?' Isoldé tried to get the conversation level again.

'Since I was ten, went for the choir as I told you in the interview.' Mark decided that, actually, Tristan was a safe topic of conversation for the time being. Anything else, he felt, was going to get him into deeper waters than he could handle as yet.

'Can you tell me about it?'

Mark paused, ate some more, thinking.

'My dad died in a fishing accident when I was twelve,' he began. 'It started as a fine evening, putting the lobster pots out with his mate, then a sudden squall sprang up, big waves hitting the side of the boat. They had to let go the pots and were trying to bring her round into the wind when a rope caught him and swept him off the deck. Jem tried to save him, threw the lifebelt and tried to get the boat to him but he was swept away. The last Jem saw of him he was trying to stay afloat but heading out to sea. They never found his body.'

Isoldé waited a moment, wanting to touch his hand but not daring to. 'I'm so sorry,' she said.

'That was a long time ago.' Mark looked up at her. 'Mum went to pieces. A few months later she died of a heart attack. I always thought she died of a broken heart. So Tristan adopted me. I'd been staying here most weekends and in the holidays since he'd got me into Exeter Choir School the year before. I pretty well lived here already. Tristan was the elder brother I'd never had. He was my family.'

Isoldé sat quiet, watching Mark. He'd lost his family twice.

'I sort of hadn't realised that it was Tristan who played the organ here,' Isoldé began, 'that he was the choir master. I never think of him doing things like that, only singing and playing the harp.' Isoldé stopped, brought the subject round again to possibly less personal things. 'Was he much older than you?'

'About fifteen years. He was twenty-seven when Dad died, just getting into his own career. That was after he did the Belfast gig that really set him on the road, got him his first recording contract.'

Isoldé sat thinking, Mark watched her.

'He never had children.'

'No. He got the HIV on the second North African trip. After that, I suppose he wouldn't even consider the idea. He'd never been a great one for women as far as I knew so it didn't seem much of a loss to him.' Mark paused, looking into the middle distance. 'It's odd that, I was only thinking about it just before you came. He wasn't an ostentatiously celibate person, nor gay, just didn't seem to be interested. He always said his music was all his passion.'

Isoldé had finished her food. Mark changed the subject back to dinner.

'There's fruit and cheese. Coffee, tea, herb teas. We could have it in the library?'

'Yes, please.'

She followed him out across the hall into a room on the other side of the house and stopped short in the doorway, knowing she had been here before. It was just as she'd seen it in her dreams; a large room with a warm feel, the dark red walls and velvet drapes setting off the books and picking up colours in the Persian carpet. The grand piano stood off to one side near the windows, an assortment of comfortable looking chairs and a sofa were scattered about and there was the huge ingle-nook fireplace with a good log fire burning.

'It's … it's beautiful.' Isoldé sent her eyes looking round the room, admiring.

'I'll get the pudding,' he offered and went off to the kitchen again.

Left alone, she went to the windows, three and a French door. She tried the handle, it opened, the scent of wet grass filled her nostrils, the stream chuckled to itself across the other side of the lawn. She shut the door, turned to the piano, it was a Bechstein. She stroked the ivory keys.

'Do you play?'

Mark's voice made her jump.

'No.' She managed a laugh. 'I can't read music. My uncle taught me the harp by ear, same as he played. I can pick up a tune very quickly but I can't write it down. We never had room for a piano in the Belfast house.'

'Umm! I suppose not,' Mark said. 'Feel free to tinkle away though.'

'Not in front of you!' Isoldé was blushing.

'Hey …' Mark began then found nothing else to follow it.

Isoldé left the piano and came over to curl on the hearthrug beside the black cat. The cat yawned, stretched and laid his head on Isoldé's knee for a stroke. She rubbed his ears.

'That's Embar,' Mark told her, 'Tristan's cat. He stayed with me.'

Mark had brought cheeses, biscuits and fruit as well as rosemary tea. She was glad of the herbs, couldn't have coped with coffee. They talked about music, about the singing master-class with Tristan that Isoldé had gone to some years back.

'I didn't know you played the harp,' he said.

'Only for folk music and only for fun, I'm not a professional.'

'Did you bring it with you?'

'No. I came to see Caergollo. And you. And it's only for the weekend anyway.'

'Would you bring it next time?' Mark realised what he'd said, held his breath waiting for her answer.

'Yes.' She turned to him, a smile lighting her eyes.

Saturday

Sunlight peeking through the window to stroke her face woke Isoldé. She stretched, luxurious and alone, rolled out of the big bed and went to the window. A buzzard called. Looking out over the garden, she watched him circle high up then slide down the air currents to land in one of the trees on the other side of the stream. Mark had left binoculars on the window seat; she took them and, holding her breath, watched the bird feed the chick. For a moment she stood at the window, looking out, seeing nothing, thinking about last night. They had hardly touched, just occasional fingers brushing. 'Not yet,' something had whispered to her, 'wait.' He seemed to feel the same. She put the binoculars down and went to shower.

Out on the cliff path the light on the grass was bright and fine, glittering with dew. She rounded a bend in the cliff trail and stopped short. A hare sat in the path. 'Hello,' she breathed, standing quite still lest she startle the creature away.

The hare came closer. Whiskers twitching, it stretched towards her until she felt the wetness of its nose as the creature touched her bare ankle below the rolled up jeans, then it sat back. Isoldé slowly crouched down and stretched her hand towards it. Again the nose came forward, this time the lips wrinkled back and she felt the teeth rub against her skin. She hardly dared breathe.

Having scented her, the hare dropped to all fours again and moved away a pace then it turned its head and met Isoldé's eyes. She felt something stab through her, almost like a recognition. The creature turned away and loped slowly up the path.

Isoldé followed, but the hare was soon out of sight. She continued along the path until, rounding another corner, she came on a girl picking herbs. Isoldé stopped short, began to speak, stopped. The girl looked up, a startled look in her wide brown eyes then she looked quickly away and hurried further down the path around a rock. Surprised, Isoldé followed but not too fast, it was obvious the girl didn't want company, when she rounded the rock in her turn, there was no-one there. The girl must have known the path and the cliffs very well, she would have had somewhere out of sight to hide until the stranger had gone. Isoldé went on towards the sea. As she came to the next bend she couldn't resist looking back. There, sat beside the rock, was the hare.

Isoldé stood a moment, watching while the hare loped off behind the rocks again, then carried on until she came to a small waterfall. There she stopped to sit on a stone, listening to its song. The morning was still amongst all the water noise, she felt herself drifting off, lulled by the continuous soft voice of the fall.

Something warm and wet blew on her hand. She froze, looked round. The hare was back and sat beside her, whiskers whiffling, nose within an inch of her hand. 'What is it?' she whispered, 'what do you want?'

The hare stared at her out of wide brown eyes then nuzzled her hand again.

A cold feeling crept into Isoldé's stomach and the hair on her arms stood up. She kept perfectly still as the hare's face began to shift, melting, flowing into the face of the girl, just for a moment. Then the creature flicked away, leaping and rolling on the bright grass, all hare again. The last Isoldé saw of her was her white scut disappearing over the rocky outcrop. Slowly, she returned to the house and the smells of breakfast.

'You went for a walk?'

Mark's smile, over his shoulder as he turned eggs in the frying pan, lit her up. 'I did so …' She hesitated slightly, unsure how to tell him. 'I went down towards the sea, as far as the waterfall.' She paused again. 'I met someone …'

Mark glanced at her, slightly down his nose, as he pulled plates of food out of the oven where they'd been keeping warm, added the eggs and brought them to the table. 'Who ... what ... did you see?' he asked as he sat down opposite her.

'I saw a hare,' she began then forked some bacon and egg into her mouth.

'You did ...?'

Isoldé hesitated again. 'It was like a fairy story coming to life ... I saw a hare begin to turn into a girl. It was only for a moment, then she was gone, as a hare, leaping back over the cliffs.'

Mark let out a soft, whistling breath. 'The faer ...' Mark breathed. He paused, then ate a mouthful. 'Tristan used to see them all the time,' he went on. 'Sometimes I do too, glimpses. I'm not good at that, like Tristan was. Seems you are though.'

He was smiling, just a slight wistful look at the back of his eyes that Isoldé could see. 'He wrote his songs for them,' Mark added

'He saw this hare-girl?' Isoldé prodded. 'Who is she? What is she? Are there more of them?'

Mark let out a long breath. 'Where to begin,' he said. 'Well ... the shapeshifters in the old stories are real. There's some I've seen in the valley here, including the hare-girl who met you this morning, but I only see her very rarely. There's the root-mother who's often out in the woods. Her face is all folds, like the petals of an old rose and her clothes fold round her in layers too, like mossy green leaves and browns with faded yellow edges like autumn leaves. Then there's water-sprite-girl, all blue-white skin and silver-blue hair, with a long pointed face and elfin ears. The air spirit, dryad-girl is all silver and green like a beech sapling, very young, thin, skinny, with wispy clothing like cobwebs, and green-gold hair. The fire-spirit is slender with creamy skin and red hair threaded through with autumn vines. They're all small, short, only about waist high on me. They're faer folk, the spirits of earth, water, air and fire.' Mark paused.

'Then there's Gideon,' Mark went on. 'He's strange. Most of the time he just looks like a good-looking Gypsy of about thirty-five, in fact that's what some people think he is,' Mark paused. 'But you see he's been looking about thirty-five since I first met him, when I was ten.'

Isoldé swallowed a piece of fried bread too fast and began to choke. Mark came round and patted her on the back.

'Ye gods!' Isoldé croaked once the coughing had stopped. 'You mean they're immortal?'

'I don't know about that but time works differently for them than us.'

Isoldé was silent.

'They are the faer folk, the woodfolk,' Mark repeated, 'the fairies of the stories. They're real. Like the little people in Ireland I expect.'

Again, Isoldé was silent for a moment. 'My Uncle Brian, who brought me up, he was a druid. He believed in the faer. I don't know if he ever met any though. I never did when I used to go out in the woods with him. He was good with animals too but not like you, although, one night, an adder came and crawled round his wrist. It lay coiled there for ages, keeping warm, before it slithered off.'

'I thought there were no snakes in Ireland,' Mark said.

'There aren't.'

They sat watching each other for a few minutes, sipping their coffee.

'Seems like there's more to you than meets the eye,' Mark said eventually.

'You too.' Isoldé grinned lopsidedly back at him.

'Hmm!' Mark decided a change of subject would be good, began collecting plates and putting them in the dishwasher. 'What would you like to do today?'

Isoldé felt relieved too, followed his lead. 'The weather's cleared, like you said, what's good for us to go and see? I'd like to go out. I've never been to Cornwall before. Can I see some of the special places?'

'Certainly can.' Mark paused for a moment, running an itinerary through his brain. 'Including a pub lunch?'

'Sounds good,' Isoldé replied.

Isoldé pulled off her boots and left them in the scullery, padding up the stairs to change. After she'd showered she pulled on fresh jeans and shirt, towelled her hair and left it hanging loose to dry out then came back downstairs. She went to the library and opened the door.

A man sat at the desk, over by the window which looked out on the stream and the bridge. He appeared to be writing. Isoldé froze. As far as she knew there was no-one in the house but herself and Mark. The man turned, looked at her.

Behind her, Mrs Protheroe came in and turned on the main light. 'Shall I bring you a cup of tea? I've took your things and put them in the washing machine, they'll be fine again for tomorrow.'

Isoldé jumped, turned, she'd totally forgotten Mark's house-keeper. 'Oh! Yes ... thank you ... a cup of tea would be nice ... and ...'

'Right you are,' Mrs Protheroe interrupted. 'I'll bring it along in a minute.' She headed back down to the kitchen.

Isoldé turned back to the desk. There was no-one there. Slowly, she walked across. There was a piece of paper on it, an old fashioned fountain pen lying across it with the top still off. The ink shone as if it was still wet. Isoldé picked it up.

My Dearest Isoldé,

When you find this note then I will be gone across the sea to the Isles of the Blest, though the gods themselves laugh to think of me as blessed. But maybe I am, the French word "blessé" means wounded and I am wounded. I would that we had been able to meet truly in the flesh but all the gods of this valley laugh to hear me thinking so.

I know you now, now it is too late. My mind puts flesh under my hands even as I write this, even though I have not touched you, known you in the flesh of the everyday world. I know in my heart these are dreams but that does not stop me dreaming them. And one day you will come to me here, in the Isles, and we will be together. That is why I have left the Moon Song for you.

Oh, Isoldé, I want you so much.

Look around my home. Look hard and carefully. I have left the song for you. You will find it amongst the music of the stones and the wind, the trees and the water, the dark caves and the sunlight. It is the moonshine. Go down to the cove and sit on the rabbit-bitten grass where you can feel the thunder of the waves at play on the cliffs. Sit on the bridge, listen to the water sing amongst the stones. Sit by the kieve and I will come to you.

Oh, Isoldé, I love you more than my life.

Tristan

Mark turned the letter over and over in his hands, read it again.

'He was sat in that chair,' Isoldé broke the silence, pointing to it. 'He seemed to turn then Mrs Protheroe switched the light on. I jumped, then looked back, there was no-one there. I went over to the desk, found the letter. It was Tristan,' she finished.

'It's incredible, crazy,' Mark began.

They were sat on the floor in front of the fire in the library. Tension grew between them, the letter was too close, too personal, the letter of a lover.

'I've never seen him since he died,' Mark spoke softly, trying to get close again. 'I hear him. I hear the piano sometimes but when I open the door, come in, there's no-one here.' Mark paused, the wistful look back again. 'There was a strange line in the will,' he went on, 'about there being more music here, waiting to be found.'

'That's like what he says in the letter.' Isoldé touched it again. 'Where he says "*I have left the Moon Song for you*". Why me? Why not you?'

'I don't know.'

'I don't want to take it from you.' She touched his hand. 'He was your master, not mine, and I can't play a note anyway. He would be much better leaving it to you.'

'But he hasn't.' Mark looked at her.

There was so much sadness in his voice; Isoldé could feel the ache in him. She touched his hand. He looked at her and again she felt herself melting. Their lips met, she didn't resist. He carried her up to bed.

Woodfolk, Hag-Stones and the Sight

Later, when the night was waning and dawn not too far away, two figures stood beside the spiral maze in the rock face by Caergollo's back door. Both were small, short, only coming up to an adult human's waist. One was round, her face crinkled into folds like the leaves of a cabbage or the petals of an old rose; her clothes folded round her in layers of mossy greens and browns with faded yellow edges like autumn leaves. When she stood still in the woods people would walk right past her thinking she was no more than a large plant. The other was slender, skinny and a little taller than her companion, smooth skinned like a beech sapling. Wisps of clothing floated round her like cobwebs, tangling with the green-gold hair. She appeared much younger than the other woman. Both had huge eyes, like animals, deer maybe, or owls, no white showing, just glowing hazel-brown with deep blackness at their centre.

The older, dumpy one put a root-like finger into the pattern and turned it. There was a clunk behind them as the lock in the door turned, they pushed it open and went up the stairs.

Isoldé was sleeping on her side, turned away from Mark, one hand stretched out from under the duvet. The dumpy woman's eyes crinkled into a satisfied smile, she extended a claw and placed a hag-stone in Isoldé's open palm, curled her fingers around it.

'Go'orn then,' she told her companion. 'You give to her now.'

The younger licked a finger and touched Isoldé's eyelids with it.

'That's right,' the old one hooted softly. 'She'll need the full sight.'

'Now we gotta take something from her too.' The young one took a single golden hair between her fingers and pulled it out.

The two women jumped as Isoldé frowned and moaned but she didn't wake up so the older one crept close again. A tear trickled out from under Isoldé's eyelid, the old one caught it on her root-claw finger, dripped it into a little bottle she'd pulled out from under her skirts.

'C'mon!' she hissed and the young one followed her back down and out into the woods.

Later still, Isoldé moaned again in her sleep. Mark held her gently.

'Oh, Isoldé, I want you so much,' he told her, burying his face in her hair so she wouldn't have to hear.

Sunday

Over breakfast, Mark held something out to Isoldé in his closed hand. She took it.

'What on earth ...?'

'It's a hag-stone,' he told her.

'A who ...?'

The stone fell out of her hand and rolled onto the floor. Mark picked it up and gave it back to her. She was goggling at him.

'Hag-stone,' Mark repeated, grinning at her. 'It was in the bed when I got up this morning. I lay on it, that's how I noticed. Where'd you get it? On your walk yesterday?'

'I don't think I've ever seen it before ...' She stopped, something tugged at her memory.

Mark watched her brow furrow.

'I think ...' she began, 'I think I had a dream. Someone ... an old woman, gave it to me.' She shook her head. 'I can't remember.'

'Hmm ... ?' Now his eyebrows went up.

She handed it back to him. He turned it over in his hand.

'It's lucky,' he went on. 'Witches use them to ward off the evil eye or hang them in the trees sometimes, to show a place is sacred.'

Isoldé stared again.

'We do ave all thicky ol customs down yere in the boonies.' He put on the accent, 'There's many as still follow the old ways, though nobody talks about it, like I told ee.'

Isoldé swallowed that. 'So ...' She smiled quizzically at him. 'Then what do I do with this sacred hag stone, oh wise one?'

'Hang it round your neck. I've got a spare silver chain upstairs you can have. And,' he said, smiling at her, 'if you don't know where it came from, if it did come from someone in a dream, then it really is special. Now,' he turned the subject, 'yesterday you said you'd like to see Tintagel, go out to the island. The weather's still good, shall we do that?'

Isoldé agreed. Mark fetched the chain, put the hag-stone on it and fastened it round her throat. The chain was quite long so the stone fell down out of sight between her breasts.

'That's good,' Mark said, watching her face. He dropped a kiss on her forehead before turning to the coat rack and handing her a warm jacket. They kitted up for walking and set off again in the truck.

Isoldé was quite unimpressed with Tintagel village, the summer shops all closed and the slate roofs of the cottages clamped down tight in the cold sunshine. But when they got to the track and she could see out to sea again she began to understand Mark's enthusiasm.

The track down to the base of the island was wild, rugged. It needed a truck to get down there. 'It's like a river bed,' she said.

'It *is* a river bed when it rains, especially in the winter.'

'Are you allowed to drive down here?' Isoldé had seen the notice at the head of the track.

'I am,' Mark replied. 'I do some volunteer work for the trust when I can, but we must go carefully as people walk here at all seasons.'

They jolted slowly down the rock-strewn way and parked at the bottom. The climb up to the rock bridge onto the island made Isoldé puff. She hung over the parapet half way up, looking down into the waves crashing around the rocks below.

'It's turquoise,' she said. 'The sea's turquoise-coloured.'

'We call it the turquoise milk-shake, the colour of the sea with the creamy froth of the waves.'

'Mmm, yes, I see.'

They continued on up and round the corner, sheltered now by the island itself rising above them. Mark stopped at the archway gate.

'Like a monastery,' Isoldé said, looking around at what

appeared to be stone cells.

'They thought it was for a long time, until they began to find the old Celtic settlement and the outline of the great hall. That's what confirmed it as a King's main place of government. Probably the most famous king was King Mark, my namesake.'

'And your name is Mark King,' Isoldé said, eyes twinkling.

'So it is!' He was laughing back at her.

They walked slowly through the remains of the walls of the small buildings that clung to the steep, grassy cliffs until they came out on the top. A pair of kestrels hovered above. They stood still watching then Mark took her to see the fire-pit.

'This is it,' he said, lifting the wooden cover which kept the weather from wrecking the ancient hearth. 'The one all the sensation was about, that says, "Arthur woz here" in ancient script.'

Isoldé laughed, peering at it. 'I don't care,' she said. 'It's still wonderful that it does, that they found it, after all the legends linking him to this place.'

'Yes, it is,' Mark agreed. He replaced the lid. 'Now, this way is the great hall.'

She followed him as they walked the outline of the hall, it really did feel enormous although there were no walls left above ground. A great king's home indeed, she thought, one who must have had a lot of influence. And she could understand why the Irish had tried to take the place; it would be a useful stronghold on the western tip of Britain.

They walked on, up over the top of the hill until they could see the sea again, shimmering under the winter sun. Isoldé stopped, stood looking at the curve of the world, a dark blue line between the paler sea and the blue sky. 'I love that.' She took Mark's hand. 'Seeing the edge of the world, knowing that beyond it is space, outer space and the stars.'

Mark squeezed her fingers. 'Tristan loved it too. You share that.'

'And you?'

'Yes …' he said softly, 'me too.'

They walked on, still hand in hand, towards the sea, coming at last to bare rocks sloping gently to the cliff edge and a large white rock sat up on the screed. 'It's crystal,' Mark told her as they arrived at it.

It was too; mostly bright white rock crystal with flecks of the darker rock running through it and the occasional spark of clear quartz. 'Sit down, milady.' Mark was laughing. 'Tristan always called this the goddess throne.'

Isoldé sat. Mark fished his phone out of his pocket and took a picture of her, the bright sea and sky as a background. He showed it to her.

'Oh! And you've got the curve of the Earth as the background.'

'Had to, after what you said.' He sat down beside her on the rock; there was just room if they huddled close. He put his arm round her. 'You're beautiful,' he said. 'Like Isoldé of the story. Isoldé Labeale, Isoldé the belle, the beautiful, that's what your name says and it was her name too.'

Isoldé turned her face away from him at first, the colour rushing into it again. Then she turned back. 'And you are Mark King, like I said,' she whispered.

'I love you,' he told her. 'I think I knew that when I first saw you, with the sparrow.'

'Me too. It was electric.'

'What shall we do about it?'

'Do we have to do anything?' she asked him. 'Can we not just enjoy it, walk each step, allow the future to unfold?'

'And Tristan …?'

Isoldé laid her head on Mark's shoulder. 'He's dead,' she said. 'Gone.'

Mark hugged her. 'After last night, the letter, I'm not so sure,' he said.

4. The Kieve & Gideon

Woodfolk – Hare Singing

Isoldé had got the hang of the journey down to Caergollo now. The A30 from Exeter to Launceston was simple and not unattractive, it carved up time. If she left work at five o'clock, with the car already packed, she was shutting the gate behind her at Caergollo by six-thirty, earlier if she was lucky. The last part, after Launceston, twisting up over Davidstow Moor was the wildest, slowest, also the prettiest, finally coming down into the half-hidden valley. But always, once she crossed the Tamar she felt she had crossed into fairyland. Cornwall was another world indeed.

Tonight was one of the good nights, just gone six and she was inside the gate, inside the temenos of Mark's home. She had flown there on fairy wings, or so it had felt, no hold-ups, no difficult traffic and clear roads in the last of the sunlight as she came up over the moors.

'It's good to be home,' she said, without thinking, as she closed the gate. Then she stopped. What? What had she just said? Her home was in Exeter … wasn't it?

She stood with her hand on the gate, frowning, wondering at herself, a slight shiver going up her spine. What was she doing? Did she really mean to commit to Mark that much? And what about him?

A rustle in the long grass by the gate caught her eye. The hare was there again, sat up on her haunches this time, looking at Isoldé.

'What …?' Isoldé breathed. 'What …?'

The hare said nothing, did nothing, just stared up into her eyes. Its own were huge, brown with a blue tinge, almost like pools of water.

'You were here when I first came,' Isoldé said. 'Then I saw you out on the cliffs. You shifted. You became a girl. Then you went back to being a hare. Are you trying to tell me something?'

Something made Isoldé look up. There, tangled in the topmost branches, was the young crescent moon. Isoldé watched it transfixed, it was beautiful, the silvery sickle shape floating upwards amongst the spidery twigs in the top of the trees, at the top of the valley, above the house.

There was a sound, almost music, a long quavering note, eerie, making her hackles rise. She turned back to the hare. Its mouth was open, the sound came from the creature, calling, plaintive, wistful. It devolved into a very simple tune, three notes up and down, da di di da da da, the first note repeated, long-short-short, then up a note, then up again, then back down to where it started. The tune sounded again and again.

'What …? What is it you want?' Isoldé asked the hare.

Still there was no response but the little beast stopped singing and dropped back onto all fours, sat for a moment then turned to disappear into the undergrowth.

Isoldé stood for a moment then shook herself, it was like waking up, had she been dreaming? The hare was gone. She crouched down. Yes, there in the soft earth was the fresh print of little paws. It had been real. She got back in the car and drove up to the house.

'I saw your lights come in the gate,' Mark said as he came out to meet her. 'Then you stayed there a while. What happened?'

'It was the hare again,' Isoldé told him, following him through to the kitchen.

He poured her a glass of wine, refilled his own. 'The hare was there?'

'Yes …' Isoldé paused, took a sip of the wine. 'It was like she was waiting for me again. She didn't speak, or shift, but she seemed to sing. Something made me look up at the woods above the house and the new moon was just rising, it was beautiful.

While I watched, this sound came, then it became a tune, very simple.' She hummed it for him. 'And when I looked back it was like the hare was singing. Her mouth was open and I swear this sound was coming out of her.'

'Strange … it's not like any noise I've ever heard of a hare making and it does sound like a simple tune.' He turned back to fussling with dinner for a moment then took his wine and came to sit with Isoldé at the table.

'Hares are moon creatures,' he said.

'That's right,' Isoldé agreed.

'And Tristan said about the Moon's song in that letter.'

'He did.'

They were both not saying it, skirting round, not coming in close, it was too personal.

'OK.' Mark grimaced. 'Is it the beginning of the song you're getting?'

'I don't know but it does seem awfully coincidental to see the hare, right at the gate, and just as the moon is rising. And then to get this tune,' Isoldé said.

'What shall we do about it?'

'I vote we have dinner, do whatever, go to bed, let it all find its own way. Straining my brain isn't working. I'm hungry. I've missed you all week. I want to be with you for a bit, not ferreting about after lost songs. There's plenty of time for that later. Can we just have now to ourselves?'

Mark pulled her hand to his mouth and gently sucked each finger.

'Will that do for starters?' he asked, grinning wickedly.

Woodfolk – Gideon

Isoldé woke in the big bed to the crepuscule light of pre-dawn. Her skin prickled, she looked up, something had passed the window but now she looked it was gone. She pulled some clothes on, went to the hall, pulled on boots, threw Mark's fishing jumper over her shoulders and slipped outside.

The air was fresh, the grass covered with dew, the sun tangling with the branches at the top of the valley above them. That way drew her; she set off up the path. The going was steep, difficult right from the start. Mark had shown her the way on the map, saying they would go up later this morning, but this was different, exploring on her own. The quiet was emphasised by the chuckling stream, the birdsong echoed in the trees reminding her of the cathedral in Exeter. A cathedral of trees. The light was indirect, sparkling off leaves moving in the almost invisible morning air. She stopped. What had she just said? You couldn't see air. She looked again, she *could* see this air, slightly, almost, by looking out the corner of her eye. It was as if the air molecules had a golden edge, like soap bubbles. She shook her head but the effect was still there. Shrugging, she set off again up the path.

Arriving at the wooden bridge by the ash tree Isoldé stood for a moment. Mark had said they always stamped three times on the planks before they went over the bridge, calling out "Permission to cross?" just in case of hungry trolls. She smiled, remembering Billy Goat Gruff.

She put one foot on the planks and tapped out three beats on the wood. 'Permission to cross …?' she whispered.

An owl hooted back at her, three times. She peered, looking for it. Hidden against the grey bark and ivy she saw the tawny owl. Behind, in the trunk, she could now see the hole where it must roost up during the day. 'Thank you,' she whispered.

The owl gave a funny sort of purring croon, stepped from foot to foot and turned its head right round and back again on its shoulders. Isoldé kept one eye on the bird all the way across the bridge.

She carried on up the path until she came to a convenient boulder where she could sit and catch her breath, watch the stream. Just below her it was shallow, limpid water flowing like silk over brown stones, rippling round larger rocks with a sort of "gollumph" noise. The birds were all quiet too, making no sound. It was as if the forest held its breath. Looking around her she guessed she was at the last stretch. The path climbed steeply above her. It must go to the rock tunnel Mark had shown her on the map. Then it would be downhill, down the steps, to the cauldron pool. And the waterfall. There was an ache within her, calling her. She got up and began to climb.

By the time she reached the rock tunnel she was out of breath. She sank into a crouch with her hands flat on the earth and hung her head down, panting. Her fingers tingled, and her feet. At first she put it down to the blood singing through them then she felt a response from the earth, a pulse, and not just the soil but the rocky bones of the planet. Her breath quieted and her eyes opened, she stayed still listening. There was a pulsing humming out of the rocks of the tunnel itself, an almost-sound she couldn't quite make out. Something leapt across the far exit of the tunnel ahead of her and the sensation stopped.

Isoldé started, shook herself and stood up. What was that? It had gone so fast she couldn't see. She took a breath, walked through the tunnel out onto the rocky platform and turned down through the gate to the steps.

The downward steps were just as strenuous as the upward path had been. Uneven, rough, sometimes sloping and often slippery, she was glad of the handrail pinned to the rock. Halfway down she passed a shelf-like path curving round to the left. For a moment she almost took it but something pulled her on down.

The sound was incredible now, deafening, the rocks

themselves shuddering in the roar. Reaching the bottom, she stopped a moment to loosen the tension the climb had put in her neck and to uncurl her fingers from the handrail. She knew what was round the corner, Mark had shown her pictures and there was a beautiful drawing of it in the library. She was savouring the moment of anticipation before seeing the real thing.

She walked around the cliff. There it was, the cauldron pool. Looking up she saw the thread of water, like Rapunzel's hair, as Tristan had called it in the song. The thin strip of white water crashed down the fifty foot of cliff into the first bowl. Spray misted the dark air above it. Then it thundered out in a bright, white fall through the hole in the rock and into the main pool, the kieve. Above the hole, on the rock shelf, sat a figure. He was laughing down at her, tossing bright stones into the pool. Light, like fire, seemed to spark upwards as each stone fell into the water.

'Isoldé! ' he called. ' Isoldé! Come up and join me.'

She stared. He was sat quite casually, swinging his legs over the vast head of water creaming its way through the hole in the rock below him. If he fell the water would thrash and mangle him on the sharp rocks below. She held her breath.

'It's OK,' he called again. Somehow his voice was reaching her over the noise of the fall and without sounding as if he was shouting himself hoarse. 'Come on up. It's magical here.'

'It's magical down here too,' she prevaricated.

Who was he? How did he know her name? This was Mark's land, Caergollo land. Surely he was trespassing?

'I live here,' he answered the question in her mind. 'I've known Mark all his life and Tristan before him. Come up so we can get acquainted.'

'I'm no good at heights,' Isoldé stalled again. 'You will be,' he said.

He was very attractive, long dark hair, olive skin, bright, merry eyes. He raised a hand, long brown fingers clicked then beckoned. Involuntarily Isoldé began walking back to the stone stairway. She half checked herself then snorted in amusement. 'You want to go,' she told herself, 'and you nearly went there first, just now, anyway. That must be where the rock shelf leads.'

She carried on up the steps and turned out onto the shelf. The path was narrow, slippery and uneven. True, there were trees beside the path, their tops coming up to her waist, which meant the drop must be at least thirty foot. Although the branches would break her fall she would be damaged. She had no confidence in the elf-man sat on the shelf being able to rescue her.

She crept along with her back pressed against the cliff, sliding one foot along sideways and bringing the other up to it to get along, glad of the trees so she couldn't actually see the drop. It seemed to take forever to go the few yards around the cliff until she could see him. He stood up lightly and stepped off the stone bridge to take her hand.

'Come on,' he said.

His touch felt warm and cool at the same time, and she got a similar pulse through her fingers as had happened in the tunnel with her hands on the earth. She looked at him.

He looked rather odd now she was up close, like a man but … those ears were slightly pointed, reminding her of Spock in Star Trek. The skin was brown but silvery-blue lines traced spiral patterns over his cheeks, forehead, hands and arms. And his eyes were golden, with vertical pupils like an owl.

'It's OK.' He smiled reassuringly. 'I won't hurt you. Nor let any harm come to you.'

For some completely crazy reason and quite unlike herself, Isoldé believed him. She let him lead her the last few feet to the end of the shelf and right out onto the narrow bridge which was the top of the hole through which the lower fall rushed. The noise was deafening and the rock trembled under her boots. He helped her sit down then sat beside her. Their legs dangled together some fifteen feet over the smooth, white curve of the water.

He clicked his fingers again and the sound lessened, seemed to go into the background, like he'd found the volume-switch. 'Better?' he asked.

It was. Her brain and mind felt less buffeted, the whole place was less in her face and she found she could think again. She nodded to him.

'I'm Gideon.' He held out his right hand, a bit awkwardly as they were sat so close together. She reached her right hand across her body to take it.

'Isoldé,' she said automatically, 'but you already know that.'

'I do.' His eyes glinted as he took her hand and kissed her fingers.

That took her breath away, she gasped. The touch of his mouth on her skin set up ripples in her belly. She felt the colour rushing up her neck into her face, looked down into the kieve and slowly pulled her hand out of his. It was hard, she felt she didn't want to lose the touch of him and knew he was smiling at her although she wasn't looking at him. It was a soft, satisfied smile, like a cat purring.

'Who are you?' she asked.

'I'm the water of life, the air you breathe. I'm the fire in your heart and the food in your belly. I'm the owl with the moon. I'm the cat on the hearth. I'm the ocean of waves and the wave itself.'

Isoldé recognised the words of Tristan's song "The Trickster". 'You knew Tristan,' she said.

'I led him to the words for the songs,' he said softly, turning to look at her. 'As I'll lead you too.'

'Me?'

He nodded.

'I'm not a singer, not like Tristan.'

'We know that, but we need you.'

'Me?' she said again. 'And who's we? Who are you?'

'I just told you that.'

'No you didn't, you recited one of Tristan's songs. I want to know who you are.'

'For that we'd better get somewhere you won't fall into the torrent. I've no desire to have to rescue you.'

He stood up. She found herself doing likewise, preceding him back along the shelf.

She looked over her shoulder. 'Up? Or down?'

'Down.' He was suddenly ahead of her, leaping down the steps like a mountain goat. She followed slowly to find him on the shingle by the kieve, sat on a stone, another comfy-looking stone beside it. Isoldé sat on it.

'You know Tristan's songs?' he asked her.

'Of course.' Isoldé was blushing again. 'I've loved him and his work, forever. Since my uncle played them to me when he was teaching me to sing.'

'Groupie …?' Gideon looked at her, eyes twinkling.

Isoldé blushed even more, looked away, then she tossed her hair back.

'I suppose you could call me that. I'm a fan and yes I went to all his concerts, even a master class once, although I was terribly scared and embarrassed as I don't read music.' She had a rueful smile at the memory. 'There were all these people, musicians, students, terribly earnest and reverent. But they did get a bit screwed by some of the exercises he gave us.' She chuckled.

'So … what are his songs about?'

That gave Isoldé pause. She sat quiet, looking into the sheet of water tumbling through the hole in the rock. It was hypnotic. Pictures formed behind her eyes; the grey flash of a buzzard's wing; trout leaping; waves crashing on cliffs or rippling softly on a sandy shore; the woods at night; the cave on Tintagel beach; the wind on the hilltop ruffling the smooth surface of Dozmary Pool. 'They're about the land here and its creatures,' she whispered.

'Yes,' said Gideon, 'that's right.'

In the pause which followed Isoldé turned towards him. He was no longer there. Beside her sat a crazy creature, a chimera, a mix of many beasts and trees. The long dark hair was like twigs and leaves, the cheeks were rosy now like apples, the legs wore fur instead of trousers and ended in cloven hooves. His arms ended in half-paws, similar to the hare-girl. Quickly, Isoldé's gaze went back to his face, he still had owl's eyes. That was still sufficiently like the original for her to cope. 'Who are you?' she asked yet again.

'Who do you think?' he said.

Her brow wrinkled. When he spoke his voice wasn't scary but warm, brown and reassuring. It was just all the rest of him.

'A shapeshifter,' she said at last, then she stopped, thinking. 'Gideon ... Gideon ...?' She looked at him.

He nodded.

'Gwydion ...?'

He nodded again. One hand shifted back from paw to fingers. They touched hers, gently curled themselves around her hand. She didn't resist. A smile began in her eyes, travelled to her mouth.

'It's ridiculous,' she said, 'me, sitting here with the master enchanter of all Britain. I don't believe it.'

The fingers squeezed her hand. 'Sorry,' he said, there was a chuckle under his voice, 'but you've got it right. I'm called Gideon around here. Some folk recognise me. To others, I'm the local man-o'-the-woods. I bring them game and sing at the local ceilidh. I dance too.' He raised his eyebrows hopefully at her.

'So do I, dance I mean.'

He was flirting with her she realised and she was responding. It seemed gentle, not having to go anywhere. He was attractive. There was a potent energy about him, if he looked at her with passion she realised he would be hard to resist. She brought her mind back to the present. The expressions crossing his face told her he had followed her train of thought.

'So ... why are we here?'

'Because Tristan is dead,' he replied.

She quirked an eyebrow. 'So what?'

'He died too soon. He hadn't finished his work, hadn't finished the Ellyon cycle.'

'I sort of gathered that.'

'There was … is … still the final song to do, the Moon Song. We need it to complete the cycle. All his images give voices to the ley lines, the land herself, the water, the rivers and the sea, all of which is good. But it's no good if the Moon is not there to co-ordinate everything.'

'What do you mean?'

'We cannot come unless you open the door.'

Isoldé stared at him. Comprehension was tickling around the corners of her mind but wouldn't come into focus.

'You'll have to spell it out for me,' she said. 'You want me to ask. You want us all to ask?'

'Yes,' he said then paused. 'OK, think of it this way. You've seen the old horror films, haven't you?'

Isoldé nodded. 'But I'm surprised you have.'

'You'd be amazed what we woodfolk get up to on the long winters' nights. Whatever, they're a good example of what I mean. Now, when the virgin goes to bed at night what happens?'

Mystified, Isoldé shook her head.

'Her guardians shut all the doors and windows, hang garlic over them,' he went on, 'tell her on no account must she open the door. Of course she does or there wouldn't be any story. But the point is that the vampire cannot come in *unless* she, the human, opens the way for him. He cannot, not with all his power, force his way in through a door which has not been opened to him.'

Comprehension was beginning to make itself felt. 'Go on,' Isoldé said.

'Well, all of Otherworld is like that, like the vampire. Oh,' he watched her begin to frown, 'we're not usually nasty, out to drink human blood or anything and anyway a vampire is an ex-human not one of us in the spirit world. But we cannot come into human space unless and until we are invited. You have to ask us to come.' He paused, watching her.

'I see … I think … just a little,' Isoldé said slowly. 'In the old days people spoke to you, the fairies, spirits, gods, often in little-seeming ways like wishing-trees and wells, special places where people left flowers, even altars in the house or the hedgerow.

'That's right,' Gideon said. 'And the festivals were always remembered, celebrated. Fire and light at Imbolc; courting and jumping through the fire at Beltane; bread and weddings and driving the cattle between the fires at Lughnasadh; the winter cattle slaughtered and the ancestors remembered at the Samhain bonfire, the good fire.'

'And all the things like John Barleycorn and the horn dances, the Obby Oss and the fiery barrels,' Isoldé added.

'Yes, all those things, and the songs themselves which everyone sang. Christianity knocked us about a lot, we had to go underground, become the little people. And the humans who stayed with us had to hide too, pretend they were worshipping the saints when all the while they were still calling to us, asking us to be part of their lives. But it's science, modern science, which has practically wiped us out. We are a major extinction about to happen which most folk are not even aware of, or only at the edges of their consciousness.'

'How?' Isoldé reached for his hand now, comforting the lost look in his eyes.

'Because so many, many believe that if science doesn't know a thing then that thing doesn't exist. It's happened with psychology too, even though the word psychology is built around the Greek word "psyche" which means "soul" the psychologists rarely, if ever, believe in the soul. There is no soul, it's all bits of sub-personality. Faugh!' Gideon almost spat. 'And we, too, have become a superstition, a figment of a disordered imagination, something to be denounced, de-bunked and ridiculed. So folk, afraid of the ridicule of their friends and neighbours, stop doing the old things, they no longer sing the old songs, no longer ask us into the world.'

'And Tristan's songs rebuild the way for people to believe again, to ask?' Isoldé said.

'Hole in one!' Gideon's grin had come back now. 'You're a quick study. Yes, Tristan's songs are part of the way back for us. And for humans. Despite your science you won't survive without us, for the Earth will change if we die. It will go barren, no longer feed you, give you water, air. And without these things your bodies will die. And,' he paused, 'if you do not call us, speak with us, relate with us, then we *will* die. When that happens the planet re-forms, shifts herself into a new way of being which may not have a place for humans any more. She doesn't like creatures that don't respect others because they don't look or act like themselves.'

'And we're only too good at that!' Isoldé said bitterly. 'Most people only care about themselves or, at least, only about human beings. Anything else is second.'

'But there are changes.' Gideon's fingers stroked hers. 'Lots of little things, folk festivals are more popular now, I mean things like the Oss and the horn dances, as well as the music festivals. People may not really know what they're doing, like children, but they sing the songs. And that's what Tristan helped us with. Dylan and Lennon did a lot but much of their work was social, about human relations with each other, about wars, poverty, hatred, race, all the things that divide you from yourselves. Tristan took it further, deeper, his songs bring you closer to the non-human, to the creatures, plants, rock even, with whom you share the planet.'

Isoldé sat quiet. The last thing she'd expected when she came out this morning was a philosophy lesson but it all made sense. Even the outlandish creature who sat beside her, who could morph parts of himself into bits of tree or goat or apples, made a strange kind of sense. She flicked her mental fingers at the modern, rational part of herself who had to have everything pigeon-holed into neatly labelled boxes which were never larger than she could handle. Her mouth grew a sneer, she could be as bad as anyone else at not wanting to think outside the box but this morning had made a huge dent in her supercilious armour. She would never be able to deny Otherworld again. Uncle Brian would be pleased if he ever knew of it. It was a big sadness in his life that she'd not followed him into druidry. She didn't think she ever would but, whatever way this strange path the woodman was offering took her, she knew she was open now to voices beyond ordinary twenty-first century reason.

She thought back. It had begun with the sparrow, when Mark had rescued it, astounding her with his affinity with birds and animals.

Gideon was smiling when she looked at him. 'That's what you have to do,' he said. 'Find the song. Tristan didn't get to writing it before he died. It has to be written and recorded; you must enable Tristan to record it.'

Isoldé felt the cold creep over her. She sat perfectly still.

'That's impossible ...' she said.

Mark

Mark sat up in bed nursing a cup of tea. He'd got up as soon as he heard Isoldé go out, but not until. Last night had been intense, passionate everything he'd ever hoped for but he could understand, appreciate, that Isoldé might want some time out now. He did himself. They had said "I love you" in the same breath as he carried her up the stairs, before they slowly and carefully undressed each other. The clothes were still there in a heap at the end of the bed, tumbled together as their bodies had been. Out of the corner of his eye he'd watched her climbing into jeans and a sweater just before dawn. She'd been very quiet so as not to wake him, not realising or – he revised the thought – not wanting to show him she knew he was awake.

The clock now said seven. He'd asked Mrs Protheroe not to come today. She wouldn't, even though she would be dying to know more of Isoldé, only too keen that he was in a relationship. Like a mother, she was always looking for, hoping for, the right girl for him. And hoping against it too. He knew she didn't want to lose her boy, that any woman would have to be superwoman and she still wouldn't satisfy Mrs P's desires. A wry grin played over his mouth. He was inordinately fond of Mrs P, she had taken care of him since Tristan had adopted him when his parents died. But he'd always kept a slight distance, even as a child when he hadn't known what he was doing she had always been Mrs P, never Gwennan although he knew her given name. Now it was more natural, as a well-adjusted former child will do with a parent, an attitude which continually reminded them both that he was an adult now. It was a way of ensuring mutual respect.

Never one to have committed affairs, Mark had been a disappointment to Mrs P on the marriage front. Now he could sense her hunting instincts rising again. She would hunt and chase Isoldé if she could, to make her into the perfect wife for Mark. Mark didn't want that and neither did Isoldé, he was sure. Oh, he wanted her, did not want to lose her, wanted to live with her, share his life with her – and all that after such a short time of knowing her, but Mrs P's ambitions were not theirs.

Tristan had never fathered him. His vibrant, restless, exciting energy was that of an older brother. When that had gone, when Tristan had died, it had left a great void in his life. Isoldé was filling that void and he realised now that it was a much older emptiness than just of Tristan's death. It had been with him all his life.

'I knew as soon as I saw her with the sparrow,' he reminded himself. So he had. But all that had nothing to do with what Mrs P understood of marriage.

How long would it take Isoldé to reach the kieve, he wondered. Not too long. The muscles he had caressed last night were long and strong, she was fit like a dancer, she would achieve the cliff. Would Gideon be there? Like in Mark's dream? Should he be jealous of the woodman? Mark laughed at himself. A fat lot of good that would do any of them. It wouldn't touch Gideon, he would do as he pleased.

No, Mark thought, no need for jealousy and petty stuff like that. After the letter it seemed strange things were afoot. How could Tristan have written to Isoldé? He was dead. But the ink on the paper had been wet when she picked it up, so Isoldé had told him.

He heard Tristan about the house sometimes, playing the piano, whistling, singing. Sometimes he smelled the scent of him, as if Tristan had just left the room before Mark entered it. It was all too like it had been before, when Tristan was alive, except he never saw him. And there were the songs. For some reason Mark had never been able to find the last collection so he could get them off to the publisher. Something always happened to stop him. He'd promised Tristan he'd get them published, out there, being heard and sung. And there was the final song to write. And to record.

Isoldé was the key, or so the letter indicated. Why? How? What if he'd never met her, what would have happened then?

A chuckle sounded in the room. Mark started out of his reverie spilling cold tea down himself. 'Damn you!' he cursed at the room generally.

Caergollo was full of the faer. Tristan had encouraged them, Mark had grown up with them, it was normal, didn't everyone? He learned very fast when he went away to the choir school in Exeter that they didn't. He'd also learned to zip up his mouth and keep his head down.

How would Isoldé get on with the faer? How was she getting on with them now? He grinned to himself, he knew she was with Gideon, he'd seen it in his dream just before waking, seen them both sat on the rock bridge over the fall. Well, he thought, that answers my question, she must be doing fine.

That settled it. He put the cup back on the tray and swung his legs out of bed, getting up. Two minutes in the shower, then he was pulling on jeans, T-shirt and a sweater. Tristan's ancient denim jacket topped the ensemble as the mornings were still nippy. Sat at the bottom of the stairs, lacing up his boots, he saw Tristan's staff sticking out of the old brass shell-case they used as a repository for sticks and brollies. He took it.

Twenty-five years of walking it meant his body knew the path up to the kieve intimately, knew where to place his feet, where the natural steps were. He arrived at the plank bridge before he knew it. Just as he made to put his foot on the bridge the owl hooted. He stopped still. She was late this morning, usually she was asleep by the time the sun was this high. He watched for her among the branches of the ash tree. There! She was looking at him.

Soundlessly, she floated across the stream to land on the post at the end of the bridge, nearly at eye level with him. She ruffled her feathers and preened around her neck, making up her mind. 'Kee-wick,' she said softly, holding Mark's eyes.

The owl had turned on his inner sight, he could see Isoldé and

Gideon deep in talk. They were still at the kieve. Gideon had shifted, his feet were hooves but the rest of him still looked more or less like a man. Mark wished he could hear what they were saying but the owl stopped him, fluttering her wings gently, bringing him back.

'Wait!' He heard in his mind.

Mark reached out a finger and the owl allowed him to caress the soft feathers under her chin. She took the finger in her beak, holding it for a moment then letting it go. Mark nodded to her then went down the bank to an old log right by the stream. It had been there ever since he could remember, the remains of an ancient oak tree whose children congregated at the top of the bank casting deep shadows at midsummer. They were just pinking up now, the leaf-buds swelling, further forward than the ash tree on the opposite bank.

'Comes the oak before the ash, then we only get a splash,' he quoted the old rhyme.

'But comes the ash before the oak, then we get a goodly soak,' Tristan's voice completed the couplet.

'Where are you?' Mark sat up abruptly, almost dislodging the owl which had come to perch on his knee.

There was no answer. There never was. He would hear Tristan but never see him, never be able to converse with him. It left an ache in his heart.

The letter bothered him. Addressed to Isoldé, it had been intimate, a lover's letter. How? Why? Isoldé was certain she'd only met him the once, impersonally, at the master-class, apart from seeing him whenever he was at the Troubadour. Would that be enough to trigger memories across the grave? Isoldé had been as startled as himself to find the letter, to read its contents. How had Tristan been able to do that, to actually pick up a pen and write? Mark had asked Mrs Protheroe if there had been any letters on the desk earlier, or pens out of the holder. She had denied it.

Mrs Protheroe was as neat as a new pin. She would have noticed if anything had been out of place. Years ago, when both she and Mark were new to living and working with Tristan, she had had to be forcibly persuaded to leave Tristan's library alone apart from basic hoovering and dusting.

He smiled as the memory of that day, of Tristan remonstrating with her, floated up before his eyes. It had been the first summer after his parents died. Living at Caergollo still felt a weird mix of strange and completely at home. And he was still somewhat in awe of Tristan.

Tristan had been composing all morning in the library, the piano strewn with manuscript, more music on the floor, dirty mugs beside. Tristan just shot into the kitchen, dumped a tea bag in a mug, splashed boiling water over it and shot back to the library again. He could never stand other people near when the composing fit was on him, would flap his arms at you, like as not splashing you with hot tea because he forgot the mug was in his hand, and shout 'Go away!' One kept clear of him at such times. Then the fit would break, the song basically written, and Tristan would shout for Mark to come down, they would be going for a walk.

So it happened that day. Up over the cliffs to the steps of Lady's Window where they sat watching the smooth lapis-coloured sea and the bank of low cloud just perched on the western horizon. Then Tristan had bounded up again, leaping over the last of the Stitches and down into Caer Bottreaux with Mark, running and tumbling and laughing in pursuit. They'd raced along the harbour where Tristan had let him win, fetching up at the fish-n-chip shop.

'OK,' Tristan had laughed, 'You win. The old man can't keep up. So I'm buying, what'll it be?'

They'd had cod and chips, squeezing tomato sauce over them along with extra salt and vinegar, then gone to sit on the bridge over the Valency river, legs dangling, joking, laughing, throwing chips to the gulls who swooped down to catch them in mid-air. After, they'd staggered back up and down the hill to Caergollo. Mrs Protheroe was just hanging up her apron, about to leave. She was much younger then, had only recently come to work for Tristan when Mark arrived, to look after him as well as the house when Tristan could not. She was as new to Tristan as he was.

Tristan went into the library. He erupted out of it. 'What have you done, woman?' he exploded. 'My papers! My manuscripts! Where have you put them?'

Mrs Protheroe quailed. Mark stood stock still, not breathing.

'Where are they …?' Tristan demanded.

'H-here …' Mrs Protheroe showed him the pile, neat and tidy, on the desk in the library.

'And the others? The scrap? You haven't thrown them away?'

Mrs Protheroe was shaking. She nodded and led Tristan to the waste bin in the scullery. Tristan turned it upside down. Paper, peelings, old tea-bags, everything compostable fell out all over the floor.

'Then you'd better find them,' he said. He sat on a box straightening and collating the papers as Mrs Protheroe and Mark disgorged them from the smelly mess. Fortunately, everything was there and not ruined by contact with the vegetable matter. Mark had been amazed that Tristan had known, recalled, every single sheet. He made a pile of them while Mark and Mrs Protheroe got all the waste back into the bin.

'Now, come and wash while I make some tea,' Tristan said, leading the way back to the kitchen.

'Thank you, Mrs P,' he said, pouring a cup for her, making her sit down while he waited on her. 'But don't you ever, ever, touch my things again. I'll clear up after myself but every scrap is important and nothing gets thrown away. That's what's in all the box-files in the studio. Mountains of paper, bits of songs that haven't so far come to fruition, but they may, Mrs P, they may.

That's why I never throw anything away.'

'I'm sorry, sir,' Mrs Protheroe began, 'I didn't know …'

'No, I should have told you but I didn't think. I'm not used to having somebody in every day. It was different when you came twice a week, I was always ready for you. Now I'm not, I'm living as I always have, as I always will. Can we manage, Mrs P? Can we cope?'

His slightly wild-eyed appearance and sweet smile caught hold of Mrs Protheroe. 'Of course we can, sir,' she began again.

'And for the gods' sake stop calling me "sir"!' Tristan half exploded again, laughing this time. 'I'm Tristan. Or if you're very cross with me call me "Mr Talorc". Then I'll know I've upset you.' He tentatively put one hand over hers. She squeezed his fingers.

'All right, sir … Mr Talorc … Tristan …' she tried them all out, smiling back at him.

'We've got that settled then,' he replied. 'Now, are you late? Shall I call Mr P and say you're on your way?'

'That's all right.' Mrs Protheroe got up to re-hang her apron on the hook behind the door and pull on her coat again. 'He'll be at the Nap. There's a darts match tonight.'

'And he'll be setting everything up and getting in a bit of practice,' Tristan was teasing.

'Now. Si … Tristan!' Mrs Protheroe protested.

'No, I know. The darts champion of North Cornwall doesn't need practice.'

He escorted Mrs Protheroe to her car.

Mark had known Tristan better after that episode than he had in all the months he'd lived there. It had brought them all to a new order of intimacy. And nobody ever cleared up after Tristan again.

Come to think of it, Mark remembered back to last night, Mrs P had left the letter on the desk after Isoldé had found it. She hadn't even put the top back on the pen.

Return from the Kieve

Somehow Isoldé's return journey was much quicker and easier than the going had been, probably because her mind was fully occupied with what Gideon had shown her. She'd just assumed things had got too much for Tristan with the HIV, and he'd walked off the cliff to end it all. It was understandable. But now it seemed he'd gone too early, before his work was finished. A bummer all round, for him and for Otherworld who needed the job done.

'I'm talking like Uncle Brian,' she told the tree she had stopped under. 'He would know all this stuff like the back of his hand. I don't. I suppose Darshan would understand it too. I wonder if Mark does?' She continued down the track.

'Damn!' Isoldé stopped again. She hadn't asked for the job of finding the lost song and apparently rebirthing Tristan, had she? Uncle Brian would say she had.

'No such thing as victims in work with Otherworld,' he would tell her, 'only volunteers.'

'I must have been drunk when I signed on for this,' she muttered, starting walking again. 'Certainly didn't read the small print.'

'What small print?' said a familiar voice, out loud this time.

Isoldé stopped, looked around. She'd arrived back at the plank bridge without noticing and down by the stream on the other side, was Mark.

'Hello you,' she called, stepping onto the bridge.

'Don't forget to ask,' he called back.

Isoldé stopped in mid stride. 'Bother! Do I have to?'

'Always a good idea.' He'd stood up now and was grinning at her.

Isoldé rolled her eyes, tapped her foot on the wood three times and asked permission to cross. The water below her did a big *plop!* making a bubble in the silky surface. She stared at it then glared at Mark. 'I'll take that as a yes,' she growled.

Mark helped her down the bank.

'Room for two on the old log,' he said. 'What've you been up to or is it secret?'

'No-oo,' Isoldé shook her head. 'I don't think it's secret but it is strange.' She looked at him. 'Maybe not to you, you grew up here, but it feels strange to me.'

'You met Gideon, didn't you?'

'Yes, but how did you know?'

'Saw it in a dream,' he said.

That silenced her. What, yes what, on earth had she got into? Mark let her find her own space.

'You know he's a shapeshifter, a real body-changer?' she asked him.

Mark nodded.

'Oh.'

Isoldé sat staring at the stream for a while.

'I don't know how to tell you so it's going to come out all splat.' She paused, swallowed. 'Tristan died too soon, too early. He hadn't finished the Ellyon song cycle. There's one last song to write.'

Mark had gone a bit pale but was otherwise taking it well. 'The Moon Song ...'

'Yes ... and ... he has to come back,' Isoldé continued, 'to write the song.' There was a long pause. 'And ... I have to bring him back.'

She stared desperately at Mark, wondering what he would say, willing him to say something. That last bit was so strange, so like things out of story books. Like the princess going to look for the bluebird, she thought to herself, just hope I don't have to scale ice-mountains. And I'm not a damn princess, maybe that makes me immune ... but she wasn't holding her breath.

Mark still wasn't saying anything ... she saw he was crying. She'd been so worried about herself she hadn't seen him. She put her arms round him now. He buried his face in her neck. After a few minutes he pulled away and sat looking at her, rummaging for a handkerchief. He blew his nose. 'Thank you,' he said.

That was the last thing Isoldé had expected him to say. He smiled, seeing the confusion in her face.

'I knew he was going to go, to die, when I went off to Japan,' he said. 'He told me so, even. And there was nothing I could do although something inside said it wasn't right, was the wrong time. Not that he shouldn't do it, I don't mean that and I would never deny him his choice, but that his timing was wrong. He was secretive, a Scorpio. No-one ever saw the songs until he was ready. Oh, I'd hear them about the house as he was making them, see post-it notes of words and phrases as they came to him dotted about the kitchen. Mrs P used to dust under and around them rather than dare move one.'

Isoldé grinned with him at the thought.

'So, you telling me he'd not finished, has to come back, isn't altogether a surprise. No.' Mark shook his head at the question on her face. 'I didn't know or not until the letter. I just knew things weren't right. What you're telling me makes sense, feels like the bits of the puzzle are slipping into place. Or some of them anyway.'

'How's that?' Isoldé prompted as Mark seemed to go off into thought again. He came back.

'I've heard him about the house since I got back from the Japan tour, after he was dead. Smelled him too, his scent and his perfume and the Tea Tree oil he used on the sores. I've never seen him though, nor has Mrs P, although she says she's heard him too. Nobody had seen him until you did that first Saturday night.'

Isoldé leaned her shoulder into Mark but looked away at the stream. 'I dreamed of him, you know,' she said at last. 'On the night he went. I saw him. I watched him climb the hill and go out across the Stitches to the tower. Watched him step off onto the moonpath. He didn't fall, just gradually became a little black dot moving against the moon-gold path, until he was gone as the sun came up over the hill behind and wiped the path off the sea.'

'But that's not the only time you dreamed of him.' Now it was Mark's turn to prompt her. He stroked her hair.

'I don't know if I can do this,' she said.

Mark continued stroking, his lips brushed her hair above the ear.

'He came to me,' Isoldé began. 'Like a lover. Wanting me. One night, in Exeter before I met you, I woke from the most amazing orgasm, like the old stories of the incubi. And then the letter ...' she trailed off.

Mark never stopped stroking her hair, his fingers never faltered throughout her speech. They didn't now. 'I'm not angry or jealous,' he said. 'Do you love him?' He paused, then went on. 'I love him. I always loved him. He was my brother. There was something about him, charisma, but it was so strong. And he was so generous despite the autocratic bits.' He smiled softly, nuzzling her hair. 'I love him still.'

It was a strange bond between them, their love for each other and their mutual love for Tristan. Brother to Mark and a role model for his life, for Isoldé he had always been an inspiration. Now it appeared he had clay feet, had got it wrong. And they would have to set it right.

'Did Gideon tell you how you're supposed to bring him back, do we have séances or something?' Mark asked her.

'No ...' She shook her head into his shoulder then pulled away. 'But I have to go there ...'

Mark stared. 'Go where? To the Isle of the Dead?'

She nodded.

'How? ... Follow Tristan ... on the moonpath ...' He answered his own question.

'Don't know yet. They're going to help me, Gideon said. You have to help too.'

Thank all the gods for that, Mark gave silent prayers. He'd been terrified she would do this thing on her own, that he would be left out. 'When do we start?' he asked.

'Soon … I think.'

Mark paused, trying to grasp all the implications. This was so soon after they had come together. He had imagined a quiet, gentle time while they got to know each other, drifting gradually into permanence. He knew, had known that first night when he sat in Cathedral Close with the mouse and the cat, that he wanted Isoldé, for always, for life, and beyond life too. But he'd thought of it as a normal, personal thing, a relationship that would grow and blossom and fruit. It seemed they were being pitched together, going headlong into an adventure which was beyond anything he knew out of the realms of story. Her too, he suspected. And how could he refuse? He loved Tristan. He loved Isoldé. And Otherworld asked it of them.

Isoldé watched him thinking. What would he do? Or she? She snuck her hand into his. 'I think we've got a job to do,' she said, paused. 'I … I love you, Mark.' She stopped again, he didn't interrupt. 'I want to be with you for the rest of my life. I've never felt this way before, I'm not used to it, I'm out of my own control. Something is lifting, carrying me. It's like falling in a river and being carried off on a journey to places you didn't know existed. It began with the sparrow. I think I knew then. But I was expecting a slow, gradual journey, not this. It's like the waterfall itself.' She waved a hand back towards the kieve. 'Tumbling and crashing down the fifty foot of cliff into the basin. I can't hear myself think with all that's happened just this morning.'

'That's how I feel too,' Mark said. 'I love you. It was instant, when we first touched hands after the sparrow. I was expecting slow too, not this helter-skelter. But I love you. That's not changed.' He stopped. They looked at each other.

Woodfolk – Calling Isoldé

If you do not come too close, if you do not come too close,
On a summer midnight, you can hear the music
Of the weak pipe and the little drum
And see them dancing around the bonfire
TS Eliot: East Coker

The light flickered and grew as the fire waxed. The wood wives crouched about the flames, feeding them with twigs and fir cones, green branches and pieces of root. The flames and smoke twined together, rising up into the sky.

The eldest one took the root pieces from her bag and fed the fire. Her round body was like a root itself, strong, full of goodness, brown-skinned. She was wrapped in robes and shawls of mossy greens and browns, their edges faded yellow like old leaves, they folded round her in layers like the leaves of a plant. Her warm, kind face crinkled into folds like the petals of an old rose.

The next wife took the green branches, threading them in to the fire from underneath. This one was young and slender, her blue-white skin shining wetly in the light of the fire, the silver-blue hair hanging down around her long pointed face, pointed elfin ears were half-hidden under it. The blue-green silky robe twisted and rippled around her like the threads of a waterfall.

The third was very young, thin, skinny, a little taller than her companions, smooth skinned like a beech sapling. Wisps of clothing clung round her like cobwebs, the green-gold hair tangled and blew around her face. She fed the fire with bright twigs and flowers.

The fourth wife was older than the young one and younger than the old one. Tall and slender with autumn-coloured vines wound through the red hair that fell around the pale cream skin of her face. Ripe cherries hung from her earlobes, her dress rustled with brown and orange leaves. She fed the fire with fruits and nuts that crackled and spat in the flames.

'I gived her the sight, Mother,' the young one said.

'Aye, and I gived her the hag-stone. Her've took it,' the old one said in her turn. ''Tis round her neck. Young Mark gived 'er a chain and it hangs there between her breasts.'

'Right over her heart ...' the young one said.

'That's right, my lover, that's right. Her've got the holey stone,' the one in blue agreed, feeding more green branches into the fire. The smoke itself took on a blue tinge.

'And we took from her too,' the young one said. 'I took one of her hairs, long, golden tis.

'The swallows took it back in time, wove a dream for Mark,' the red one added.

'So they met,' the young one said. 'And a tear trickled out from under her eyelid. You took it, Mother, caught it on your claw.'

'I did.' The old one fished in a pocket and held up a little bottle she'd pulled out from under her leafy skirts.

'And what is us to do wi' that?' the blue one asked.

''Tis the water,' said the green one. 'The moon's fluid. It comed from her sight, she will see.'

The red one fed more fir cones into the fire. 'Aye ... she's a good girl and she will see, but she don't know what she be doin', not yet she don't. Nor she don't know what we do neither.'

'That'll come,' the blue one finished up.

The old one put out a wrinkled claw-finger and pulled a burning root out of the fire. It was shaped like a tiny spiral, a wriggling worm, a wormlike child. She blew on the glowing root-coal, it whistled out a weird cry, singing, spinning outwards. The wood wives blew against the root-coal, blowing the sound back inland, towards Caergollo.

Isoldé stirred in her sleep, found herself within a dream, stood in the kieve. A wild, weird whistling sound spun around the bowl of rock, making it sing. There was a cry within it, almost a human cry, almost but not quite. It reminded her of a seagull, or a cat, making the strange call that reminds of a baby crying.

Isoldé stood, turning her head to catch up with the cry as it sang round the rock-bowl. With a final whistle it was gone, seemingly sucked up into the waterfall. Her ears were ringing with the silence now the sound was gone, even the roaring of the fall was out of her hearing spectrum, it made her dizzy. She turned back to the fall. There, on the rock arch where the water fell from the cauldron into the pool, were sat four women. They seemed to be of different colours. The oldest was all moss-browns and green. Next came a silvery-blue one, younger than the first, not old at all; as she sat on the arch she seemed to blend with the thin waterfall behind her. Next was a gold-green figure, like a young beech tree growing out of the rock. At the end, a figure coloured all the fires of autumn sat coiled on the arch. She crooked a finger to Isoldé.

'Come!' they all whispered to her.

Isoldé heard the call inside her head.

'I am coming,' she replied.

The women all seemed to smile.

The roar of the waterfall came back to Isoldé then. She stirred out of sleep, woke, sat up abruptly. It was daylight, just, with the old full moon hanging in the turquoise sky. The two lights, the sun and the moon in the sky together ... twilight. She got up softly and went out.

Hare Song

Isoldé crept out again early on Sunday morning. What was all this stuff, having to creep away without Mark first thing in the morning? She liked mornings in bed with her lover, why wasn't she getting any now? It's this damned song, she muttered in her head as she strode out down the path to the sea.

She got to the open cliffs and the waterfall and there was the hare again. Once more the hare came right up close, sniffed her, then it sat down beside the waterfall. Isoldé sat down beside her and the hare shifted again, Isoldé watched it happen. The hare's face changed shape, her eyes stopped bulging in the way that rabbits and hares eyes do and became human; her ears shrank, her paws began to turn into hands and her body became human.

The hare-girl smiled at Isoldé, then she realised she hadn't done her teeth and looked away, putting a paw-hand in front of her mouth. When she looked back the transformation was complete. 'I need my song,' she whispered.

Isoldé was speechless.

'Listen!' she said. Then her paw-hand reached up and touched Isoldé's right ear and suddenly the woman could hear a song-thread in the sound of the waterfall, an almost-tune. Isoldé tried really hard to concentrate and remember it and found she was watching the waterfall. It was as if she could see the actual drops of water. They looked like a bead-curtain. Isoldé pulled out her notebook and tried to draw it.

The hare-girl patted her hand chuckling and leapt up to run away up the path towards the sea, turning back into a hare as she ran to go rolling over the grass and bounding over the rocks out of sight.

Isoldé sat staring for a moment then shoved the book back in her pocket and headed for home.

'You know,' Mark said over his shoulder as he prepared the

coffee, 'I really like making love when I wake up in the morning
…' He turned, bringing the coffee pot to the table and pouring for
her.

'So do I,' she replied.

'Odd how we're not getting to do it,' he said, 'seeing as how
we both like it …?'

Isoldé sipped at the coffee, then made a face at him. 'I can't
help it,' she growled. 'It's them! Otherworld, Gideon, whoever,
and this morning it was the hare-girl. They keep calling to me as
soon as I wake up,' she paused, 'well before actually, in a dream.
And I have to go. Do you understand at all?' She put her hand
over Mark's, willing him to smile.

His fingers gripped hers. 'Yes,' he grinned lopsidedly, 'unfortunately … or perhaps fortunately … I do. They do call. Up to
now, for me, it's always been about music.'

'This was about music …' Isoldé fumbled in her pocket and
brought out the notebook. 'The hare-girl spoke to me, told me she
wanted her song. Then she touched my ear and I could hear it in
the sound of the waterfall. And I could see, really see, each actual
drop of water in the fall so I drew them.' She pushed the pad over
to him, open at her scribble-drawing of the fall.

He stared at the lines; they did seem to imitate the pattern of
a waterfall. Then an idea struck him, he turned the page on its
side.

'Yes!' Isoldé cried, 'you've got it!'

They could both see rough scratches in the paper, five lines,
with the marks of the water-beads Isoldé had drawn on them.

'It's a musical stave!' he was grinning incredulously at her.

'It is so,' she agreed. 'It was the hare-girl. She traced her claws
across the paper and showed me. I was writing music without
even knowing it. She giggled at me then. It was like we were
sisters, or best friends, I felt so close to her. Then she ran off. I
watched and, as she ran, she turned back into a hare again,
leaping and dancing up the cliff. I sat on for a while, watching the

water patterns then I came home … to breakfast?' she ended with a hopeful query, the early work had left her hungry.

'Boiled eggs.' Mark got up and began to do them while Isoldé made toast.

Later Mark sat at the piano and slowly began to play the simple tune. It worked. It was a beginning.

'But I can't write it,' he told Isoldé.

'Neither can I,' she replied. 'It must be him. Only Tristan can write it. I think this is just encouragement.' She paused, looking at him, brow slightly furrowed and eyes worried. 'I have to live here, with you …'

'I know.' He was smiling. 'I want you too, so much.'

5. Caergollo

Darshan & Isoldé

Darshan waited for Isoldé to return. He knew she would, this time, but for how much longer? He was surprised to find himself wishing for her return quite so fervently. He had deliberately stayed late in the shop, stocktaking and accounts he told the staff. Hilary had eyed him as she left, a sly smile creeping over her face. It seemed they knew better than he about how it was for him with Isoldé.

So far, she'd told him practically nothing about her visits, just a short 'Great weekend!' and the subject would be dropped, she would ask him about work, about setting up a new project, new CD, whatever, but nothing about herself or her time in Cornwall. This time, Darshan wanted to learn more. She was different, ever since Mark had done the Imbolc concert.

She arrived late, after nine, looking flushed and tired, yet exultant. He saw her through the plate glass of the window. She waved. He got up from the desk and went over to let her in before she got her key out. Her face showed surprise, and then delight.

He could scent the sex on her. She was like a vixen. It was strange, when they'd been together in London she had never been like this. Passionate, yes, and full of generous love, but not wild as she appeared now. Perhaps the ancient Cornish earth was getting to her. It seemed Mark had touched off a spark he had never managed to light, had not even realised was there, he thought sourly.

'Hi … I didn't think you'd still be here.' She smiled up at him with the innocence of an animal.

'But I am,' he said, the irritation dying in spite of himself. 'Catching up with the stocktaking. I'm stiff and hungry.' He stretched, grinning down at her. 'How about you, after your drive?'

'I am so,' the Irish was back in her voice, she stretched like a cat.

'Shall I get a take-away?'

'Hey ... that would be good. I can't face cooking and I don't want to go out.'

'What d'you want? Indian or Thai?'

'You choose, it's your treat.'

'Thai then.' Darshan grabbed a coat and headed out.

Isoldé watched him for a moment then went up the stairs to her flat. It had always amused her that, despite his Hindu background, he loved Thai food. He had introduced her to it when they were first together and there were only a few Thai restaurants in London. She turned from the window back to the kitchen, found some candles, put mats on the low table in front of the sofa, got cutlery and set plates to warm in the oven. Going back to the window, she watched him return. She was still there, looking out across the square, when he came in.

'Like the old days ...' a half-smile slid across his face.

He took the bag into the kitchen. She came to help him serve up the meal.

Later, finished, satisfied and with Muddy Waters on the hi-fi, he got onto the subject that burned his heart. 'So ... you're with Mark?'

He was watching her. He'd never looked at her quite like that. She looked back at him, wary, cautious, hopeful, eyes half-hidden. 'I am so,' she said softly. 'I think I'm going to be with him for a very long time.'

Darshan stared at her, startled, nonplussed. He found his voice. 'After just a couple of weekends? A month?'

She turned to him, the warmth in her eyes was huge but it wasn't for him. 'Uh-huh ...' She nodded. 'I think I knew when I first saw him, when we first shook hands. Something happened. Electric.'

She was sitting curled up at the other end of the long sofa. It might have been miles away, he thought, rather than just a couple of feet. She looked complete, whole. Darshan looked at her, looked away, feeling as if he'd been hit in the stomach with a cricket bat. He'd known her for years, they'd been an item for several of them until it had faded and she'd moved out, moved on. They had enjoyed each other, remained friends. Memories poured over him, through him.

He got up and went over to the window, looked down into the Close. The cathedral clock began to toll midnight. He hadn't realised it was so late. He stood, staring out, seeing nothing, as she had been earlier when he came in.

He could feel her watching him. She hadn't thought about it like this, he realised. Neither had he. He was acting as though they were still in a relationship, as though she was leaving him. And they weren't, although he was sure she would be leaving to go live with Mark, he didn't think she'd want to continue at the bookshop once she was with him. It was years since they'd made love and never since she'd come down to Exeter. Part of him wanted to go to her, touch her, he could feel the chemistry. If he did, they would be in bed and, he realised, she would enjoy it as much as he would, but it would wreck their friendship. The temptation was nearly overwhelming.

What was going on? He had never felt her so electrified this way, not even when they were together. He could sense she was holding herself still, like an animal in hiding, trying to pull in her feelings as close as possible so he wouldn't notice, wouldn't see she was actually hot for him. He knew she was trying desperately to turn herself off and, after a few moments, he could sense she had succeeded, she was breathing normally again. She sat quiet, unmoving, waiting for him, detached at last.

He couldn't bear that. He felt a chill wash down his spine, but he pulled himself together and turned back to look at her at last. He perched on the window seat to keep a distance between them. 'OK,' he said softly, keeping the feelings out of his voice. 'I'm glad for you. I really am. But you've got to tell me about it, all of it.'

Isoldé curled back into the sofa, making herself small, her arms around her legs and her chin on her knees, not looking at him. Got to? What was this? He wasn't her parent.

'I don't know myself, yet,' she temporised. 'I know I love him. It's deep, deep inside, I can't explain ...' she paused. 'I have to go ... you know that, don't you?'

Darshan nodded.

'Do you understand ...?' she stopped again.

Darshan was silent. This was it. This was the end. He knew for certain there would never now be a future for himself and Isoldé. He felt as though the world had stopped. This quickly? How had he not seen it?

He went over to her, sat beside her, put one hand firmly over her wrist so she would look at him. She turned, not pulling away. They were silent for a moment, staring into each other's eyes. 'It's real, this time, isn't it?' Darshan said. 'Not like us. You know it in your bones.'

Isoldé looked away then turned back. 'Yes, I love Mark.'

She gently took his hand off her wrist and got up, went to the window, stood looking out, seeing the trees of Nectan's wood not the jumble of Exeter roofs. 'I have to leave you,' she said. 'I have to go live with him.'

'I know ... I'm sorry. You're good. And fun. I've enjoyed our brief partnership.'

'So've I.' Isoldé turned back to him. 'Darshan, I'm sorry ...' She meant it for everything she could see in his face, not just the splitting of the book-shop partnership, she hadn't realised how much he felt for her.

Somehow, Darshan twisted his face into a smile. 'Things happen. Life happens. I saw it when I first saw you and King together. You can't stop things like that. Go! Be happy. Paul will carry on for me. He has his own plans and they fit fine with me. You go do what makes your heart sing.'

Isoldé gasped softly, he'd said her mother's words. She wanted that, oh so much.

The Move

Isoldé flew down the stairs, arriving at the shop door just as Mark opened it. She was in his arms, kissing him, despite the fairly full shop. A ripple of applause came from customers and staff.

'You're here!' She peered over his shoulder at the big transit van drawn up outside. A traffic warden was bearing down on it, she dived out the door. 'It's me!' she called out. 'I'm moving. We won't be long, is that OK? There's some big stuff to come down.'

The warden looked at Isoldé. 'OK ... I'll be back in half an hour, how's that?'

Mark came out beside Isoldé. 'I think we can manage that,' he said.

'It'll be a good half hour,' the warden said kindly, turning round and taking herself off towards the High Street.

'I've got the boys organised and everything's packed.' Isoldé headed for the stairs again.

Jamie, Paul and Darshan were already heading down them armed with boxes. Mark flung the van doors open and began stacking. Isoldé came down with smaller stuff to pack in corners. It was all done within the time. To Isoldé it felt like a whirlwind of which she was part. In twenty minutes she was standing in the empty living room remembering seeing the flat for the first time.

'Don't worry about the birds, Zoldé, I've got a student who wants the flat and she'll be feeding them.' He stopped. They turned to face each other, both finding it hard to say anything. Darshan reached for her, she went into his arms, hugged him. He hugged her back.

'It's been good,' she said. 'I hope it was for you too.'

'I'll miss you ...' Darshan replied, 'and not just as a business partner.'

They stood looking into each other's eyes, so much unsaid. Isoldé could sense the cords that had brought them together wrenching free now, now that Darshan had given up all hopes of her at last. She squeezed his arms, then reached up to kiss him. Letting go, she hurried down the stairs, not saying another word.

Mark met her at the bottom.

'Let's go,' she said, slightly snuffly.

Mark gave her a quick squeeze and went to start the transit van. Jamie and Paul hugged her. She climbed into her own car and started up to follow Mark out of the Close. Glancing up, she saw Darshan leaning on the open window-ledge, he waved and there was a wistful smile on his face. She turned the car out into the Fore Street.

Mark led the way. Rather than go down the motorway they'd decided to take the scenic route, stop for a pub lunch and get home to Caergollo in the late afternoon. Isoldé followed Mark through Exeter and out onto Cowick Street and so under the A30, her usual route, and onto a B-road that led up onto the moor.

The road was quite good but winding and steep as it rose onto the moor; the transit van touched both hedges at times. She enjoyed the countryside and the little villages. A couple of miles out of Moretonhampstead Isoldé got her first real view of Dartmoor as they climbed a hill and the land opened up all around them. The wide skies gave her a whole new feel for the country; it was wild but differently wild to the Cornish Bodmin moor she was more used to. Mark slowed right down so she could look and after another mile he pulled in to a solitary pub, Isoldé pulled in beside him.

'You'll like this.'

A long bar opened in front of her, a couple sat at a table off to the left and a bright fire crackled in the stone hearth to the right, with a trestle table and bench right by the fire. Isoldé headed straight for it then stopped, turned and followed Mark over to the bar.

'Aha!' Mark's eye had spotted a favourite brew of his. 'Can you do a pint of Jail Ale,' he pointed at the pump, 'or shall we just stick to halves and some coffee?'

'Better be halves,' she replied, eyeing the chalked-up menu on the blackboard. 'And a local ham and pickle sandwich for me.'

'Make that two halves of Jail Ale please and two ham sandwiches.'

'Coming up,' the jolly, middle-aged woman behind the bar replied. 'You sit yourselves down and I'll bring the sandwiches over when we've made them.' She drew the beer into a couple of handled half-pint jugs and passed them to Mark.

He followed Isoldé over to the trestle by the fire. It had a window behind it so they could see the moor.

'Dartmoor is impressive,' she said after a first sip of beer. 'What's that huge circle over there?' She pointed out the window.

'That's Grimspound,' Mark announced, there was a note of pride in his voice. 'It's a late Bronze Age settlement. All those little circles you can see inside it are the twenty-four hut circles, the big one is the surrounding stone wall.'

'Cool ...' Isoldé breathed, staring at it over her half-pint. 'Why Grimspound? It makes me think of the Grimpen Mire in The Hound of the Baskervilles.'

Mark chuckled. 'Very likely! Although it was probably Fox Tor Mires that were Conan Doyle's inspiration but he may well have thought up the name from Grimspound. And, a bit further down the road, if you turn off to the left you'll come to Lower Merripit Farm where Seventh Wave Music hang out. I'm sure he used that name for the villain's house because he knew the place.'

'Oh I love their stuff. I'd forgotten they're on Dartmoor. Maybe, one day, I'll go make a drum with them.'

'Or a flute,' suggested Mark. 'You could, indeed you should, play that from the heart, not from written music.'

She smiled, touched his hand. 'Why Grimspound?'

'Grim is one of Odin's names,' Mark told her. 'A local vicar,

Richard Polwhele, gave it the name back in 1797. Later, in 1893, the Dartmoor Exploration Committee got a dig together. They recorded lots of stuff about Grimspound but they also, and very controversially, did a reconstruction of the site. Goodness knows how good that is!'

Isoldé rolled her eyes. 'Hmmm ... yup!' She laughed. 'You know, we should come up and walk up here. I love this ancient stuff and the tors themselves are incredible. And I want to visit Ted Hughes' stone. I've wanted to since Darshan told me about it when I first came down but I never got around to it.'

'We will, now you've got time. Round toits are notoriously hard to find but we have a good supply hidden away in the old mines in north Cornwall.' Mark chuckled.

'Oh! You!' She made to slap him, he pretended to duck. Her face changed, became serious. 'That's a point though, what am I going to do with myself now I don't have a job?'

'What do you want to do?' Mark put his hand out to just touch hers.

'I don't know. Except I have to find this song. And Tristan. The gods know how long that will take or how much of my time.'

'I'd guess you don't want to be a housewife ...?' Mark was grinning.

'The gods forbid!' Isoldé spluttered. 'And I'm no good at it. Mrs P will stay, won't she? We can afford her?'

'Oh yes. She'd hate to leave, it's part of her life. And yes, I'd be affording her anyway, you don't make any difference to that, not economically.' His fingers squeezed hers.

'I just don't know what I want to do, Mark. All my training is in writing, journalism, books. And music, and the CD sales side now from working with Darshan. Goodness knows if there's anyone wants me to do that in Caer Bottreaux. And, you know, I don't want to be commuting somewhere. I want to really be based in Caergollo, not have to go out to work each day.'

'Doesn't lots of journalism happen through the internet now?'

Mark was not one for reading, watching or listening to the news, he just about managed to catch up on a daily weather forecast and read the odd musicians' magazine, usually when he was flying somewhere.

Isoldé chuckled. 'Yes, it does, but I don't know if I want to go back to that again. Being with you, not having the news in my face every day, has changed me. The world still goes on even if I don't know all the details and the latest. The world of Caergollo, of the woodfolk, of the people in Caer Bottreaux has its own rhythm and events, I find that far more interesting than the idiot world politics.' She paused. 'I dunno! I'm sure something will turn up. My only thing is being financially independent.' She scowled. 'I know you've said it's OK but it sort of isn't, not to me! Makes me feel like a child again. I must earn a bit of money for myself.'

'I know, love.' Mark let go her hand as the sandwiches arrived. Isoldé earning her own money was the only fly in the ointment. It would work out, he felt that, but he'd no idea how.

'First of all, we've got to get ourselves set up together at home.' Mark was practical after eating his first sandwich. 'One step at a time. We're going to have a busy time getting you moved in.'

They finished up the sandwiches and gave the coffee a miss. Back on the road, Isoldé followed Mark across country again and the moors rolled along on either side. He turned right after a few miles and headed for Tavistock then headed down the lanes to cross the Tamar at Gunnislake. The transit van creaked its way down the steep hill, round the hairpin bend and squeezed over the bridge to climb up the other side. Isoldé followed trepidatiously although her car was much narrower than the van.

Coming up to Callington, Mark turned off again and headed out to Kit's Hill. He pulled up in the car park, Isoldé drew in beside him. They walked up to the trig point and stood looking out, sipping water and glad of the break. The wind blew her hair around her face, it felt good.

'It's the site of King Arthur's last battle, so they say,' Mark told her. 'We'll come up again soon so you can explore, see what you think.'

'Feels wild,' she said looking round and down at the surrounding land.

They went back to the vehicles and Mark led the way on the last lap of the journey across country towards Launceston and down the back ways to Caergollo. Isoldé was glad to get there, shut the gate finally behind her own car and follow the transit up to the front door. She'd enjoyed the journey but it was good to come to the end of it too.

Mrs P was waiting for them with four stalwart lads from the village, including Mark's gardener and his teenage son. They were already wrestling boxes out of the van by the time she'd put her own car away and brought in the bags and bits it contained. Isoldé took one look and decided not even to think about it for the time being. Mrs P steered her through to the kitchen, parked her at the table with a big mug of coffee and a plate of Cornish fairings.

'You let them all do their bit, you hear? There's no need for you to worrit yerself over what goes where. Nial and the boy will be here again tomorrow, they can fetch and carry for you so you get sorted. The main thing's to get that dratted van unloaded and back down the garage tonight. And Nial can see to that so Mark don't have to fret neither.'

Isoldé had to laugh. She wasn't used to having help, still, despite Exeter where there'd always been someone to lend a hand. It was all so unlike London where nobody was ever available except for a fee. Country folk, it seemed, did still help each other out, or most of them. She liked that.

New Home

The bay window looked out down the valley. The room was full of light and the sound of chuckling water from the stream, and the tree-echoing music of birdsong. This was the place for the desk, she thought but she also laughed softly … she might well spend a lot of her time looking out the window rather than working.

Was she going to write? Yes, she couldn't see herself without writing, but what the outcome of the writing would be she didn't know. She was trying to get herself not to look for outcomes but just to do things, do the writing, allow it to find its own way to wherever it was going. For Isoldé that was hard, she was used to knowing where she was going, even if the direction might change later.

"It's good to have an end to journey to, but it's the journey that matters in the end." Ursula LeGuin, Isoldé remembered, from "Left Hand of Darkness". Not a way of thinking she was used to but one she felt it would be good to get her head around. It fitted with what she was beginning to learn from the woodfolk, how they allowed the forces of nature to find their way and influence all forms of life. Not being in control but being part of a team. Hmmm! She was undoubtedly going to trip over her feet learning those lessons.

She and Mark had chosen a couple of interconnecting rooms on the west side of the house that would be Isoldé's own, her place to be, to work, her own space. Mark would knock before entering here. Nial and his son had set the bookcases and desk where she had indicated. The next room was her sitting room, it also contained a sofa bed so she could be completely independent if she ever wanted to be. The big double door that connected the two rooms also made it possible to open them up into one big space and, in any case, she didn't need to go out into the corridor to go from one to the other. It felt good. They'd redecorated so the walls were a primrose yellow and the ceilings blue, her own bright rugs glowed on the waxed wood floors. She went through to the sitting room to try the window-seat. Embar was already there, sat with all four feet precisely together and his fluffy black tail neatly coiled around the whole. He was looking out the window but glanced back over his shoulder to her as she entered.

'Hi,' she said softly. 'Looks good, don't you think?' Embar purred enthusiastically. Isoldé sat down beside him and rubbed his ears.

Outside, the wide lawns stretched down to the stream and up to the woods and the path leading up to the kieve. The grass was full of sunlight, a blackbird hunted worms and grubs, a robin carolled from the ash tree by the bridge. Peaceful.

Beside her, Embar couldn't help clicking his teeth in excitement, watching potential lunch strutting about on the lawn. 'Birds are *always* out of season,' Isoldé whispered to him. He stopped clicking and butted her hand. 'I know,' she chuckled. 'Butter wouldn't melt in your mouth!'

She'd enjoyed Darshan's cats but Embar was something else. At Caergollo, she lived with him all the time rather than visiting as she had with Darshan. He had been Tristan's companion, familiar spirit, he adored Mark and it seemed he liked her a lot too, he certainly followed her about the house, twined round her legs, got under her feet and asked her to feed him. She would find herself talking with him, confiding in him, and she always felt better after doing so.

It would work out here, she knew it, even if she couldn't see how, couldn't see what she would be doing as gainful employment.

'Stop hurrying so!' she told herself, 'You've only just arrived here on a permanent basis, you still have savings in the bank, you don't need to ask Mark for pocket money for a while yet. Give yourself a break! And, you seem to have a job – even if it's not

Elen Sentier

gainful employment – in finding the song, and finding out what the hell is going on with Tristan. That's going to take some time and energy. Then you have to learn how things work out here in the real countryside.'

She'd fairly grasped that although Exeter was a lot more laid back than London it was still a city, a metropolis. This was "the sticks". You had to get in the car and drive five miles to the nearest post office, ten miles to the nearest bank and best part of fifteen to a supermarket, while Waitrose was a jaunt to Plymouth. It was deeper into the wilds than she'd ever lived before! It meant thinking and planning your shopping, menus, toiletries, everything. It also meant much more buying on the internet too. There wasn't a Body Shop that she knew of nearer than Plymouth. She didn't like Plymouth much so it would be buy on the net for soap, shampoo, creams and perfumes.

Did that mean more time for the things she wanted to do? An unknown factor as yet. She wanted to explore Caer Bottreaux, there might even be a job for her there although she wasn't holding her breath and, anyway, the local people would need to get used to her, accept her, before any openings on that front were going to come about.

A call up the stairs announced lunch. Embar leapt straight down, she followed, they went downstairs together.

'Settling in?' Mrs P asked as she served up a bowl of homemade leak and potato soup.

'The things are set out. I'm sort of getting used to them,' Isoldé replied. 'It's odd, not being at work. Probably be a while before I get used to that.'

'Ahhh, likely it will,' Mrs P agreed.

Mark came in, hooked a chair with his foot and accepted a bowl of soup. 'You done your rooms?'

'I have so.' Isoldé smiled at him. 'They're really nice. And Embar approves, he came and inspected, sat on my window seat. The view is wonderful, I could just look out there forever.' She chuckled. 'Don't know how much work I'm going to get done!'

'You will, once it starts. You're just getting settled.'

'What's your regular routine? I've never been here when you're working.'

'I have to practice every day. I do piano practice, keep up my repertoire on the music side. But I need to practice on an organ too. I use Tristan's for that, up at St Symphorium's on the cliffs at Forrabury, above Caer Bottreaux. You could come and listen if you like, you've not been there yet, it's quite amazing and the organ itself is painted.'

'And she could see the Stitches an' all,' Mrs P put in.

'So she could.'

'What are the stitches?'

'Aha! They're a mediaeval field system. The old strip system, still extant and used. The National Trust owns them now and rents the fields out to local people who farm them in the old ways. Want to come?'

'Sure do. And I love to hear you play.'

Mark coloured up. Mrs P snorted softly, hiding her grin behind a tea towel as she pulled apple pie out of the oven for pudding.

Tristan's Organ & the Moonpath

The church was high on the top of the cliff above Caer Bottreaux. St Symphorium's was an original, a seaman's church, hanging above the sea to which it prayed for mercy.

Entering the church itself, Isoldé was struck by the simplicity and beauty of the place. The altar was made of old planks from pew seats, fantastically carved. The organ, as Mark had said, was painted, all the pipes coloured and beautiful, twined with vines and fruit. Mark went straight to it and began warming up. She went slowly round the church, examining all the different strange carvings and inscriptions. There was a soft breathing then the organ began to hum softly. Mark began to play. Isoldé sat down to listen.

An hour later, Mark was done with practice. He shut the organ down, patted it, whispered something and came to where Isoldé sat.

'That was amazing,' she said. 'I used to go to hear the organists practice in Exeter, it was good. But this was so personal. And you don't mind me being here, listening?'

'As long as you don't mind me grumbling and swearing when I get it wrong, going over it again and again.' He grinned down at her.

'No, I don't mind.' She reached up, kissed him.

He kissed her back. They left the church, walked up the path towards the sea.

'Oh!' The exclamation burst out of Isoldé. There, falling away below the graveyard, were the long strip fields just burgeoning with the first shoots of corn.

'That's The Stitches,' Mark said softly.

'They're amazing. I did all this in history at school, I never thought to see the real thing, and still working.'

They stood still, just looking. Mark, too, was always impressed by the old fields.

'When I was a kid,' Mark began, 'I used to come up here with Tristan when he did organ practice. Quite often I'd go ahead, down through the Stitches to the Lady's Window.'

Isoldé followed where he pointed. A stark finger of stone, like a tooth with a hole in it, clung to the very edge of the cliff below them.

'Can we go there now?' she asked.

'I hoped you'd want to.'

Mark took her arm, walked her down through the strip fields and out to the stone tooth. She'd been right, it did cling to the rock. She walked up to it slowly. Three stone steps rose out of the grass and led up to the hole in the tooth, it was a big hole, a person could step through it but where would you go? She peered through. It was right at the edge of the cliff, going nowhere. She stood staring down.

Mark came up beside her. 'It's called the Lady's Window because it's said that's where the Lady, the goddess of the land looks through to the human world and, sometimes, humans can look through into Otherworld. And it's where the moonpath comes down to meet with this world at the full of the moon each month.'

She looked at him, questioning. Mark pulled her down beside him. They sat looking out to sea.

After a moment, Isoldé pointed out to the horizon. 'What's that? Is it a front coming?'

'That's the Lost Land,' Mark said softly, 'not a front. You watch, it never moves.'

'Is it always there? Is it a real island?'

'Sort of. When it's there, it never moves. It's a magic land, it comes and goes as it wills.'

'Is it where the Faer Folk live?'

'It is. One of their places. You can only go there when the moon stretches a pathway out across the sea from our land to theirs. The moonpath.'

'What's the moonpath?' Isoldé asked.

'You've stood at the edge of the sea at full moon?'

She nodded.

'So you've seen the silver road the moon lays down over the waves?'

Isoldé nodded again. 'Like the road to Fair Elfland in Thomas the Rhymer?'

'That's right.'

'And the Lost Land is Elfland?'

'The old Cornish stories call it Lyonesse, or the Isles of the Blest. In Brittany they call it Ys. The story is that the land was swallowed up by the sea. Some stories call it West-Over-the-Sea. Round here it's known as the Isle of the Dead.'

'Some of those are in the Arthurian legend.'

'That's right. We're right at one of the centres of Arthurian legend here, you know that. Remember when we went up to Tintagel?'

'It was your namesake's castle too,' Isoldé reminded him. 'I feel like I'm living in a legend,' she whispered.

'Maybe we are.' Mark stood up, reached down a hand to help her up. 'When I used to come here with Tristan we'd often race down the cliff path into the village and get fish-n-chips. You want to do that too?'

'Won't Mrs P be upset if we don't eat her dinner?'

'I told her I was going to take you into the village, we might end up at the Nap and not to bother with dinner. That's partly why she gave us a big lunch with pudding.' He rolled his eyes. 'She doesn't trust me to feed you up well.'

'Ha! Forethought and planning on both your parts! C'mon then, where's this path?'

They arrived, helter-skelter, on the harbour quay, laughing and out of breath, Isoldé was just ahead by inches. She turned to him. 'I won! I won!'

Mark crouched into a wrestler's stance, Isoldé matched him,

they squared up to each other. 'Fight you! Fight you!' she shouted

'I'm betting on the little lady,' a voice reached them from one of the boats moored at the quay.

Mark stood up. 'What? You'd bet against me on this little squirt?'

Isoldé saw her chance and went for Mark who staggered back and crumpled on the stone.

'See? I were right.' A grizzled head stuck up over the side of the boat. 'You get him, my lover. An' you keep that up I'll be havin' you on me boat next season. You'm quite wily enough for a lobsterman.'

Mark leaped up and grabbed Isoldé in a bear hug. 'Fish-n-chips?' he asked her.

'Fish-n-chips,' she agreed.

'You mind he's buying!' The lobsterman called after them.

Mark waved. They swung off down the quay towards the town and the chippy.

Sat on the bridge, eating out of the paper, legs swinging over the swirling water of the Valency below, Isoldé had never felt like this before. There was something so deep there between them, in such a simple thing like sharing fish-n-chips, even more than making love. She'd never thought of it like that before. Always, like most people, she'd thought making love was the ultimate expression of love, now she had another sense to compare it with … sharing food. They'd shared experience over the afternoon too. And they were sharing a house, each of them looking at the other, watching, listening to the other. It was like dancing, being in step, moving to enhance the other's movement, moving so as not to be in the way, moving as one unit made of two whole parts.

Mark touched her elbow softly. 'Hey,' he said, 'you gonna eat that thing?'

She realised she had been sitting there while enlightenment rolled over her with a chip half way to her open mouth. She began to laugh, popped the chip and jumped down from the bridge. 'You were talking about a pint earlier …' She danced across the road, making for the hill up to the Nap. 'What about it?'

Mark stuffed the fish papers in the waste bin and followed her up the hill.

Ceilidh at the Nap

'Oh my! It'll be good tonight,' Mark exclaimed as they made their way up the crowded street to the pub entrance. 'I forgot Mrs P said there was going to be a sing! All the locals will be here and some visitors too. There's even someone from Exeter I think she said.'

They squeezed into the bar, it was absolutely jammed with people and Isoldé felt a bit scared. A tall, thin man climbed off his stool and offered it to Isoldé. He looked just like Aragorn in Lord of the Rings. She stared at him in half-recognition.

'I hope that you'll sing too,' he bowed to her, his smile captivating.

Mark clapped him on the shoulder, his eyes lighting up. 'Gideon!' he said. 'Didn't know you'd be here tonight.'

'Didn't know meself 'til I arrived.'

The man grinned at Mark then looked Isoldé up and down with speculative, hungry eyes. He looked quite different from when she'd seen him at the Kieve. She noticed he had the most perfect set of teeth she'd ever seen.

Mark bought a round and they took the drinks outside into the car park. There were no cars tonight, the whole place had been opened up for music and dancing. Torches flared from poles all around a wooden stage that held pride of place at the centre-back. Musicians were tuning up and the benches set all around the central dancing area were filling up with people, many of them dressed in bright costumes with wreaths of leaves and flowers in their hair.

'It'll be starting soon,' Mark told her as he slid onto the bench beside her. 'This do is the spring festival, for the equinox, and a sort of warm-up to the big Beltane festival at the end of April, with the Oss. Singers and musicians come from all over. I'm really glad you're here.'

'I am too,' Isoldé tucked her hand into his. 'Will they really want me to sing?'

'Yes, if you don't mind. Nobody will press you but they would like to hear you.'

'What have you been saying about me?' she demanded.

'Nothing! It's just that everyone knows about you and they want to know you better.'

'And how do they know I sing?'

Mark had the grace to colour up. 'Well ... I did sort of mention it,' he said ruefully.

'Ha!' She glared at him, then relented. 'OK, if I feel I can. But don't push me.'

'Good.' He hugged her.

A riotous drum-roll thundered, a quartet of cornettos split the air like shrieking trumpet ghosts and a man dressed all in green with leaves stitched into his hat and costume, his face painted like a bird of prey, leapt onto the stage with a feral yell.

'Now come on my lovers!' he cried. 'Tonight's the night we stop time and teeter at the balance. From tonight, we get more light than dark each day up until the standstill of midsummer.' He capered about, leaping at the cornetto players and banging his hands on the drums. 'Tonight's the change, the going from winter to spring, the coming of the Spring Maiden. Aha !!!' he yelled and leapt off the stage right in front of Isoldé.

'And here she be!'

He grabbed Isoldé's hands and pulled her up then he lifted her in his arms and put her on the stage, leapt up after her. 'And here she be!' he shouted again.

There was a great roar of approval from the crowd.

'All hail to the Spring Maid!' yelled hundreds of throats. 'All hail! All hail!'

Mark stood just below the stage smiling encouragement up at her but it had all taken Isoldé's breath away.

'Sing! Sing! Sing!' yelled the crowd.

The green man sank to his knees in front of Isoldé. There was complete hush.

'Will you sing for us, lady?' he asked her, taking her hands in his, all supplication. 'Will you sing for us? Will you sing for us, sing us from winter to spring?'

Isoldé's head was in turmoil but he was speaking to her heart. She found herself taking on the role he had given her. She looked down straight into the owl-eyes and realised this was Gideon in another of his guises.

'I will sing for you, Woodsman,' she said. 'I will sing for you. I will sing for all of you.'

Gideon let go her hands but continued to kneel at her feet. Isoldé took a couple of deep breaths and found, surprisingly, that her heart was beating steadily and her breathing was easy. She took a final breath and launched into song.

I will go as a wren in spring, Isoldé began the Fith Fath song.
With sorrow and sighing on silent wing.

Behind her, a fiddler struck up, picking up her tune, followed quickly by a flautist. The drums caught the rhythm and gave a heart-like beat under the tune.

And I will go in the Lady's name,
Aye til I be fetched hame.

Gideon took up the god's part, still on his knees. His voice was near as pure as Tristan's.

And we will follow as falcons grey,
And hunt thee cruelly for our prey.
And we will go in the Good God's name,
Aye to fetch thee hame again.

Isoldé began again, this time with the voice of summer.

I will go as a mouse in May
In fields by night and cellars by day.
And I will go in the Lady's name,
Aye, til I be fetched hame.

Gideon continued.

And we will follow as black tom cats
And hunt thee through the corn and vats.
And we will go in the Good God's name
Aye to fetch thee hame again.

Isoldé took up the voice of autumn.

I will go as an autumn hare
With sorrow and sighing and mickle care.
And I will go in the Lady's name
Aye, til I be fetched hame.

Gideon followed her.

We will follow as swift greyhounds,
And dog thy track by leaps and bounds.
And we will go in the Good God's name
Aye to fetch thee hame again.

Isoldé's voice dropped into the deep minor key of winter.

I will go as a winter trout,
With sorrow and sighing and mickle doubt.
And I will go in the Lady's name
Aye, till I be fetched hame.

Gideon took up the final verse.

And we will follow as otters swift
And snare thee fast ere thou canst shift.

Isoldé's voice joined his for the final lines of the song.

And we will go in the Good God's name,
Aye, til we be fetched hame.

Their voices spun out the last line of the song, Isoldé harmonising over Gideon. There was a moment's silence as they finished then the crowd went wild. Flowers showered onto the stage. The musicians did a fast gallop through the tune finishing on a huge drum-roll.

Isoldé was feted. Gideon lifted her up on his shoulder then leapt down into the crowd and carried her back to her seat on the edge of the dancing square. The crowd yelled and hooted and clapped the whole way.

'Thank you!' Gideon kissed her cheek.

The landlord of the Nap appeared with a jug of beer.

Mark wrapped her in his arms and hugged her. 'You're brilliant,' he whispered. 'That was just amazing, perfect, awesome!' He kissed her soundly. 'And no, before you ask! I didn't know it was going to happen. Nothing to do with me at all.'

'That's right,' Gideon said. 'He didn't. It was all our idea, wasn't it?' He looked at the landlord for corroboration.

'It surely was!' the landlord agreed. 'And a proper job you did of it too, young lady. Just like you was always one of us.' He poured their beer and went off.

'I think,' Isoldé was just getting her breath and her act back together. 'I think that was quite a compliment.'

'Uhuh.' Mark nodded. 'It was.'

'Proper job!' Gideon put on the local accent even more strongly. 'Proper job!'

Isoldé and Mark were left alone then for a little while as the musicians struck up again with a fast dance tune. Lots of folk came out into the open square, whirling and stamping feet. It was the wildest thing Isoldé had ever been too despite being on the folk scene all her life. There was a lot of unaccompanied singing as well as a couple with squeezeboxes, a girl with a fiddle, another with a set of Breton pipes, a tall, bald young man with a mandolin, lute and whistle, and an incredible person with a set of drums, including a djembe. He was tiny, a dwarf, about four foot tall. When he got behind the djembe you could hardly see him, just his hands flashing over the skins.

The locals were very good and Isoldé knew many of the songs and joined in. They even got her to sing Thomas the Rhymer. She did Tristan's version and it was well received. A man with a beautiful voice sang The Twa Magicians. It was a fine night, people wanted to dance. The fiddler girl and the one with the pipes plus the man with the mandolin set off with some fast tunes and people began to whirl. The couple with the squeezeboxes spelled them after a bit and then the dwarf came out with the djembe. Somebody set up a platform across a couple of barrels and he was off. Isoldé had had a couple of turns of jigs and reels with Mark but she could feel the drums getting into her blood.

Gideon came across.'D'you mind?' He smiled at Mark.

Mark grinned and shook his head. 'Go on Zoldé, you'll enjoy this,' he told her.

Gideon pulled her onto the floor and they were off. He was an amazing dancer, as he'd suggested when she met him at the kieve, and she found he gave her feet wings. The dwarf's hands flew so the djembe pounded, thudding through the air. Gideon lifted her, swung her round, a mix of jiving and salsa, things she'd never tried before. Eventually the pounding rhythms stopped and she fell into his arms. For a moment he held her, then ducked his head and pressed his mouth on hers, he tasted of blackberries and the sea. After a moment Isoldé struggled slightly and he let her go, laughing, looked into her eyes.

'I'll be seein' of thee,' he whispered as he steered her back to the edge of the dance floor where Mark stood watching. He handed her over with a bow.

'Well ... did you enjoy that?' Mark's eyes were laughing, open, he didn't seem at all jealous.

'Yes, I did!' Isoldé felt reassured. When Gideon kissed her she had, for a moment, completely forgotten about Mark. 'Very much. It's the best sing I've ever been to.'

The band struck up with a slow ballad. Mark stood up, took her hand.

'Come on, let's dance,' he said, catching her in his arms and pulling her close. 'Gideon is a far better dancer than I am but I can do this slow stuff real well,' he whispered into her hair. She snuggled against him as they smooched around the dance floor.

The evening finished after midnight with a Tintagel resident offering them a lift home.

They stood in the road waving the car goodbye then Mark opened Caergollo's gate and let them in. A rustle in the bushes greeted them and the hare came slowly out, sat up on her haunches and looked at them. As Mark watched, she began to shift. Now the fae figure of the hare-girl stood in front of them. She reached one paw-hand up to the sky where the moon hid behind a cloud.

'I need my song,' she said softly. 'Please find my song.'

6. Finding the Songs

Tristan's Hideaway

'How did you know to do the Fith Fath song?' Mark asked over breakfast the next morning.

'I've always known it …' Isoldé began tentatively. 'Uncle Brian taught it me, told me about it, the meaning of the seasons and the chase. And the "Good God" is what the name of the Dagda means in Gaelic. It's the eternal story of the Spring Maid bringing the seasons to life again after the darkness of winter.'

'That's right,' Mark was smiling. 'You know, I'd forgotten – if I ever knew – about the meaning of Dagda, the All-Father, the Good God.'

'The chase isn't about chauvinism,' Isoldé went on. 'It's the goddess testing her mate, her guardian, to see if he's up to it, capable of looking after her, fetching her home.'

'Yes, that's how we tell it here too. The old way.' He laughed. 'In the old ways the woman was in charge, led the way. The man is guardian, keeper. It's what the Morris men are too and their dancing comes out of old martial arts exercises, hidden from the overlords in dance.'

'I didn't know that,' Isoldé said, smiling at him. 'But it makes sense.' She began to collect the breakfast things and put them in the dishwasher. 'But … again … we were reminded last night that we have a job to do. You said Tristan's manuscripts are up in the cottage at the head of the waterfall … right?'

'Ye-ees …'

'And that you can't go there, not at the moment?'

'Yes …'

'So, I will.'

'OK …' Mark watched her, a frown on his face. He got up. 'I've got to practice.' He left the room, heading for the library and the piano.

Isoldé watched him go. He might not be jealous of Gideon but he was certainly crotchety this morning. He didn't like the idea of her going where he could not.

'I wanted a job,' Isoldé muttered to herself as she finished loading the dishwasher, 'and now I've got one. And he's cross because he can't help. Men!' she muttered. The job wasn't anything she'd ever dreamed of doing, it sounded like what Uncle Brian called a soul retrieval, but there was no way she either could, or wanted to, turn it down.

The sun was shining, time for a walk. She would go to the cottage. It was what had set Mark off, when he'd stomped out of the kitchen. She sighed. Relationships were like that. You had a fabulous evening and the next day things went all to pot. It was only temporary, she knew that. It would be good to keep out of the way for the time being. Yes, she would go to the cottage. She might see Gideon there too, a warm flush flowed through her as she said his name over in her mind. Hmmm! After last night, singing and dancing with him, that's how it was, was it?

She went to the hall and pulled on walking boots. Listening, she could hear Mark practising; he seemed to be all thumbs today and by the sound of the swearing quite crotchety. Isoldé was already learning to duck and run when her beloved had problems with himself. He was well used to sorting them without assistance, a very independent soul, as she was herself. That was good, they fitted that way and, she hoped, they wouldn't get in each other's way.

The birds were quiet, post-prandial snooze after breakfast, she thought. She walked in the soft, green-gold, dappled sunlight of spring and got to the bridge almost before she realised. Setting her walking stick, Tristan's stick, on the planks she knocked three times. A groan of moving wood, along with three loud plops in the water, answered her.

'I'll take that as a yes,' she said out loud.

She managed the path better this time, pacing herself well, and arrived at the top not too out of breath. She pushed her way through overhanging branches and found a gate. The latch creaked and the hinges groaned with all the vigour of a horror film as she pushed it open to find herself in a courtyard. Wisteria hung all round the walls along with the remains of last year's Old Man's Beard. The wisteria was in flower already, that was the Cornish climate for you. It was scenting up the courtyard along with bulbs and forget-me-nots crowded amongst the ragged paving. To her right, the white walls and black timbers of a cottage showed through the undergrowth. It was beautiful. A hideaway.

She made her way towards what must be a door hiding under a rickety wooden porch that was probably held up only by the wisteria itself. She lifted the latch … it opened. This door creaked suitably too and she had to shove quite firmly to get it open as it had swollen with lack of use and the winter rains.

It opened directly into a large living room, full of light. The wall opposite was all window, floor to ceiling, and looked as though it opened onto a balcony. She could hear the rushing of the water now and guessed the cottage must be right above the falls. Faded, antique furniture was scattered about the room, tables covered in paper, a crusted coffee mug beside a lovely velvet-covered nursing chair. White cotton drapes were pulled back and tied with sashes to the sides of the long window. Off to the left was a doorway that seemed to lead to a kitchen. Another closed door stood to the right. Isoldé picked her way across the faded Turkish carpet to the long window, tried a handle, after a couple of rattles it jerked open and she near fell onto the wooden balcony.

She pushed herself backwards. The rail at the edge looked ancient and she realised without seeing that she really was right over the waterfall, a potential seventy-five foot drop into a cold, boiling cauldron. Sliding one foot after the other she crept forward to the rail, peered over. Yes, there it was, half hidden in tree branches.

What a place! What a view! She stood gasping until, gradually, her heart quietened down. She could see why Tristan had made it his hideaway, a place to which he would disappear to work. It was gorgeous, she wanted it, wanted it to be her own hideaway too.

She turned back into the living room. Now she saw the upright piano against the side wall. Lifting the lid she read the name Bechstein, another beauty. She tried a few notes; it was still just about in tune despite having probably not been touched for ages. She felt the wood, it wasn't damp. Going over to a chair she tried the cover, the velvet wasn't damp either. Odd, especially as the place was hidden in a Cornish jungle at the top of a waterfall.

She went into the kitchen, an old Rayburn stood proud against one wall, a bucket of coal and a basket of logs beside it. There was a dusty copper kettle on the back-plate and a row of steel utensils hanging above. A Belfast sink was slung across a corner with a wooden plate rack above it containing a motley crew of assorted china of various ages, from Wedgewood to Woolworths. A broken china jug with a William Morris robin on it held a similar varied assortment of cutlery. Spiders had decorated the whole with webs, ancient and modern. It reminded Isoldé of Miss Haversham's wedding feast.

She crossed the living room to the closed door. With her hand on the handle she felt a slight hesitation to opening it. Silly! She turned the handle, this door opened easily. It was a bedroom. Not as big as the living room but still a fair size. A big canopied bed held centre-stage on the right wall, facing out through another huge French window onto an extension of the balcony over the fall. A pair of low, elegant, ash chests of drawers stood each side of the bed. An ash tallboy stood on the wall opposite her, a pair of basket chairs and a low table occupied the end of the room to her left. The tallboy door was open, a pair of white flannel trousers had half fallen out of it, a heavy cotton shirt lay at the end of the bed. It was just as though the owner had left it that morning.

Isoldé stood transfixed in the doorway, then she shook herself and went over to the bed, picked up the shirt. The rosemary scent came to her. Mark had told her Tristan used rosemary oil. There was a faint masculine smell too, his own scent. She held the shirt to her face, breathing deeply.

Still holding it, she went to the window, opened it and let herself out onto the balcony. This part of the cottage was built at a slight angle, she could see the fall better now, hear it too. Somehow, although it was loud, it wasn't the deafening, thundering, mind-numbing roar it had been down in the kieve, perhaps because she wasn't surrounded by a rock sounding-box but was above the fall.

She turned back into the bedroom, closed the French window, laid the shirt back on the bed and went out, closing the bedroom door behind her. That was somehow a very private place, she felt easier in the living room. Going back into the kitchen she tried a tap, it coughed and choked, spat some brown sludge at her, gave a couple more gurgles then settled to a good flow of clear water. She washed a glass, filled it with water and took it back into the living room, stood looking around. There was an order here despite the apparent chaos, definitely a touch of Tristan as she had come to know him through Mark's eyes. She went over and sat in the nursing chair. It felt as if it had been his main perch. Sitting there, she was surrounded by papers and music manuscripts. Carefully, she picked up a sheet and tried to read it. The notes staggered in her brain but there were words too, strung along the notes, they told of the sun rising in the morning, climbing up the sky to his zenith then rolling down again to fall into the sea. The verses told of the sun swimming through the dark waters to rise again out of the sea the next morning and do the whole thing over again.

This must be part of the Ellyon Cycle, Isoldé realised. Mark had not been able to come here since Tristan's death. And here they were, where Tristan had left them, scattered all over the floor and every place else. Isoldé wondered how many songs there were.

'Seven,' said a familiar voice from behind her. 'Plus the one he hadn't managed to write, the one for the Moon that you must help him find and write.'

Isoldé nearly fell off the chair as she swizzled round to face him. It was Gideon.

'Ah! Wha...! Arrgghh!' she mumbled. Then, getting control of her voice again she said, 'What the hell? Why d'you have to scare me like that?'

Gideon chuckled. 'I'm glad you found your way up here,' he said, not answering her. 'I've been trying to attract your attention since we met down there when you first came. You can be damnably focused at times, and on things I don't want you to be. You make life very difficult.'

'Tough!' Isoldé spat back.

'Now, don't pretend you weren't thinking of me when you decided to come for a walk,' he countered.

Isoldé flushed, decided to make out it was anger and began to turn on him, then she saw the funny side. 'Oh, damn you,' she said. 'Let's drop the sparring! Tell me about this place.'

'I think you've worked it out pretty well for yourself,' he said, crossing the room to sit in the armchair across from her. His eyes went to the glass of water. 'Oho! You've drunk the water here. That's good. It will help. You should be able to find Tristan if you keep taking the water.'

'How's that?'

'It comes from a sacred spring. All sorts of wisdom hides in sacred springs, you know. This one even has a salmon in it, or so they say. Tristan certainly thought so, he wrote one of the songs to the salmon of wisdom. There's a bell hides in the fall too, or is it the kieve itself, the cauldron pool?' Gideon mused, pretending to look puzzled.

Isoldé wasn't fooled, she could see the twinkle in his owl-eyes. 'He wrote you a song,' she said, on a sudden hunch.

Gideon sat up, faking startled. 'Now why ever would you think that?' he asked.

'Just a hunch.' Isoldé grinned at him. 'Call it intuition.'

'Mmm! I think I will at that,' he said, leaning forward to sniff at her. 'You and Mark are getting along well by the smell of it,' he said, grinning back.

That brought a real flush to Isoldé's face. She didn't know whether to be angry or just to let it go. Sexual innuendo was always difficult for her and here, with him, even worse, considering how he affected her. She got a slight rush of desire every time she thought of him.

'You always find a way of avoiding answering questions that are important to me,' she told him, trying to turn the subject back the way she wanted it to go.

'Yes, I do, don't I?' he replied.

Her face fell, she sighed resignedly.

'OK, yes, he did.' Gideon relented. 'It's the Trickster Song, you knew that already from our first meeting, when I quoted it to you. The original will be about here somewhere and it's rather good. Tristan had a fairly good grasp of me, understood a lot about me. That's unusual, for humans, but I've a feeling you may be that way too.'

He reached out and touched her hand. As she looked down it shifted into twigs, then into a wolf's paw. Before she could withdraw it was just a hand again. She gasped.

'It's just flesh,' he said softly. 'It can be any shape you choose. Like your genius, Einstein, said, matter is just compressed energy. And energy is always in constant movement. One can get stuck in thinking it always has to be only one shape. That's a very human illusion.'

Isoldé blinked. What? The philosophy of physics now? 'I thought we were talking about Tristan's songs,' she managed.

'So we are. Did you think they had nothing to do with physics or shapeshifting?'

That stopped Isoldé in her tracks. 'I think I need to go at this very slowly, one step at a time,' she said. 'And there's so much I want to ask you. This place. Tristan's songs. What you want of me. After last night ...'

Gideon chuckled again. 'You're right there,' he replied. 'I certainly had a hand in getting you to be the Spring Maid. It gave you a feel of what we are, your relationship with us.'

'Can we talk about that? What does it all mean? What am I to do? How does it help?'

Gideon blinked, again feigning startlement at the barrage of questions from her. She wasn't taken in.

'You will be the Lady's representative in the land, Mark is your guardian. That means you learn to hear the land, listen to it, ask it what it needs. That's what the shaman does, walks between worlds and brings back goodies to share with her people. Mark's got to do more of that too, as a musician. Like Tristan, he gives out the goods through his playing. Yours will likely be more practical work.'

Gideon got up and went over to the window. Isoldé's eyes followed him; she saw that the sun was drawing down the sky, twilight coming on. Where had the day gone? It felt to her as though it was just after breakfast still.

'You'd better head off for home now, the path is dangerous in the dark until it knows you well.' He paused, turned to look at her. 'Dangerous in all sorts of ways. Go on now. I'll come with you as far as the bridge. You'll be all right after that.'

A chill settled round Isoldé's shoulders as he spoke. She put the sheet music down just where she had found it and went to the door. Gideon closed it behind them and led her back through the gate, down through the tunnel and down the steep path. At the bridge he stepped out onto the planks and stamped his foot three times.

'Let her pass!' It was a command. 'I say this. Let her pass. Let none try to trip or trick her on pain of my displeasure. Let her pass.'

There was a grumbling, rumbling noise and a little vortex of water slithered noisily under the bridge as though someone had just emptied a bath into the stream.

Gideon reached back a hand and drew her up onto the bridge. He kissed each of her cheeks and between her eyes.

'Go now,' he said softly. 'Tell Mark. He will be pleased. But don't let him go up to the cottage, not yet. You need to be there alone for now, unless I'm there too. Come back to the cottage as soon as you can. Hurry home now, Isoldé, run!'

He gave her a little push and she found herself running, leaping, agile as a hare, going down the path at speed. In moments, so it seemed, she was running across the lawn and into Mark's arms. He swept her up and took her inside.

Finding the Songs

Isoldé brought lunch with her this time. And Embar. The black cat was very much at home in the cottage. He sniffed around at first and bottled once or twice – Isoldé thought it was where Gideon had been – then found himself what was obviously a cat-niche on one of Tristan's old cardigans on the chaise longue and curled up to watch her over his tail. The cardigan was covered in a felt of black fur, Embar must have been using it for years. She'd been a bit worried when he'd first insisted on coming up to the cottage with her, would it be too far for him? He'd soon disabused her mind of all that, bounding up the path, turning at corners to give an imperious yowl telling her to hurry up. When they got to the cottage he'd gone straight in through the cat-flap. She'd never even noticed there was one on her first visit. He was obviously well at home. A look through the cupboards in the kitchen had brought to light three elderly, but still good, unopened tins of cat food, it looked like he had regularly accompanied Tristan when he came up here.

Mark, however, had not wanted to come. He was delighted she'd found the manuscripts, all his crotchetiness of the previous morning gone. He had been to the cottage occasionally, as a child, exploring the woods and the kieve, but Tristan had soon made it clear the cottage was private, people came there only by invitation and that included Mark. He'd been up once since Tristan's death but had found the experience so emotional and freaky he'd quickly left, thinking to come back later, when time had put some cushioning between himself and his loss. Somehow, the time had never been right and now Isoldé had found it for herself. He was content with Gideon's prohibition. 'You go on,' he said. 'It's what they want you to do.'

So here she was, with a thermos of coffee, an avocado sandwich and an apple. And a massive curiosity.

Looking at the place, it really was a mess. At first glance, there seemed no rhyme nor reason to any of the piles of paper, however, Isoldé was sure there was a system to it somehow. The stories of Tristan from Mark and Mrs P told her he was methodical and organised even if it didn't look so.

'The "heap" system!' Isoldé chuckled to herself, using the old computer phrase. There really was such a system but she was sure Tristan hadn't known about it, he just worked in heaps.

Against the side wall was a long, elegant ash dining table. Something struck Isoldé then, most of the furniture, the good stuff anyway, was ash. Brow furrowed, she stirred her brain, "Nuin", that was the ogham name for the ash tree and it was the tree sacred to Gwydion, the master magician of all Britain. And that, for the gods' sake, was Gideon wasn't it? Ha! So this whole place was tied up with him, with the trickster, the shifter. And likely all the songs were too.

She pushed her hair back out of her eyes and went over to the table. There was rather less clutter on it than on the floor and chairs in the rest of the room. She cleared it of filthy crockery which she dumped in the sink, filling it up with water. A day or two of soaking should release the china and cutlery from the encrusted food. Not to worry about that now, now was for looking for the songs. The piles of paper she laid carefully, just as they were, on the floor in front of the long window. There'd been cobweb-ridden J-cloths under the sink, she took a couple, shook them out and dampened them then wiped the table down. In the bathroom that led off the bedroom she found towels and dried the wood. OK, here was a work surface some eight foot long by two and a half wide, she ought to be able to make some order of things on there.

The nursing chair had obviously been Tristan's favourite perch. Apart from another old cardigan hung over its back it had no other adornments, unlike the rest of the seats which, apart from Embar's nest, were all covered with papers. The piano had more papers on its closed top, but nothing hiding on the rack inside. Although the stool was overflowing with yet more stuff it was all old and much of it not Tristan's but other music he must have loved, including classical stuff.

She sat down in the nursing chair and took up the pile of paper beside it. Might as well begin here as anywhere, probably this was where Tristan had been working last.

The pile was a very motley heap of notes, receipts, scraps of paper with the odd line written on them and then, at last, a piece of music. This one was just music, Isoldé sighed, it really might as well have been in Greek as far as she was concerned. She took it over to the piano, opened the lid and perched on the stool. She knew which note was middle C but had to count her way up and down from there. Sharps were to the right of the white key, weren't they? And flats to the left? That was as good as it got for her. Slowly she managed to pick out the tune. It was subtle, haunting, reminding her of water flowing. There were no words, so far, to help her. She took it back to the ash table and set it to one side, went back to the nursing chair. She didn't immediately get back to work but sat thinking.

Not being able to read music had never worried her because her ear was so good, along with her ability to pick up a tune from a single hearing. Lazy! She had a good ear and that hadn't encouraged her to struggle with a discipline she found ultra-boring. However, Mark would be able to read it, and play it.

The sheet music was the only definite goody in this pile so she decided to find a home for the rest of the stuff for the time being until they could decide if any of the bills and receipts and lists needed keeping. Some of them went back to the late eighties she saw incredulously from the dates. Did Tristan have squirrel genes? She got up to look for a box to keep all this stuff in, found one in the corner cupboard in the kitchen beside a vacuum cleaner that really should have been in the Victoria & Albert museum. Perhaps Tristan had given the place a clean once a year for some feast day or other, definitely not more often.

The ash table now held the three sets of music and a small pile of scraps that looked like potential words for songs, some seemed related and others were very indeterminate. Isoldé took up a pile from by the window and went again to sit in the nursing chair to go through it. She felt she was getting something of a method to the work now, a feel for Tristan. There were more scraps with words on them in this pile, along with a half sheet of music. This one had a few words under the notes, the same as on the scraps of paper, so Isoldé felt confident she was on the right track.

After a couple more piles Embar got up and climbed to paw her lap. He was definitely asking for a drink and a snack for himself. Isoldé found a couple of clean dishes, put some cat food in one and water in the other, put them down for him. He wolfed the food down then took a long drink. She took her thermos and sandwich out onto the balcony and curled into one of the basket chairs. Embar followed her out and sat on the low table. Together they contemplated the rushing water.

She now had seven piles on the ash table, five pieces of music along with scraps of words and two heaps of notes. Gideon had said there were seven songs written and done, so she had pretty well got those. Then there was the one that Tristan hadn't yet written, had left this earth before he'd done, the Moon Song. That was the one she must find Tristan for. From the look of what she'd found she had five songs and two more potentials, bits and pieces, but not the manuscripts as yet.

What a mess, she thought, and why? Why hadn't he got it all together and sorted? Especially as he knew he was going to die, to go to Otherworld and leave his sickly body behind. That was odd, inexplicable. It seemed unlike the man she remembered, and the man Mark knew. Disorderly he might be but he had been thorough as far as she could tell from Mark and Mrs P. Not the sort of person to leave all in a state and just bugger off, leaving the mess for others to clear up. She finished the coffee and packed her stuff back into her knapsack, went back to the living room and the work.

Clouds came up the valley later in the afternoon; a patter of rain against the long window soon became a torrent in one of the sudden spring downpours that Cornwall enjoys. Glancing at her phone Isoldé saw it was already half-past three. Where had the time gone? And, surprisingly, there was a signal on the phone. She tried calling Mark, he picked up immediately.

'Everything OK?' His voice was slightly anxious.

'Yes, we're fine. It's raining here, where are you?'

'In Tintagel. I went to the post. The contract for the European tour arrived and I thought I'd get it straight back. They want me to do a recording as well.' There was a pleased note in his voice now.

'That's great,'' she responded.

'It does mean I'll be gone a bit longer though,' he added tentatively.

'Very long?'

'Maybe another week.'

'But that's OK, isn't it? It's good they want to record you.'

'It's just … we've only just got together and I have to go off and leave you.'

Isoldé chuckled. 'We always knew how it would be, didn't we? You have a career to run. I don't want it stopped or held up just because of me.'

'Mmm!' Mark almost purred. 'You're good for me! How're you doing though? Found anything?'

'Lots! But I need you to read the music, see if they are different or more bits of the same. And it's all mixed up with old bills and notes about shopping and laundry, for goodness sake! I'd never have believed he was so disorderly.'

'Strewth!' Mark exclaimed. 'That's not like he was here at all. Wonder what happened up there. It almost sounds like another person and yet, from your description of the place, it's really him.'

'And Embar's really at home here. There's even old tins of cat food in the cupboard. He had his lunch with me on the balcony before it began to rain, Embar I mean, not Tristan.'

'Are you OK? You want me to come up and get you? I can drive most of the way up and you could come back on the path to the old well at the end of the lane.'

'I've not finished yet. There's still light and I brought fuel for the tilly lamp, so I'm good.'

'OK, but if I don't see you come supper time I'll come and find you. You won't be able to reach me down at the house I expect, with the signal coming and going like it does down there.'

'OK. Hey ho! Hey ho! It's back to work I go ...'

She put the phone back in her pocket and lit the tilly lamp. The cloud and rain made it dark inside the cottage, she needed to see what she was doing. Working steadily through the piles she didn't notice the time at all, and Embar didn't remind her. He had resumed his watchman's post on the chaise longue and dozed intermittently in between bouts of watching her intently. When she next looked up it was black dark outside.

With a shock, she realised there was no way she could safely find her way back down to the house and she recalled Gideon's admonition that the path was not safe until it knew you. Mark had said something about a path to the well and the lane that led up to it from the road. She'd not been that way but she knew it from the map. Was there a map here? It was the sort of thing Tristan might well have had. She got up, muscles creaking a bit from the crouched position she'd been in for some time, and went over to the bookcase. Yes, there on the top shelf was a little pile of ordinance survey maps. Stretching, she could pull them down. They fell on her, scattering her with dust.

One was of the local area though very old, from the fifties by the date on it, but the lane wouldn't have changed, it had been there forever, like the well. She took it over to the ash table and spread it out. There was Caergollo and the path leading up to the kieve. Here was the cottage, clearly marked and, over to the side, about half a mile away, was the well, in a grove with a standing stone marked. The metalled track led up to it from the road and there was a footpath marked between the cottage and the well.

'Do you know this path?' she asked Embar.

He stood up, arched, stretched and came over to jump on the table, putting his nose down onto the map just where the cottage was. Isoldé blinked. She hadn't thought about it at all, had just spoken to the cat as she would to Mark or another person. And the cat had responded, apparently understanding just what she'd said. He sat down now and looked her in the eye. She looked back. Hmm! It seemed he did understand. If she told Mickey or any of the others at the paper they would say she was off her head. But she knew she wasn't. Was this part of learning to know the land and its creatures?

Still holding her eyes with his own brilliant green ones, Embar nodded slowly, once.

There was a chair beside the table. Isoldé was glad of it as her legs wobbled and she sat down heavily in it. 'Oh ye gods! What have I got into?' she muttered, more to herself than to the cat. Embar leaned towards her, gently butted her hand then licked her fingers. 'Oh ye gods …' Isoldé muttered again.

Getting a grip on herself, she looked at the cat. 'I suppose we'd better head for that path, get to the well and down the lane back to the house. Looks like it's a couple of miles,' she said.

Embar chirruped softly in his throat.

'At least it's stopped raining,' she said, glancing at the blackness on the other side of the glass. The cottage felt strange now, in the dark, now she'd come out of the work-space she'd been in while she was going through the papers. The ash table held seven separate piles now and the junk-box was near full of the odds and sodderies that had all been mixed in with the work.

Part of Isoldé didn't want to go outside. It felt like another world out there. She could sense things moving, not all of them physical, she was certain. There were strange sounds sometimes, just on the edge of hearing. Suddenly a something flashed past the long window. Isoldé let out a strangled squeak and half leapt out of the chair. Embar put a paw on her hand. She sat down again. He began to purr.

'Oh hell's bells and buckets of blood,' she muttered. Embar carried on purring.

She got the phone out of her pocket. There was still a signal, she tried calling Mark. The phone told her his phone was either switched off or out of range. 'Damn and blast!'

She sat still for another moment. Either she was going to spend the night here in the cottage or she was going to find the path, the well and the lane and get herself home. Very likely Mark was on his way up the lane right now to fetch her. She was being ridiculous.

She pulled her jacket on, donned the knapsack, picked up the tilly lamp and followed Embar to the front door.

Outside, the night closed in on her. It was warmer than she'd thought, sticky almost, clammy. The trees dripped on her. In moments she was quite wet despite that it had stopped raining. The lamp showed her the ground a few feet ahead, she tried to orient herself but Embar was already leading her in what looked like the right direction. She followed.

Leaves dripped on her, on the map, on Embar's fur sparkling in the lamplight ahead of her. It looked as if the path was used by animals but taller, human traffic had probably been scarce since Tristan's death. Half a mile shouldn't take very long she kept telling herself, but the footsteps continued, same on same, seemingly marching on the spot.

'Embar!' The cat stopped, turned to face her.

She could sense the question in his eyes, what was the matter? Then, suddenly he sensed what she had felt too, his fur bottled, he sprang in the air turning back the way they had been going.

Lights flickered amongst the moss-covered tree branches, bright shadows stretched between the lights. They looked like the outlines of Arthur Rackham's fairy folk. Both cat and woman stood stock still, staring. The lights danced around them, Isoldé could see them out of the corners of her eyes, in front the shadows danced more clearly, they were little people, slender, translucent, sharp noses, pointed ears, fine fair hair and expressions that were interested in the two newcomers to their woods, almost to the point of being predatory.

Embar stood guard in front of Isoldé although both cat and woman were well aware that the faer folk were all around them, behind as well as before. He backed carefully towards her until his huge fluffy tail touched her legs.

Isoldé relaxed, very visibly, allowing her shoulders to slump and her knees to buckle slightly. She turned her hands palm-outwards.

'We come in peace,' she whispered, feeling as if she was in some sci-if B movie and glad the faer folk didn't look in the least like the victims of Roswell.

The lights came down from the trees, coalescing into Rackham-like forms. On the edge of sight were some very strange ones, more on the lines of John Anster Fitzgerald's beasties, part animal, part human, part demon. One of these slid down a branch to land at her feet with a little bounce, making Embar flinch and emit a slight hiss. The cat checked himself immediately. The little demon stood looking up at Isoldé, he reached about to her knee.

She slowly squatted down, coming nearer to eye level with it. Him. He was rather obviously male. As she noticed so he grinned, seeing her looking at him. He pushed his hips forward and backwards at her, like Brad Pit in "Thelma & Louise". That made her grin too.

'Hello,' she said softly. 'What might I be able to do for you?'

The creature gave a crackly hissing noise, like a wet fire just getting going. She realised it was a chuckle.

'Ssss! It'ssssssssss what we can do forrrrrrrrrr you,' he replied.

'And what might that be?' she countered, then, remembering what Uncle Brian used to say. 'And what will it cost me?'

'Ssssss … ssssssssss …' the little creature chuckled again. 'Ssss–she thinks, she thinks!' He turned to his compatriots smiling all over his face.

There was a rumbling grumbling of agreement, amused, approving.

'You want the songs. The Trickster told you to find the songs.'

'That's right,' she replied.

'We want the songs. The Moon wants her song so she can direct all the songs so they synchronise … harmonise … match up.'

Inspiration smacked Isoldé in the mouth. 'You mean so we all sing from the same hymn sheet?'

More hissing and rumbling, grins spread across the sharp, pointy faces surrounding her.

'I sssss–said ssss–she'ssss ssss–sharp' hissed the little demon.

'So, I'm smart,' Isoldé tried to steer back to the point of their conversation. 'So what's your help going to cost me?'

'First I'll stew and then I'll bake, then I will the queen's child take …'

'No! I'll not play Rumplestiltskin with you,' Isoldé told him. 'There may be prices I will not pay, that are too high.'

There was a hush for a moment. Just the dripping of the leaves punctuating the silence.

'Tell me what the songs' purpose is, what they're for, what will happen if they're not found. And what will happen if the Moon doesn't have her song,' she said.

The strangest thing began to happen. The grass began to draw back from the surface of the soil revealing a flat area of level dirt. A silvery vertical line stretched up away from Isoldé. Two lines crossed it at a point making three angles of sixty degrees to each side of the vertical line.

'A ... a six-armed cross ...?' Isoldé asked tentatively.

'Yesssss ... watch ...'

More lines grew, threading themselves together into more six-armed crosses, becoming a web of silvery lines. The edges of the pattern reached out into the grass, disappearing under it. The demon looked at the pattern then looked pointedly at Isoldé.

'I get it ... I think ...' Isoldé said softly. 'This is the web of life, yes? Like the ley lines. Like the wyrd. It connects everything to everything.'

'And the Moon ...?' There were no hisses from the demon this time.

Isoldé was silent for a moment. She thought of how the moon governed and presided over the tides in the sea, the flow in a woman's body and many other rhythms under her direction.

The little demon watched her face, nodding slowly. 'That's the sort of thing,' he said, again without the hisses. 'We need her to direct the flow. She enchants us. She sings us into life.'

Isoldé sat back on her heels, staring off into nothing. 'And I must find the song that enchants.'

'Yes ... please,' the demon replied.

'You know where it is?'

'In a manner of speaking.'

'In Tristan's mind ...' Inspiration struck Isoldé again.

'And you must tap that mind to find it.'

'Just how do I go about doing that?'

'We can show you.'

'And that brings us back to the price again,' Isoldé said, a slightly sour note in her voice.

The demon sighed, shrugged. 'It's complicated,' he began. 'We don't know what the price is either. If Tristan had just gone on and finished the job the price would have been his life. He was quite willing to pay that. Too willing, in fact. He jumped ahead of time. That's what screwed everything up.'

'Ha!' Isoldé snorted softly. 'Is it likely to cost me my life?'

Again there was a hush. 'We don't know that either,' he answered her.

'So, I go into this without knowing what I'm doing nor what it will cost me. Or Mark.'

'That's about it,' the demon agreed.

'But you'll all help me?'

'We will.'

There was a soft rumbling of agreement from all the faer.

Isoldé began to try thinking then realised what a complete waste of time that was. She had no parameters to work with, no idea, just a gut feeling that this was what she had to do. She took a deep breath. 'OK,' she said. 'I'm in.'

The little demon reached out a long, silvery claw and took her hand in his. He pulled her fingers to his lips and kissed them. She felt a fire course through her hand, quickly filling her whole body.

'Come,' the demon said. 'It's time to get you home.'

Return with Mark

Mark was sat on the step of the truck at the far edge of the grove when Isoldé got there. He got up as she appeared, holding out his arms to her. She went to him. They stood holding each other without saying anything for several minutes.

'What happened?' he began, pulling a little away from her so he could look at her.

'I met the faer,' she told him.

Mark's eyes opened wide, he watched her. 'Tell me,' he said.

'At home,' she answered, taking his hand and pulling him back to the truck. They climbed in, Embar jumping into Isoldé's lap. Mark drove fast down the bumpy, twisty track. Isoldé hung onto the cat in case he fell. At home, they tumbled into the kitchen, Isoldé collapsing into a carver-chair with Embar sat on the table beside her.

Mark had left soup on the back of the stove before he came to get her. He brought the pot, got dishes, spoons and bread, made coffee. Isoldé was as glad of the respite as she had been of the journey home. Her mind was all at sea, she needed time to pull herself together. Mark served the soup, poured coffee, put a shot of brandy into both mugs, put out a plate of cat-food for Embar then sat down opposite her.

'Now, tell me?' he said.

'I found lots of the notes and manuscripts,' she began. 'Tristan's working stuff for the Ellyon Cycle. Got them sorted. It was absorbing work, I never noticed the time, nor the change in the weather, not till it happened.'

'That's when you called me?'

She nodded. 'I carried on working, sorting, then I suddenly realised it was pitch dark outside, that it must be late. It was weird ...' She stirred her soup ate a couple of mouthfuls. 'I thought I saw something fly by outside. Yes, I know, it could have been an owl, there are lots up in the woods, but there was a frisson. Embar was with me, it felt like he was watching out for me. Anyway, I realised I must pack up and try to get home. I tried phoning you but your phone had no signal, left a message on the landline but I supposed you were already on your way up here. It felt strange, I didn't want to go outside, prevaricated a bit, got a map, looked up the path and eventually got my ass outside and started off to meet you. All the time I was hoping you'd suddenly appear and everything would be all right. Didn't happen like that though.' She stopped again, ate some more soup then got back to her story.

'I sensed something. Then Embar got it too, bottled up and sprang round to face up the path, staying close to me like he was trying to guard me. At first it just looked like flickering lights then the lights took on form, like the folk Arthur Rackham drew, all pointy faces and ears, thin, spindly, beautiful. Except they felt like predators. Embar backed right up against me, I could feel a sort of growly purr vibrating against my legs, like he didn't want to threaten them but did want to tell them he'd stand up for me.' Isoldé stroked the cat who still sat on the table beside her. He purred softly back. 'Well, I tried to relax. There were a lot of them, all hanging in the trees around us, far too many to fight and, anyway, I didn't know that fighting was what they wanted either.' She began to giggle, Mark raised an eyebrow. 'I came out with the standard line in every old sci-fi-movie, "We come in peace", well the second standard line I suppose. The first is "Take me to your leader" isn't it?'

Mark managed a chuckle himself. 'Yeah, I suppose it is.' He stroked her fingers across the table.

'At least they looked beautiful, not like those Roswell things from the X-Files. Nor Richard Dadd's faer folk, they always seem a bit weird too. Whatever, one of them slid down a branch and landed at our feet. It was so fast we both jumped and Embar hissed but shut himself up again. Some of them now looked more like Fitzgerald's half beast-creatures, especially the one that had landed in front of us. I crouched down to get nearer eye-level with him and ... do you know ... the little thing got all sexy with me, wriggled his hips at me! It's funny now, looking back, but I couldn't raise a laugh at the time. I did manage a grin though, it sort of broke the ice. We got talking. I asked what I might be able to do for him.'

Mark broke in. 'You didn't promise anything?'

'No, I do know better than that.' She smiled at him, squeezed his fingers back. 'The little creature's voice was sort of like a soggy firework, hissing and spitting, rolling his "rrs". He told me he, they, could help me. I asked what that would cost. We had a bit of argy-bargy then, he was sort of testing me, anyway, we got through that and began to talk sense. They want Tristan's songs, like Gideon said, particularly the Moon Song.'

Isoldé crumbled bread into the last of her soup and ate it.

'Do you know anything about ley lines, energy lines?' she asked Mark.

'A bit. Tristan knew a lot, taught me to dowse. I can find them and I know where there's lines hereabouts.'

'Well, the little demon-creature drew me a pattern.' She dipped her finger in her coffee and drew the pattern in wet lines on the beech table. Mark got the pad and pen from beside the kitchen phone.

'Thanks.' She smiled at him, redrew the pattern, the six-armed cross.

'Yes,' said Mark. 'I know that. Not exactly ley lines, it's the pattern of everything or so Tristan always said.'

'That's what the demon said too. He said each of the seven songs that I've found go with each of the points of the star, with Earth, this world, Middle Earth at the centre. Then the Moon's Song goes over all, directing the whole.'

Mark thought about that. 'Yes, that makes sense, I think. Like the moon directs the tides and the water within our bodies and the flow of sap in the plants. And loads more things too according to Tristan. He was well up in all that. I know a bit but it wasn't my thing. Has it got to become that now, for both of us?'

'I don't know that we need masses of knowledge,' Isoldé said. 'Just to know how important the moon is may be enough. What they need, so the demon impressed on me, is the song. That will do the trick without having to have all the academic-style knowledge.'

'Mmm … I sometimes wonder if we humans aren't natural head-cases,' Mark said with a chuckle. 'We spend lifetimes talking *about* things and very little time actually doing them.'

'You've got a point,' Isoldé agreed. 'You and I seem to be more doers than talkers, at least in this field. Darshan was a bit of a head-case, always off on courses, could talk the hind legs of whole beach-fulls of donkeys on spiritual stuff, probably bore for England on the subject. I think that's why I never got into it while I was with him. Uncle Brian was a doer too. I used to love going out with him, even though my teenage self got a bit rebellious later, wanting boys and "reality" rather than magic.'

'I expect we all mostly go through that,' Mark said.

'Anyway,' Isoldé got back to the story, 'the demon impressed on me that they, we, everything, needs this song. He said "We need her to direct the flow. She enchants us. She sings us into life," meaning the moon. And that I must find the song that enchants. In fact he even said "please" at that point.'

'Does he know where it is?' Mark asked.

'So he says …'

'But what …?'

'It's in Tristan's mind and I must tap that mind to find it.

'And just how do we go about doing that?'

'Precisely what I asked,' Isoldé said. 'The demon said he could show me and that brought us back to the price again.'

'So … what is the price?' Mark still had hold of her fingers, his own tightened on them.

'It seems the demon doesn't know.'

'Oh shit!' Mark exploded, letting go of her hand. 'What's the use of a bloody demon if he doesn't have all the answers?'

That made Isoldé laugh. 'I think, you know, that while they're different from us, can do things we can't, it's like Gideon said, they can't do everything nor are they omniscient.'

'Damn it! Yeah! I know you're right. I'd just rather it was like in the simplistic Victorian stories, where they do know everything and sort it all out for us.'

'No you don't, you don't really want that. You're not that dumb!'

They sat across the table from each other grinning. She took both his hands and held them. 'There's us,' she said. 'Us! We're together. We have each other. They can't take that away.'

Mark's face clouded over. 'Can't they …?' he said.

That put a chill up Isoldé's spine. Was that the price? She wouldn't pay it. No! She wouldn't pay that. She got a grip on herself again, shook Mark's hands, bringing him back to her.

'They told me they'd show me how to get the song,' she went on, remembering now what the demon had said when she'd asked about Mark. She was not going to tell Mark that. And she'd renege on the deal if it looked likely they'd lose each other. She sent a mental message to the demon telling him just that. There was a spike of pain in her head, she flinched.

'What?' Mark gripped her hands again.

'Nothing. Just a bit of headache. Not surprising really.' She blinked, picked up the coffee cup, drank. 'And they promised to help me. I agreed to look for the song,' she told him. 'Then they led me to the grove and there you were, thank the gods. Had you just arrived?'

'I'd been there a while,' he said. 'I tried to come to you but I couldn't get out of the grove. Every time I tried I seemed to come against some invisible barrier, my foot wouldn't move, not until I turned back to the truck. I gave up. It felt as though something was happening out there, with you, but I couldn't get to you.

Something didn't want me to. Makes sense now. It was scary though, I was sat in the truck trying to work out what to do if you didn't come soon. I've no idea how long that went on for. Time seemed to go weird. It felt like it was only a few moments, and the clock in the truck didn't move much, but it also felt like ages.'

'What time did you set out to get me, do you know?'

'Around eight-thirty, just gone, I think.'

The both looked at the kitchen clock, it said a quarter to eleven.

'I think it was ages,' Isoldé said softly.

'They can freak with time …' Mark added.

'Looks like it …'

Isoldé was still very shook up after her meeting with the fairy folk. Telling Mark about it had been both harder and easier than she'd expected. Getting going at all had been difficult but it got better as she got going.

'I've seen them too, just occasionally,' Mark told her, 'especially in the grove up there. It's special, you saw it, there's a spring there, by the carved stone.'

Isoldé remembered. It was a little grove of ancient, twisted Scots pine trees, all low and bent with the wind that swept across the top of the hill direct from the Atlantic. They coiled and spiralled round to not even ten feet high in most cases, very different from the tall slender stems and wide flat branches she was used to. In the dark, at first, she hadn't even been certain they were trees, they looked more like Tolkien's Ents. Perhaps they were, she thought now. After last night, anything was possible. Now, here, in the daylight she wasn't sure she wanted anything to be possible, had a strong feeling she just wanted to crawl back inside a nice, small box and not know about anything that wasn't completely mundane. She sighed. Fat chance of that!

The carved stone was strange, a picture of it came into her

mind's eye, sticking up out of the ground, looking like a flattened head, as she'd followed the faer folk down the path. Last night it had looked almost alive in the crazy half-light that came wherever the faer folk were, it was like they emitted the light themselves. There'd been no moonlight, heavy cloud filled the skies like a thick, black blanket, enclosing her in the world of the faer, claustrophobic almost.

'Like a bubble in space-time,' Mark had said when she told him how it had felt on the way back to Caergollo in the truck. Then, when they'd finally looked at the clock in the kitchen, it seemed that was true.

It had frightened her when he'd told her he couldn't come any further, had had to stay there waiting for her.

'I couldn't go any further, I just had to stay there and wait,' he told her again over breakfast. 'I tried, tried to get to the cottage, but my feet wouldn't move, not beyond the edge of the grove. It was like they were paralysed, I couldn't even feel them. The waiting was terrible, not knowing.'

'Didn't you know?' Isoldé asked him suddenly.

Mark stared at her for a moment, frowned. 'Yes ...' he said. 'I suppose I did.' He thought about it some more. 'It was like I knew you were there, coming. And, yes, I did, I knew the faer were with you. It made sense of me not being able to get to you. But part of me didn't want it to be that, didn't want to know. I wanted it to be ordinary, just a wet night and you not knowing the way home.'

Isoldé took his hand. 'It's hard, isn't it?' she said. 'This living in two worlds at once. I'm not used to it either, despite Uncle Brian. I used to go with him, learn the stuff, but it was all still a sort of game to me.'

'This is no game,' Mark said.

'No ... it's not.'

Little Folk

Slowly, Isoldé followed the traffic out of Exeter airport and back round the A38 and A30 to the Moretonhampstead road. Mark would be in the hotel on the Isle St Louis as soon as she would be home to Caergollo, like as not. She wanted to go home over the moors, the way they had gone when she moved to Caergollo. Mark could call her on the mobile and, as long as she was on the tops, there'd be a signal.

'This is a treat for me,' he told her as they waited for his flight to be called. 'Until now I've been on my own, driven myself up here, left the car in the car park and sat reading music magazines over a coffee all on my tod.'

They were sat together in the café enjoying coffee and Danish pastries. It felt odd to her, him going away and, at the same time, quite normal. She knew his calendar, the dates of performances, recordings, his life was mapped out for the coming two years. Oh, there was plenty of time at home too, and she wanted to go with him on some of the trips, in fact there was a semi-journalistic idea growing on the back burner of her mind about a series of articles on musicians, their travelling and international performances. She'd tried it out on Mickey over the phone, he'd thought it could be a runner, said he'd try it out on the features editor at the paper. But there was no way, as yet, she could be gone from Caergollo, with all that was happening between worlds there she wanted to get back. It would be the slow way, over the moors, today. Something there was calling to her.

'I don't think I'll stop off at the bookshop,' she told Mark as they finished their coffee. 'Doesn't feel right.'

'What about Darshan?'

'I'll text him, he'll understand. Say I need to get on, get home.'

'Do you?' Mark eyed her, knowing her, he could tell there was something else.

Isoldé rolled her eyes and quirked a smile. 'You know me too darned well!' She squeezed his fingers. 'I think … I think I need to go back over Dartmoor, not decided yet. I'll see where the car takes me. You can call me on the mobile when you get there.'

Mark sighed. 'You'll love the hotel … when I ever get you there. I think it's on the site of the building Bacon lived in when he studied in mediaeval Paris.'

Isoldé laughed. 'You're an incurable romantic!' she told him. 'And you're throwing out lures!' He knew Bacon was another of her favourites.

'I am so,' he laughed back, mimicking her accent.

'I'll come, I will, but not now. There's too much going on and my head feels full of mush about most anything else except that wretched song.'

'Yeah, I know. I have to keep focused myself to do my concert and recording work. The song presses down on both of us.'

'Good job you know what goes down then,' Isoldé snorted. 'I've got to learn my part.'

'And everything that goes with it,' Mark added.

Once through Moretonhampstead she was out on the moor and it opened up around her. She took the left at the top of the hill and went slowly along the narrow road until she saw the lay-by. She drove straight into it, the car jouncing a bit on a pothole, and stopped the car. Up to her left was the path Mark had told her about that led up to Grimspound. She locked the car and set off up the three steps and onto the track beside the brook that chuckled its way downhill.

Coming to the wall she looked up at the remains of the huge Bronze Age village. Mark had said the gate was up on the higher side, she could see it from down here and set off widdershins to go to it.

It was impressive, even after four thousand years. She tapped her foot on the stone, asking permission to enter. It felt like an invisible barrier disappeared. She set out across the wide expanse. Scattered remains of round houses were to either side but she was heading for the best kept ruin, Mark said it was impressive and well worth sitting in to get a feel. As she got close she saw he was right. The entrance was curved, probably to keep out the wind, again she tapped the stone for permission to enter, felt a welcome and went in to stand looking round. A chill wind whipped up around her, catching her scarf and blowing it tight over her face. She felt herself begin to choke, grabbed at the silk and pulled it away, then she really did have a fright. All around her were a mass of little folk, again just like out of the Victorian fairy painters minds, and similar to the demon's friends up above Caergollo. These didn't look overly friendly and stood around her in a circle, grinning, their little sharp-pointed teeth shining white in the dull light under the purple cloud that had suddenly come up. Isoldé froze to the spot.

'Tis 'er,' the oldest and ugliest of the little gnomes told his compatriots.

'So tis ... so tis,' several agreed.

'And she don't know what she be doing.'

There were chuckles all round at this.

'Is we be goin' to tell 'er then, maister?' said one of the others.

'Do y' think we should then, folk?' the old one asked generally.

'I thinks we should,' one old dame with very long teeth said as she reached out to touch the cloth of Isoldé's trousers.

That unfroze Isoldé, she let out a scream and jumped back, only to find herself amongst even more of the gnomish creatures. They hung onto her trousers, her coat, a couple of the little ones swung from her sleeves, one climbed to her shoulders and sat pulling her hair.

Trying to get control of her breath, Isoldé managed, 'What? What is it? What do you want?'

Suddenly there was silence. The little folk dropped off her to stand again in a circle round her. She turned to find Gideon standing right behind her.

'Oh! Thank the gods! It's you,' she exclaimed, collapsing in a heap on his shoulder and sobbing dryly into the male-scented leather of his jerkin. He stroked her hair, mumbled comforting noises into it.

'That's very sweet of you, I am of course delighted to have you in my arms again, but whatever would Mark say?' he said, chuckling but still holding her close as the shaking gradually stopped and she pulled away. He led her to a stone seat at the side of the roundhouse and sat down beside her, holding her hand.

The circle of gnomes stood motionless around them.

'Now,' he said. 'Just what do you think you're doing up here?'

'I thought they were going to eat me!' she muttered. 'Like in the stories. All those sharp, pointy little teeth …' His teasing was beginning to effect a feeling of security that had gone right out the window when she'd been alone with the gnomes.

'No, they won't do that,' Gideon assured her. 'They know who you are, what you're needed for. But they are wicked teasers and they know the stories about them, play up to them. And you've met their relatives before.'

'I have? When?'

'When you've done the stirrings with Nial.'

'What? Biodynamics? You're joking! He never described them like that. He said we were doing it to get the soil going for the spring plantings.'

'So you are but the energy you're working with is still the gnomes, the earth elementals. That's what this lot are too but these are wilder, they live on the moor, not in your garden, and they don't have the same contact with people. These are used to daft tourists, or even dafter new-agers prancing about in the circles pretending to be pagans.'

Isoldé frowned at Gideon then. 'They make you cross, the new-agers?'

Gideon sighed. 'Yes, the idiot ones do. They get a load of stuff from some fancy foreign shaman out to make his name, and, or, a buck, and try to plant it here. They never bother to listen to the land herself. They don't understand the culture of this land, my land, your land. They don't feel they have a tradition so they must import someone else's. It doesn't fit and it upsets the land.'

Isoldé looked at him, put a hand on his. 'It really does make you cross, doesn't it?'

'Yes.' He sighed again.

'I can understand … I think,' she told him. 'And … I think that's part of why you need the Moon Song, isn't it? To try to re-enliven the traditions of here, of Britain?'

Gideon's face broke into a smile. 'Yes, it is. It's about the energy lines, the threads that connect everything. Moonpaths, if you like, as the moon does activate them.'

'Are they not always active? I've read Watkins now, and Paul Devereaux. It seemed to me that the lines, once they're … there? Seen? Known about, like people recognise the alignments of the hills and things …?' She hunted for words, Gideon nodded. 'Once they're there, they're always there.'

'Yes they are. But they work differently at different times of the month, partly because of the seasonal energies but very much because of the moon. What have you learned from Nial?'

'What? Gardening you mean?'

Gideon nodded.

'Well …' Isoldé frowned. 'I've done a couple of stirrings with him and Mark. On root days he said, for the soil and the roots. That's when he told me about Steiner calling the earth elementals gnomes.'

Gideon nodded again.

'He said, Nial said, it would help the michoriza get going with the roots, help them get the nourishment out of the soil and improve the soil, get the worms going and all the beneficial bugs and stuff.'

Gideon chuckled. 'Nial's a good teacher,' he said. 'Doesn't fart about with a load of cosmic crap, just gets you going with the basics in the physical. But what did he say about the moon?'

'Oh … well …' Isoldé tried to remember. 'It's about the moon being a lens,' she said, her brow clearing as it came back to her. 'The moon's a lens for the energy of each of the constellations as she passes in front of them during the month.' She found she'd got it, was in the element again. 'The moon spends two or three days in front of each of the twelve constellations each month, so she goes through them all, through the astrology, every month. Each time she's in front of a constellation she sort of magnifies and focuses its energy onto the Earth and that helps the relevant bit of the plant.'

'Mmmm! Not bad.' Gideon encouraged her. 'Tell me about how it helps each bit of the plant.'

Isoldé thought for a moment. 'The constellations are in four types, earth, water, air and fire,' she said. 'Like Scorpio's water, Leo's fire, Gemini's air, Taurus is earth. And there's a part of the plant for each of them.'

Gideon helped her out. 'Earth is roots, water is leaves, air is flowers and fire is fruit.'

Isoldé nodded. 'Yes. So … so if you want to help spuds you work on an earth day, like when the moon's in front of Taurus or Virgo or Capricorn. Cabbages are leaves so you wait til the moon's in front of Pisces, Cancer or Scorpio. For cauliflowers, and all garden flowers, you work when she's focusing Aquarius, Gemini or Libra and for fruits you do it when she's in front of Aries, Leo and Sagittarius.'

'Pretty good.' Gideon had his arm round her still and gave her a squeeze. 'Now … how do you think all that works with the energy lines?'

Isoldé frowned again, sat up straighter. 'Oooo …! It must work the same way, but …' She turned to him, 'I don't know what the effect would be.'

'Why would it work the same way?'

'Well the moon's shining onto all the Earth, isn't she? All the time. Well all the time while the Earth's not between her and the sun.'

'Hmm! Good! You do know a bit about how things work.'

'Of course I do! The moon reflects the sun, of course. That's how she gives us light. As she goes round the Earth there's a few days, a week, where the Earth is between her and the sun so no sunlight can fall on her. That's the dark of the moon.'

Gideon was nodding, grinning. Isoldé frowned, he was pushing her to take the idea further. She sat back thinking.

'This is getting complicated, I think I need to go home and draw and write and make patterns for myself, so I can get a handle on it. Is that OK? Do I need to be here for anything else? And why did I get the urge to come this way anyway,' she added.

'Gnomes calling to you,' Gideon said. 'I don't suppose you'll forget this encounter.'

'I certainly won't! It was very scary.'

She looked around. The gnomes were still there, sat down now against the stone walls, teeth neatly folded inside their jaws, looking like little bundles of rags or leaves. If she'd not known, had not seen them earlier, she would have thought they were just bits and pieces blown in from the moor. That made her think again, how often was it truly the woodfolk when people thought it was just rubbish and dead plants lying about? And what happened to the woodfolk if they got swept up and put in the rubbish cart? She thought about the compactors the local council used and shuddered. 'O! Ye gods ...!' she muttered.

One of the gnomes, the old dame, unfolded herself and waddled across to Isoldé, took her hand. 'Thank y', lady,' she said, the huge brown eyes regarded Isoldé. 'Thank y' for thinking of us.'

'I'm so sorry,' Isoldé said, squeezing the small claw-like hand in hers very gently. 'Can you not get out of the way?'

'Mostly we does,' the dame told her. 'But the old folk may be sleepin', hard to waken when we's old and off in the dream-world. And the youngsters don't always know the dangers, though we tries to tell 'em. They gets scooped up and put in the crusher. Tis an evil death.'

Isoldé shuddered. 'I'm so sorry. We're an ignorant species, we humans, and think we know best all too often. I'm sorry we kill your folk, and not even know we do it. That feels terrible.'

'So it is, lady, so it is. Maybe, if you can bring the Moon Song home, things can begin to change. Humans may begin to see there's so much more in the world than they've known for many a long year now.'

'We used to know,' Isoldé said.

'Yes, humans used to know. Tis time you knew again, well time.'

'So it is,' Isoldé agreed. 'I promise you I'll do all I can to get the song, begin the change.'

'We thanks you, lady.'

Gideon escorted her back down the track to the car. The gnomes came with them, the old dame holding Isoldé's hand. As they arrived at the layby the little dame let go her hand and waddled off. Unlocking the car she saw they had hidden themselves as rags and leaves again.

A breeze came up suddenly, whipping round the lay-by, gathering up the leaves and twigs and other bits and pieces, sweeping them off back up the hill towards the Bronze Age ruins. In moments the place was new-swept and clear. Isoldé stared.

'The winds help,' Gideon said softly. 'And the little ones live under the hills.'

'I'm glad,' Isoldé said. 'It's well time I got myself off home, I've got a lot of work to do.'

7. Moon Paths

... Keeping time,
Keeping the rhythm in their dancing
As in their living in the seasons
TS Eliot: East Coker

Embar purred steadily as Isoldé's pen scribed drawings and diagrams and scrawled words all over the A3 sheet of paper on her desk. This was more complicated than she'd thought when sitting with Gideon in Grimspound. One idea led to another, led to another, there seemed no end to it. Were all these moon paths? She knew they were, even if she didn't know how or why or much else about them. Mark had reminded her how many, many rhythms the moon was involved in. Although she'd known, taken it in at a mental level, this doing, drawing, scribing, working one thing from another was making a different, deeper, sort of sense to her.

If the moon affected everything, and she was certain it did, then she was beginning to see why the song was so important. And she was also wondering what had possessed Tristan to bugger off out of his life before he'd finished. What the hell had got into the man? He knew all this, must have done, or most of it. Nial had been his gardener, been working at Caergollo for over twenty years. He'd brought biodynamics to Tristan and, in return, Tristan had given him the pagan outlook. Nial thought it a very fair exchange, said it had broadened his outlook no end from how he'd been when he arrived, fresh from college in Sussex.

'I was all took up with it then, when I first came here,' Nial had told Isoldé as they sat in the old shed and he showed her the preparations. 'Thought I knew it all, thought Steiner had known it all. Then I got to working here, with Tristan, and found how much more there was, all hidden deep within the land and the people.'

'Didn't Steiner know that?' Isoldé asked him.

'Oh, I don't know. Steiner knew his own land, I dare say. And there's those lovely stories of him on the train, meeting this ... this person. I think that was one of the wyzards he met, one of the old wise ones. They say he got a lot of the old lore from him but you don't hear about that too much at Emerson College. They tend to stick to telling you it all came from Steiner.'

'Didn't it?'

'Well ... I think it's more complex than that,' Nial had said thoughtfully. 'I think Steiner put it all together, got an "aha!" moment probably, but I don't think it was all suddenly invented then. Probably the putting together of the preps, like cow shit in cow horns and such, came about then, maybe. But once you start to get into the old shamanic practices you see how alike all that stuff is to many of them. That's what Tristan showed me. It certainly changed my outlook on paganism. Before then I'd been rather heavily Christian. Many Steiner folks are really, down inside. It's because Steiner's supposed to have had some revelation or other of the Christian variety. And, anyway, the Christian box is small enough not to scare most folk.'

'I know that one!' Isoldé had laughed back. 'Confession before you go to mass on Sunday every week, get absolved from all your wickedness, and then you can be wicked again for the whole week, knowing the slate'll be wiped clean again at your next confession. Makes killing and kneecapping and hating people who are different from you real easy.' Her voice had been bitter by the end.

'Aye, I guess it does. I was forgetting again where you come from. You always seem to be so much a part of us down here, even though you're a real newcomer.'

'An emmet?' Isoldé queried.

'Aye, that's so, that's the word for foreigners down here, below the Tamar. And I was one myself for many a year. But somehow you're not.'

'I don't want to be. I want to be part of this place. I've never felt so at home anywhere in all my life. Caergollo fits me like a glove.'

Now, sat here at her desk, Embar beside her, looking out over the grass to the woods, Isoldé knew it was true. She was part of this land.

She pulled herself back to the work in hand.

'The Moon reflects the sun,' she repeated to herself as she'd told Gideon up on Dartmoor. 'It's how she gives light. And as she goes round the Earth there's the week where the Earth is between her and the sun so no sunlight can fall on her ... the dark of the moon.' She paused, chewing the end of her pen. 'So there's the usual quarters of the moon to think about as well, even if they don't seem to mean so much in biodynamics.'

She drew a circle on the paper, divided it into four and shaded each quarter differently, one black for the dark of the moon, its opposite quarter she left un-shaded to show the full moon. The other two quarters she shaded with diagonal lines, right to left for the waxing quarter, left to right for the waning one. 'Four again ...' she told herself out loud. Embar chirruped encouragement.

Isoldé took a pencil then grabbed a rubber just in case. She began to write in the elements by the quarters. Earth she put against the dark of the moon, it felt right, like a womb-space under the earth where things could begin their growth, their shifting from a single cell into a complex being. And ... it was the Earth that caused, enabled, the Dark Moon? Without the eclipse there could be no womb?

Opposite, at the full of the moon, seemed to be the place of flowering, where everything pushed and burgeoned with beauty, like the month of June in a garden when everything flowered and seemed so perfect. That gave her another idea. Beside the dark she wrote "midwinter" and beside the full moon she wrote "midsummer". Yes, that made sense – then the waxing and waning quarters were like the equinoxes? Was that right? Embar butted her hand encouragingly.

'If that's so,' she told him, 'then the waxing quarter is about the first growing of the plant, the leaves coming up out of the soil. And the waning quarter is about the fruiting, the culmination of the plant where it does it's phoenix stuff of dying and giving birth at the same time.'

Embar purred loudly, stood up and shoved his nose in her face, licked her. She laughed. 'That good, eh? You think I'm getting it?' The cat sat down again, satisfied.

'Oh Embar, there's so much.' She sat back, pushing her hands through her hair, releasing the tension from her shoulders.

She certainly felt she had a handle on it now. The moon related to the plant kingdom very efficiently, keeping the rhythm of its cycles through the constellations as well as through her own monthly rhythm of birth and death, from the dark of the moon round to full and back to the dark again. And that monthly rhythm linked to the sun's annual one of solstices and equinoxes. And both worked with the growing seasons of the plants.

She picked up the pencil and doodled again around her circle of the moon's monthly cycle. Then she drew a stylised plant, giving it roots, leaves, flower and fruit all at once. Beside the roots she drew a dark moon; by the leaves she drew the waxing moon; at the flower she drew the full moon and by the fruit she drew the waning quarter. It made sense. Yes, she'd already done it one way round, from the moon's perspective. This was from the plant's perspective.

'And it works for animals too?' she asked Embar.

He gave a chirrup.

'I'll take that as a yes.' Isoldé got up. 'I need some coffee and a break. My head's awash.' She headed for the kitchen, Embar following.

Over coffee and a piece of Mrs P's ginger cake, Isoldé began to get a feel for why Tristan had copped out. It was huge, this whole thing about the moon and how she worked. How did you go about making that simple?

'Needs a bloody symphony, not a song!' Isoldé muttered as she rinsed her plate and cup, left them to dry on the draining board. 'And I need a walk. Coming?' she asked the cat.

IIe leaped down and followed her. They headed up the path to the cottage. Gideon had been trying to get her back up there for a while. OK, she thought, I'm coming.

At the Cottage

It was different at the cottage. During the times Isoldé had been there, as well as sorting Tristan's manuscripts, she had put her own stamp on the place, even she could feel it. The kitchen was now clean and tidy and there was more cat food in the cupboard along with tins of biscuits, coffee and a filter jug for herself. She'd dusted, even in the sacred bedroom, but she'd not put the shirt away nor altered any of his clothes. Opening the windows had given the place a fresher feel but had not taken his scent away from the rooms.

Entering now, Isoldé had ambivalent feelings towards Tristan. He was still a figure of awe to her, holding great attraction, her loins stirred every time she caught his scent, but she loved Mark. Her hormones gave her gyp when she was with Gideon too, he really brought out the lust in her but she'd never done anything about it nor wanted to. With Tristan she wasn't so certain. If she met him in the flesh it might well become a thing of the flesh.

The piles of paper were all still neatly stacked on the ash table, the seven songs, the manuscripts and the words, and a pile of fragments. She'd brought solicitor's tape with her and spent time tying each of the bundles neatly and labelling them. When that was done she brewed coffee, took a mug to the nursing chair along with a saucer of milk for Embar.

The cat finished his milk then stood staring over her shoulder back into the living room. He was so intent it was unnerving. Isoldé turned to see he was looking at a fine corner-cupboard hanging out of his reach by the door.

'What?' Isoldé asked him sharply.

Embar chirped softly.

'There's something there? You want me to go look?'

'Prrowww!'

Isoldé got up and went over to the cupboard. She stood staring at it then opened the door. There wasn't a lot in there but right on top of the pile on the lower shelf was a CD. There was no label but she was suddenly certain she knew what it was … he *had* recorded the songs after all. She took it. Her fingers tingled as she touched it. On the upper shelf was an ancient radio-cum-CD player, battery powered. She took that too.

'The batteries will be all dead and rusted,' she told the cat.

He butted her leg, purring.

She dusted off the ancient relic, it didn't look so bad once it was clean, and took it with her back to her coffee and the chair. Then she pushed the button to open the CD player, it worked. She put the CD in and pressed play.

The room was suddenly full of Tristan, his pure voice lilting through the space. She found herself sat still, sipping the coffee but at least half in Otherworld, listening.

The cycle began in the darkness of Lowerworld, womblike, full of memories and all the things people had ever done. How Tristan conveyed this sense with the simple words he used Isoldé had no idea but it got to her, straight through any surface levels of expectation or superciliousness.

The second song took her from the nadir to the zenith, to Upperworld, bright, sparking with life and colour and light, too bright to see clearly. It gave her the feeling of being prickled with light, and with ideas. The rhythm pounded out like a black-smith's forge.

The third song pulled her into the world she knew, into the woods. Tristan must have written this one in the kieve, magical, fairy but also intensely alive and real. It had a full-on feel of all the elements, the rocks, the water, the wind in the trees and the strange bright-soft light that always filled those woods.

The music changed. It was as if the first three songs were a set apart. Isoldé stopped the CD, grabbed paper and a pen, drew a vertical line and marked it with a circle at each end and one in the middle. She wrote Lowerworld, Upperworld and Middleworld beside each corresponding circle and rapidly jotted her feelings for each of the songs. They had to be about the vertical axis of the six-armed cross, the world-tree, but now, here in the cottage, listening to Tristan sing, she knew it in her bones.

Another thought struck her. She drew three circles and wrote the name Brighid above them. Then she added the name Ffraid beside Brighid. Brighid came from her own Gaelic Irish culture but down here, Mark had told her, in the Brythonic Cornish tradition, she was Ffraid. Isoldé put the word Brighid in brackets, honouring the goddess's name in the country where she was.

'Frayde, Brighid, is the goddess of the three faces,' Isoldé said aloud. 'Maiden, mother and crone. That's what Tristan is singing too.'

She was remembering some of the words of each song now and quickly drew herself a table with three columns … maiden, mother, crone; Upperworld, Middleworld, Lowerworld … and so on.

After a couple of minutes she had several sets of three words in her list. Frayde's jobs were smith, healer and poet; those words were in the songs. She put the first song on again, listened carefully. It spoke of wisdom, the cauldron of wisdom, of the poet who told that wisdom as stories so that none should forget it, and of the crone, the old wyzard, who had seen all things and held them in her heart, in her cauldron, so that all should remember. It told how she would give a drink from her cauldron to those who came and asked.

'Remember … Remember …' The words spun out, holding her in their long, subtle, minor notes. 'Re-member …'

Isoldé heard it in a different way this time.

'It's about putting things back together,' she muttered as the song faded. 'About putting the members, the limbs of a body, back together. About re-making the body, making whole.'

The second song began again, taking her attention. It told of a maiden dancing, a tower spinning, about climbing the branches of the tree to find yourself amongst the stars. The rhythm was like that of a blacksmith hammering iron in his forge … daa-da-da, daa-da-da … the blow of the hammer followed by the double judder as it bounced after each stroke. The song sang of newness, ideas unformed being forged, new stars birthing in the universe.

The third song sang of the mother who walked through the forest, sat amongst the ancient rocks, drank from the stream, listened to the wisdom of the birds and the beasts and the trees. The children followed at her heels, playing, growing, learning to know themselves and the world around them. The mother found a plant that sickened and gave healing energy to it, the same with a beast. The mother healed and nourished.

Yes, the first three songs were about the vertical axis, the three worlds. She let the CD continue into the fourth song.

Tristan sang first of the stones, the rocks in Rocky Valley, the bones of the Earth, of crystals and the sand on the beach in Bossinny Cove. Then he sang of the gnomish earth-folk tinkering with the soil, drawing together the threads of life, the fungi and the soil beasts to make a perfect ground to nourish the seeds and roots so the plants could grow and flower and fruit again. It was a mischievous song, full of laughter, with a strong rhythm that made your feet want to dance.

Isoldé was smiling, her fingers and feet tapping, by the end. 'Next time I see the gnomes I must dance with them,' she told Embar. He didn't move his nose from under his tail but his eyes smiled.

Tristan began the fifth song with a twisting, flowing melody on the harp. It seemed to be pushing its way up through darkness. Just as Isoldé was certain the twisting was going to make it his voice joined the harp in a soft cry. 'Water of Life,' he sang, 'Water of Life …' spinning out the wide vowel-sound in the last word. Isoldé found herself almost holding her breath. The song called to the ondines, the water-folk, told how they spun the clear water with the sunlight to make the leaves that feed the plant. She realised he was singing about photosynthesis and yet it was beautiful, not dry and scientific but like the fairy story of spinning gold out of straw. The song was a wild twisting melody, it reminded her of the way the water twisted down the fall outside in the Kieve, like the fall of a woman's long hair.

The sixth song blossomed immediately. Tristan sang of the scent of May blossom. The words hinted at its powers of life and death, of courtship and of the burgeoning summer being born. He sang of the sylphs, the air-folk, who guard and nourish the flowers, how they work with the bees to turn the pollen into the sweetness of honey. He sang how the sylphs shift into butterflies and Isoldé thought how Arthur Rackham had seen that too when he painted his faer folk. The song told how sylphs ask the help of the bees and butterflies to take the pollen from flower to flower, mixing the sexes, enabling the plants to birth fruit and seed.

The last song was fire. Isoldé didn't know how he did it but from the very first note she was on fire. The rhythm pulsed through her like her blood when she was dancing. It twined and spiralled through her body, up her spine, to explode in her head with a soundless flash of light. Tristan sang of the fire-folk, how they wove the strands of male and female energy together and bound them in the seed, a little bomb waiting to explode when the soil and rain and sunlight called. The song began fast as the seed was built, forged out of the life of the plant. Then it sank into darkness, only a soft pulse reminding that life was still there waiting for the call. It ended with an irresistible rhythm that got Isoldé on her feet and whirling round the room, singing along with Tristan, to end on a final high note that the singer held for an impossibly long time and then suddenly cut off.

As it finished Isoldé collapsed in a heap on the floor next to the cat. Embar sat up and stared down at her as if she'd gone nuts. She began to laugh as the word "nuts" and the idea of fruiting caught her.

'Oh Embar! I did go nuts, my darling cat,' she told him as he butted her nose with his. 'And nuts is what's meant to happen, you know, at the end of the cycle, when it all comes together in the seed, in the fruit that is the next generation.'

Embar stared at her. She knew he knew. She also knew he considered humans to be impossibly thick at times, like her realisation now of what the songs were about, but tolerated their slowness.

'We *will* do better, we truly will,' she said. 'But I see how Tristan's songs will help. Subtle stuff, subliminal almost, but that gets through to us humans you know, better than preaching, better than logic and science and all that "reality" stuff. We like stories and pictures and being fired up through the imagination. The songs do that.'

Embar gave a purry growl and coiled himself back into the old cardigan.

'But we still don't have the Moon's song ...' Isoldé said to the room in general.

Lady's Window

Isoldé stood in a place full of light and darkness. She was asleep, she knew it was a dream, but it was a very lucid one.

'I'm journeying,' she realised. 'This is what lucid dreams are about. I'm in Otherworld.'

Something silent and large, like the spirit of the place she was in, agreed with her. There were no words, just a knowing inside her, an undeniable rightness. She was journeying.

She turned slowly around. There was no definition in the place, dark colours swirled, sometimes she thought they were trees, at others it looked like curtains of water, then they cycled into slick sheets of rock, only to shift into shimmering air. She made up her mind.

'Hello …? Is anyone there?' she called out. 'I'm here … waiting. Will somebody please tell me where I am, what's going on?'

The light shuddered, held, began to solidify. She stood on the edge of a cliff, looking out at the endless ocean and the curve of the Earth through a window of rock. It was the Lady's Window.

Isoldé went cautiously towards the person-sized hole in the tall tooth of granite, standing up like a spike out of the edge of the cliff; she climbed up to peer through. As she did so the view changed, she was no longer looking out to sea but into a circular grove, like the grove with the head-stone at the end of the path from Tristan's cottage. Perched on the stone in the centre of the grove was Tristan himself, staring down at his feet.

Isoldé pulled back, afraid that he would see her. She could still see him through the window. His head came up as though he had noticed something, he looked about the grove.

'Isoldé? Is that you? Are you here?'

Her throat tightened, she couldn't answer.

'Isoldé …?'

Tristan stood up now, turned, looking all round. Isoldé backed further away from the stone. What was going on? Was she supposed to meet him here, now, in the dream?

'Watch!' the large presence inside her head told her.

She watched. Tristan stood looking around the grove then he shrugged and sat down again on the head-stone. She saw now that his harp stood at his feet. He picked it up, began to play, a tentative thing, just beginnings. He tried the tune several times but it obviously wasn't going right. He put the harp down on the ground again, sat looking disconsolate.

'Isoldé … if you can hear me … I need you. I can't do this without you. This song just won't come to me. It can only come through you.' He paused, waited, at first looking hopeful then a resigned expression came over his face again. 'Isoldé, if you can hear me, I need you but I can't come to you, not properly. Please come to me. If you come to the Lady's Window there'll be someone who will help you, you can come through the window. I'll be here. I know now, we have to make the song, the Moon Song, together.'

Isoldé woke with a start. She was in bed, in Caergollo, Embar curled into her side and just woken with her, his green eyes staring into hers.

'I dreamed …' she told him, 'of Tristan and the Lady's Window. Do you know why that is? Am I to go there?'

Embar chirruped, jumped off the bed and headed for the door, he ran down the stairs and made for the kitchen, Isoldé following. The grandfather clock in the hall said it was near six o'clock, rather than going back to bed she followed the cat into the kitchen and brewed some coffee, made toast. Embar sat on the kitchen table, watching.

Sat with him, munching toast, Isoldé said, 'I'm to go there?'

Embar put a paw very deliberately on her hand and purred loudly.

'You want to come?' she asked the cat.

Embar jumped down and stalked off to his usual sleeping

perch at the back of the Raeburn and curled up, turning his back on her.

'That,' Isoldé said, chuckling, 'is definitely a no!'

She went back upstairs, took a quick shower, pulled on jeans and sweater. It was spring but still parky of a morning and the wind was from the west, from the ocean. It would be fresh and breezy out on the cliffs.

Isoldé parked the truck half in the ditch at the end of the lane by Forrabury Church so any early morning traffic, like tractors and such, could get by. She climbed out and took the path up through the churchyard to the gate that led onto the rough moors of the headland and the Stitches. An ancient ruin of a bothy stood just to the left of the gate, a shepherd's hut perhaps, maybe even someone had lived there once. She climbed over the gate and went to look. There had been a loft, still was a bit of it left, with some fresh hay stacked up there and a new-looking ladder leaning by the wall. It was dry and sweet smelling inside, a metal hay rack on one wall with half an oak manger still useable below it. Someone still used the hut for food for the beasts but not to live in.

A soft, low whicker startled Isoldé. She jumped and turned. A small black pony stood in the doorway, tossing her head and watching Isoldé.

'Phew! You made me jump!' Isoldé told her, turning to fully face the pony, the hairs on the back of her neck all standing up. She fumbled in her pocket to see if she had anything the mare might like. This was not just an ordinary pony, she was sure it was one of the woodfolk, shifted into pony-shape.

The pony stamped a foot and tossed her head again then stood looking at Isoldé, barring the way out of the bothy. Isoldé stood looking back at the pony, wondering what she should do.

'I need to go there,' Isoldé said after a moment, pointing towards the headland and remembering the troll-bridge and how you should always ask permission to cross. 'I have to go to the Lady's Window. May I pass?'

The mare snorted and tossed her head again, then backed out of the doorway. Isoldé followed her. Outside, the mare stood beside the path leading down to the cliff edge. She whickered again, tossing her head towards the path.

'Yes, I'm going down there … you want to come with me?' she asked the mare.

A soft whicker answered her and the mare fell in beside her. Tentatively Isoldé reached out to touch the long, silky, black mane. The mare leaned towards her, Isoldé put her arm over the mare's neck and they went towards the cliff edge together. The path went down into a slight dip then up again, as they topped the rise there was the tooth, straight ahead of them.

Isoldé stopped still. The mare stopped beside her, let her be still for a moment then blew softly through her nose. Isoldé shivered. The mare nuzzled her. Isoldé began walking again. She couldn't explain what she'd felt and, remembering Gideon's advice, didn't try to. It was enough just to feel. Her skin was tingling, the hair on the back of her neck stood up again. She took a handful of the silky mane in her hand, the mare didn't object and it seemed to help. There was nothing to see, to be scared of, the sky was bright blue, no clouds, a soft wind rustled the soft grasses and heather, the scent of gorse was on the air. But Isoldé was scared.

As she watched, the grass rippled at her feet sending a pathway of silvery light ahead of them. The mare began to walk forward, pulling Isoldé as she went. Isoldé stumbled, got her feet together and managed to keep up. The silvery grass led them towards the tooth.

In one way it took ages to get there. In another it felt like only a couple of steps. An impossible shadow stretched backwards from the tooth towards Isoldé and the mare, yet the sun was behind them both, rising as always in the east. They faced west, yet the shadow of the tooth stretched back towards them as though there was a sun in the west to cast it. Isoldé stopped, staring. It was cold.

The mare stood beside her, both of them covered in the shadow then she nudged Isoldé making her walk forward again.

The hole itself was too high up the stone for her to see through. At her feet were the steps, cut roughly into the stone and leading up to the hole. The mare shook her head, loosing Isoldé's hand from her mane and butted her gently towards the steps.

'Are you sure?' Isoldé turned back to the mare.

A rough snort answered her and the nose pushed her again.

Isoldé put a foot on the first step. It felt strange, as though she wasn't altogether in the everyday world any more. As she mounted the last one she could see through the window … or could she? It wasn't the sea as she had expected, although it did look like water and ocean. The colour was different, turquoise green with a slivery sheen, sky and sea merging into each other. The light itself came from behind the sea, from behind the shadowy land on the horizon, a kind of glow hung above it. Was it this that threw the tooth-shadow eastward back across the land?

The names came into Isoldé's mind … the Isles of the Dead, Isles of the Blest, West-Over-the-Sea … that was where she was going, as Gideon had said she would.

She looked at the stone under her hand. It seemed different to how it had appeared while she was still standing on the ground, now it looked silvery too, slick, almost like it was damp but it didn't feel wet. In fact it felt warm under her hand. She looked back … and could see nothing. The black mare, the grass and heather on the cliff and the cliff itself were all gone. It was as if she was suspended between a grey mist and an endless ocean. Out of that ocean something dark moved towards her. It grew, became a figure, a person, a woman in a long dark robe like the midnight sky, her long, silky black hair flew out behind her. In a moment she was beside Isoldé.

'Come,' she said, holding out her hand.

Isoldé took the hand and stepped down out of the hole in the stone onto the sea. Immediately she felt herself being carried along, like on a moving walkway but this one was completely smooth, effortless. The next instant they were somewhere. She couldn't tell what sort of a place, the light was fractal, shimmering, never staying still long enough for Isoldé to make out shapes. The dark woman led her forward. The light strobed, flickered, then steadied up. They were in a grove just like the one near the cottage, even down to the head-shaped rock.

'Yes,' said the dark woman, 'it's the same.'

'So why am I here?'

The woman said nothing but something, someone, was coming through the twisted pine trees towards them.

The man was tall, skinny, rangy, his grey-blonde hair fell in a long forelock over his face, the long fingered hands swung at his sides against the flapping grey flannel bags. His shirt, open at the neck showed some bare pale skin, a paisley bandana was loosely tied around his neck. He looked up as he entered the grove, stopped short on seeing Isoldé and the dark woman.

'Rhiannon!' he said, softly. Then he looked towards Isoldé, pushed the hair back from his face.

The dark woman, Rhiannon, stood still on the edge of the grove. Isoldé could feel Rhiannon wanting her to go on. She took a deep breath and stepped forward.

'Tristan …?' she began as she came towards him.

'Isoldé …?' Tristan whispered. 'I wanted … I hoped … I need you to help me finish it …'

He stopped, looked around then folded himself up to sit cross-legged on the grass beside the stone, he patted a spot beside him. Isoldé came over and joined him. All the charisma was still there, her body reached out, she wanted him. Looking into his eyes she could see he wanted her. She looked away quickly. This was ridiculous! He was a ghost, wasn't he? Or was she? If this was Otherworld then she must be the ghost, it would be his reality. How could a ghost and a reality make love?

Tristan's hand was on her shoulder, his arm slid round her. 'What's the matter?' he turned her to face him.

Electricity shot through her, her whole body on fire. She leaned towards him, found his lips with her own, parted them with her tongue and kissed him deeply. After an instant of surprise he kissed her back, long and hard then they were on the ground, pulling at each other's clothes. In moments they were naked, his hands stroking her, opening her flesh. He licked slowly down her body, opening her. She parted her legs then reached down pulling his head back up to her. He slid up her body, between her legs and deep within her.

She moaned softly. They moved together as one being full of ecstasy. After forever the climax came, softly at first, rushing upwards, filling them until they knew nothing else. For a long, bright darkness they held still, not breathing, then consciousness fumbled its way between them. His hand was no longer her hand, his eyes looked into hers, they knew each other again.

Tristan slid sideways so his head rested beside her. She turned to face him. For long moments, years, neither said a word.

They were still naked, still glued together with the sweat of their passion, the slick joy that had bonded them in their lovemaking. Softly, Isoldé pulled herself away from him, looking down their bodies as they slipped apart. His fingers traced down her flesh. She shuddered, her body flicking back against his then sinking back to lie on the grass. He took his shirt and gently wiped down her body then lifted her, helping her back into her own clothes. Slowly still, they dressed each other then sat together with their backs to the headstone.

'I'll help you,' she said finally. 'I'll help you find the song.'

'As a shaman, you can cross between the worlds and bring back the goods.'

'Am I shaman?'

'I think you are.'

Isoldé was silent.

'That's what shamans do, isn't it? Isoldé said at last. 'Be conscious in both places at once. What you sang about in Thomas the Rhymer, about walking between worlds.'

'Yes ... yes it is.'

Isoldé climbed back through the Lady's Window, down the steps, onto the grass. There was a different feel as her feet touched down on middle earth again, she felt more solid and, at the same time, cut off from the world she had been in with Tristan.

The black mare nuzzled her. She stopped, took the long horse-head in her hands, no longer afraid. 'It was you, wasn't it?' she asked the mare. 'You *are* Rhiannon too.' The mare's head nodded in her hands, the dark, liquid eyes held hers.

The lovemaking came back to her again. It had been perhaps the most passionate lovemaking of her life. She loved Mark. The episode with Tristan had been passion, ecstasy, but not of this world. Although her body was on fire again as soon as she thought of him, she was not at all sure she wanted a repeat performance. 'Oh ye gods! What am I to do? Do I tell Mark?'

The mare poked her in the ribs gently. Isoldé came back out of her head into the world around her and began walking back to the truck. The mare accompanied her. At the stable-bothy, the mare stopped. Isoldé paused, watching the mare, waiting.

'Go home,' came a voice in her head. 'No need to tell Mark. Wait. Watch. You'll know what to do.'

'Will Tristan be there?'

'No.'

Isoldé let out a sigh of relief.

'Not yet anyway,' the mare added. Isoldé could have sworn there was a chuckle in the voice in her head. 'You have work to do. You have planted the seed of the song.'

Isoldé stared. 'You don't mean I'm pregnant?' she gasped.

'No ...' The chuckle sounded again in her head. 'He is!'

If a horse could grin, Isoldé would have sworn the black mare did. With a flick of her tail she gave a little jump and galloped off toward the cliff. Watching, Isoldé saw she didn't slow down but leapt up and out over the sea.

Tristan

Isoldé was getting used to being in the house on her own. She was used to living alone but living alone at Caergollo was different. The house was alive with energy, with invisible things – well mostly invisible – that she could sense. The flats in London had not been like that. And there was always Embar. He had completely taken to her, would be with her whenever he could. He still went to Mark – Isoldé was glad of that, she didn't want to take anything away from him – but she was included in Embar's life, like he was her familiar spirit.

'He was Tristan's familiar,' Mark had told her.

That thought, now, felt uncomfortable. She didn't want to take Embar away from either Mark or Tristan. But … the cat seemed to have made up his own mind, he wanted to be with her.

It had been three days now since she'd been through the Lady's Window. The house was quiet, the days dragged. Embar had been with her for most of that dead time, sat with her in her study or down in the library, under her feet in the kitchen. Mrs P kept a weather eye on them both, with the odd amused snuffle as though she suspected something or other. Isoldé had told nobody anything, not even where she'd gone, and she'd skilfully avoided any questions.

'Damn the song!' Isoldé exploded.

Embar mewled softly, wrapping his tail round her legs. He'd been trying to get her to go back up to the cottage, she'd refused. Even after everything that had happened it still felt very odd to know exactly what a cat was thinking, no possibility of being wrong, mistaken. 'I probably ought to be sectioned,' she muttered.

Uncle Brian would have understood. He always knew what animals were thinking, what they were saying to him, trees too. Isoldé had never been able to properly believe it. She knew it was so, at least with Uncle Brian, but ... how? Perhaps it was just some people who were able to hear that way. Not her ... except now it was.

She sat down. Embar jumped into her lap. They sat together in the window seat looking out across the lawn. 'I know, Embar, I know. I have to go up the cottage, but I can't. I can't. Not yet. He'll be there. I know he will. I can't face him yet.' She paused, stroking Embar's long dark fur. 'Perhaps not ever.'

A sense of warmth crept over her, a confidence she hadn't felt since before she went to the Lady's Window. Embar's purring was having an effect. Maybe she could face Tristan again. If she was to get the song she'd have to. She looked out across the lawn. He was there.

Isoldé jerked upright. Embar dug his claws into her leg. It stopped her. She sat still watching.

Tristan was on the other side of the lawn, at the edge of the trees. He stood at ease, weight into his right leg, his thumbs hooked into his trouser pockets, jacket tucked behind them, his shirt open, bandana fluttering slightly, along with the birch leaves of the tree he stood under. How was he here? Was he here? Was the place he stood even in the same world as the place she sat?

He looked up, saw her at the window. A hand came out of the pocket and waved dreamily to her. Without thinking, Isoldé waved back. Embar got up, went to the door, she followed him. It seemed events were making up her mind for her.

Down in the library, standing at the French windows, Isoldé saw Tristan hadn't moved. The mare had told her he wouldn't be at Caergollo. No ... that wasn't quite what she'd said. She'd said 'not yet, anyway' and that had been three days ago. Damn! Damn them all! Isoldé was angry, felt out of control, not something she was used to. 'And I don't want to get used to it either,' she muttered.

But there was Tristan, stood across the lawn under the trees, watching her. Embar brushed past her ankles and stalked out across the lawn, tail straight up like a mast and purring fit to bust. Tristan saw him immediately, crouched down, his face breaking into a smile. 'Oh! Embar! It's so good to see you again.'

Isoldé heard the joy and wistfulness in his voice and, despite her crossness, it pulled at her heart. Was it possible to be lonely, to miss your friends, when you'd passed over? Perhaps it was. She followed the cat across the grass. Tristan got up, they stood looking at each other, the cat purring and doing figures of eight around and between their legs.

After the silence had gone on for too long, Tristan began to speak, his voice croaked, he tried again. 'How are you doing with the song?'

'I'm not,' Isoldé replied. She paused a moment, then went on, realising she'd sounded more brusque than she'd intended. 'I've not tried. I don't know how to try.'

'Hmm!' Tristan folded himself onto the grass. Isoldé sat on a log a pace away from him. Tristan's rueful smile told her he understood why she didn't want to get too close. 'I don't know if I want to do all that again either,' he said, after a moment. 'Not that I didn't enjoy it,' he added quickly. 'I did. I … I'm just not used to it. Not with people. I mean real people …' he trailed off, watching her.

Isoldé thought for a moment. 'You mean … you mean you … your lovers … they're the gods?'

Tristan chuckled. 'I don't think they call themselves that.'

'No,' Isoldé snorted in her turn. 'That's sort of what Gideon said … I think.'

'But the answer to your question is yes.'

'Rhiannon …?'

Tristan nodded. 'You met her as the black mare, didn't you?'

'Yes.'

'She was, is, my muse, my inspiration.'

'She told me you're pregnant with the song …'

They stared at each other.

'So I have to give birth …?'

Isoldé took a deep breath. 'I suppose you do ...' Her eyes narrowed as she studied Tristan.

'How are we going to do that?'

Isoldé sighed. 'I haven't the foggiest,' she replied. 'In fact, since you're here … and have been there … and have far more experience than I do, I'd rather hoped you would know. Or at least have some idea how to find out.'

'Well I don't.' Tristan almost sounded sulky.

'Oh! For the gods' sake!' Isoldé exploded at him. 'I'm the neophyte here, not you. Why couldn't you have hung on, finished the job. I don't want the damn job. I don't want to do this. All I want is to love Mark, to be with him. I don't want all this stuff with you. All I want is him.'

She buried her face in her hands, shaking with dry sobs. Tristan wanted to comfort her but something about her stopped him, like a force field around her. He looked again and realised that there was a field there, like an aura around her, he could feel it repelling him. Isoldé stood up suddenly, ran back across the lawn. Embar leapt up and ran after her.

Tristan sat still, watched her go. As she got to the French windows there was a bright flash and she was gone. Tristan shook his head at the soundless noise, his ears ringing. He was no longer at Caergollo, he was back in Otherworld and Isoldé was in the everyday.

Gideon

Back in the library, Isoldé came to a halt, panting, angry. Tristan was useless, she told herself. How the hell was she going to do what Otherworld wanted with a helpless creature like him? What the hell had happened to him when he passed over the moonpath? It was like being with a wet rag, a sulky brat. She hated him.

Slowly, her breathing calmed down, she began to be able to see further than six inches in front of her nose. Gideon sat on the piano stool watching her.

'Problems?' he asked, a quizzical look in his eye.

'Oh damn you!' Isoldé muttered, walking away from him, over to the fireplace. 'He's a useless piece of shit! What the hell am I supposed to do with him? All he wants now is to get his leg over again and, good as that was that one time, that's not what I'm here for. I want Mark, not Tristan. I'm here for Mark.'

'And to do the job,' Gideon reminded her.

'Ha! I've a mind to say no, renege, let it go. It's too hard!' Gideon looked at her. She felt herself colour up.

'You promised ...' he said.

'Oh damn and damn and damn and damn!' Isoldé turned to the fireplace and stood there with her head on her arms, sobbing.

Gideon came over to her, turned her about and enfolded her in his arms. Despite his attractiveness Isoldé didn't feel any sexual urge as he touched her this time, she just folded against him, sucking in support from him and letting her feelings go, just for once. Gideon held her, rocking her gently like a child and humming softly into her hair. Slowly the sobs subsided, she began to pull away from him. He led her over to the sofa, sat down opposite her. 'I know it's hard,' he said.

'Why doesn't Tristan know?' she asked him. 'Why is he so thick, stupid, childish? Why have I got to carry it all myself?'

Gideon studied her for a moment. 'Well ...' he began, 'Tristan shouldn't have passed over the moonpath when he did.'

'I know that,' Isoldé interrupted crossly. 'But did it fry his brains as well or something?'

'In a word, yes.'

Isoldé stared. 'You mean … he's not all there? Because he died too early? Something got lost?'

'That's about it,' Gideon told her, his mouth quirked in a sour smile.

Isoldé thought about it. 'Is that what happens to suicides then?'

'No, not always, it depends on why they do it, and if they should know better.'

'Ha! And Tristan should certainly have known better.'

'Yes, he should, did. But he thought he could get away with it. He rejected us and so rejected a part of himself, the part that can stay focused, write songs. You have to get that back to him.'

'You mean I'm holding it, that part of him?'

'You are. That happened when you made love. It came into you rather than wither in the wilderness where he had left it.'

'Oh shit …' Isoldé struggled with the enormity of the job. 'Thanks for not telling me all this before,' she told Gideon sourly.

'You wouldn't have said yes, would you?'

She looked at him. Suddenly she began to smile. 'Of course I wouldn't. I'd have been so ultra careful of my personal self but that's not how things work across the worlds is it?'

'No. You humans call us tricksters and so we are but our concern is with the Earth, with everything here, not just one little human incarnation.'

'And I've plenty more of those to do, haven't I?' she paused, thinking. Ideas were sparking in her mind. 'Had Tristan walked the moonpath before then? That's different than what I did with Rhiannon to find him in the grove, isn't it? I know I went through the Lady's Window but there was no moon and no moonpath, she just floated me there somehow.'

Gideon chuckled. 'I said, when I first met you, you're a quick study. Yes, that's right, she did float you over. And yes, Tristan had walked the moonpath and come back, several times.'

'So it's possible for a living human to walk the path and return?'

'It's what shamans do, what we want you to do.'

'He said that, Tristan did, about shamans,' Isoldé paused then continued. 'Are you certain of the return bit?' She glared at Gideon.

'Tristan did. If he did, you can.'

'Are you saying I'm better than him?'

'Aren't you?'

That was hard. Tristan had been her hero all her life, to think herself better than him was almost sacrilege.

'He doesn't see clearly, not now,' Gideon went on. 'You do. But he has the song even if it's stuck somewhere inside him and he no longer has the tools to create it. The lovemaking stirred it in him and gave you the connection, as well as a home for his rejected soul-part, through the passion. But we need him to sing it here, in Middleworld, and to record it so everyone can hear it. His voice is part of the enchantment. Someone else's voice, however good, won't have the same effect. Not until Tristan has sung it and been heard. After that, everyone will be able to sing it as the threads will have been made, the pattern begun.'

'So he has to be here. Damn!' She looked out the window; there was no sign of Tristan under the birch tree. 'He was just here! I ran away from him. I should have held onto him.' She looked at Gideon. 'I screwed up, but I didn't know what was happening and he was so different from when I met him through the Lady's Window. Oh damn!'

'That's because he's missing the soul-part that enables him to function here. It's not the end of the world. You'll just have to go get him. We always thought you would have to.'

'Cross the moonpath … gee thanks!' Isoldé glared again. 'And return ...?'

'And return,' Gideon told her firmly.

'I think I need to know a lot more about this stuff. I'm not usually like this, I mostly don't care about the knowledge stuff. I suppose it's because I'm now up to my neck in it I want to know more. What are these patterns, are they like ley lines? How does it all work?'

Gideon looked at her. She meant it; he could see it in her. 'Everything is everything,' he began.

'Shit! You sound just like Darshan,' she said.

He laughed. 'Even new-agers can speak true now and again, and even when they don't really know what they're talking about.'

'OK, so go on, tell me.'

Gideon sat quiet for a moment, looking inward. 'There are three worlds, you know that. They're on what we call the vertical axis. It's like the warp, the threads you weave the pattern on when you're weaving, they hold the structure so the pattern has shape.'

'Yes ... I can see that. I saw that when I heard the songs. The first three are about that, the threeness, the vertical. Then the next four are about the four elements and how they work.'

'Yes. And that structure is in everything, Isoldé, from the smallest atom to the largest creature, to the planet herself. On that warp the pattern of life is woven. That's the vertical axis, the warp of the universe. The horizontal axis is made up of the four elements, they are the weft.'

She remembered what the demon had shown her. He had drawn a silvery vertical line then two horizontal lines crossing it making a six-armed cross. More lines had grown, threading themselves together into more six-armed crosses, making a web of silvery lines. The edges of the pattern had reached out into the grass, disappearing under it.

Isoldé looked at Gideon, he'd been following her thoughts. 'I get it ... I think ...' she said softly. 'The web of life? Ley lines, the wyrd. It connects everything to everything.'

'That's right.'

'And the demon told me about the Moon, directing the flow. Tristan must get the song that enchants, that sings it all to life, back to Earth.' She stopped, staring off into nothing. 'So, I'm made up of hundreds ... thousands ... maybe millions of those six-pointed stars?'

'Yes,' Gideon replied. 'Just like everything, including me. Including the little demon you spoke with that night. And including Tristan.'

'Every plant, animal, insect, bird, atom, molecule, mineral, everything.' Isoldé told them over aloud. 'And the planet herself,' she added.

'That's right.' Gideon said.

First Crossing

Isoldé was sat on the cliff again by the Lady's Window, on top of the steps that began the moonpath. Tonight was full moon, the sea green-grey, only the slightest breeze rippling it with silver, the scent of grasses and the spring flowers was strong in the air. Isoldé was alone, no Mark, and no black ponies nor black cats either. She wanted it that way.

The Moon ... the Moon ...? She'd brought the notebook, the drawings she'd made about the moon, the lines, the six-armed cross, the plants, all the things she'd thought about the moon. Would they help?

It was the half-light of evening. She'd left the truck by the church and walked down over the Stitches. Wrapped up in warm clothes with a waterproof rug and a lantern, a thermos of coffee and a packet of sandwiches, she was prepared to stay all night if necessary. What should she do? She felt strongly she should do some sort of ritual, ask the moon herself for help, but she'd never done this on her own and had no real idea what was required. She pulled the notebook to her, opened a new page and began to write.

What do I want?
to learn what the moon wants me to do
to know how to do it

'Yikes!' she muttered, 'and I need to know if I can do it. No bloody use if it's something I can't do. I know Gideon wants me to cross over the moonpath. And come back.' She frowned. 'So what do I want?'

to meet the moon
to ask the moon what she needs

'And if I can't …?' Isoldé went on talking to herself.

'Then you gotta find a way you can do it,' an earthy-soft voice answered her.

Isoldé turned. There, on the other side of the rug sat the woodfolk; the hare-girl she'd seen when she walked down Rocky Valley the first weekend she'd come to Caergollo and, beside her, was the root-mother Isoldé half remembered from the dream where she'd been gifted with the hag-stone. The three of them sat and stared at each other for what seemed like forever.

'Uh … err … h-hello …?' Isoldé began.

'Ullo …' the root-mother replied. After another moment she went on. 'This be the moon-child, the hare-girl. Her's none too good with words, not yet she ain't. She be needing you fer that. You be needing her too. She'm real good at crossing the moonpath, her can help you.'

'Err … err … yes …' Isoldé could think of nothing to say. She sat staring at her two companions. These were woodfolk. They were real. They were fascinating. The flower-like folds of the root-mother's face caught her eye like Leonardo's drawings, lovely, strange, like a plant, a flower. She had hands and feet, a humanoid body, but her hair was more plant-like and the fingers were long, twisted and root-like, so were her feet.

The hare-girl was much younger looking and still half animal, the paws were definitely paws, not hands … long, soft-furred ears stood up out of her fine hair … her nose was half human and half animal, trailing into the upper lip. But she, too, was beautiful. She sat silent now, watching Isoldé intently. Both women's eyes were large, deep and strange, like the eyes of deer.

Suddenly, on impulse, Isoldé reached out her hand towards the girl. The girl shivered slightly, then her paw came towards Isoldé. They touched.

Electricity sparked through them both. They let go, jumped back slightly, sat staring.

'Go 'orn, then,' the root-mother whispered to them both.

She pushed the hare-girl gently towards Isoldé. Isoldé reached out again, just letting one finger touch the soft fur of the paw. The hare-girl twitched but didn't withdraw this time.

Had she already given birth? Isoldé turned the idea over in her mind, looked up to see the root-mother grinning at her.

'You'm made it possible for her an' you to be together in the same world, like you is now.'

'But I saw her before, in Rocky Valley, when I first came here.'

'You did?'

The hare-girl nodded, confirming.

'Twas you,' the root-mother whispered. 'You must've known, somehow.'

Isoldé thought about that. 'I knew something,' she said. 'Even if I didn't know what I knew, or even if I knew it. Was that enough?'

The two woodfolk nodded. 'Soul-knowing …' the root-mother said. 'Now you gotta do it, make it body-knowing, make it real.'

Isoldé nodded. It sort of made sense, although she wasn't sure how, it had that same sort of rightness she'd felt before.

'Do I need to call the moon?' Isoldé returned to her thoughts before the woodfolk had arrived.

The root-mother and hare-girl looked at each other, they looked back at Isoldé. 'Aye … aye … we need to call the Lady.'

'The Lady …? I thought that was the goddess of the land.'

'So tis … so tis … but tis also the way we speak of the Moon-Lady.'

'How do I do it?'

The two woodfolk stood up, they went and stood beside the stone steps. Isoldé got up and followed them. They took her hands so they all stood in a circle, the two woodfolk began to hum, the root-mother low and ground-shaking, the hare-girl higher sounding, like a flute. Isoldé found herself joining in, her voice somewhere between the two.

It had grown dark. A soft light spun around them, coming

from nowhere. Did it come out of the sound they made together, Isoldé wondered? The light grew as the humming grew.

Isoldé stood facing the steps. As she watched, a brightness grew on the horizon, it got brighter, dazzling, she screwed up her eyes in an attempt to continue watching. Suddenly it flashed as a pathway rolled out across the sea. She shut her eyes tight. When she opened them again a figure stood on the top step.

The humming stopped. Isoldé and the woodfolk were silent. The figure too was silent, slowly it came down the steps, stood beside them. It was a female figure, not young but not old either, tall, beautiful, golden hair falling down her back almost to her feet. Her robe was silver, like a fall of water and it rippled.

'A-are you the moon?' Isoldé asked. It felt a stupid question but she had to know.

The figure turned to Isoldé, a half smile flickering across her face. 'I am ...'

'I have to bring your song to life ...' Isoldé said. 'I don't know how to do it ... I know, now, the hare-girl is part of it. She's the child ... have I somehow given birth to her already?'

'She was born when Tristan began the songs, conceived in the idea of the song. It was too early, she was not fully formed. And then he abandoned her, left her unformed and she cannot shift as the others can, cannot be all in one piece at one time,' the Moon-Lady indicated the hare-girl's paws and ears, 'or speak, or sing. The seven songs he wrote were the beginning, they seeded her birth but she's not complete, not whole, she can't be whole until Tristan has sung her. You must bring him.'

Same old story! Isoldé thought sourly.

The Moon-Lady nodded agreement.

'And that means crossing the moonpath ... and coming back,' Isoldé said.

'With Tristan,' added the Moon-Lady.

'With Tristan,' Isoldé agreed. 'So ... how do I do that?'

The Moon-Lady pointed up behind Isoldé. Looking, she saw

the full moon had risen. Turning back she saw it had begun to spread the pathway across the sea. This was very different to the firework display that had heralded the moon goddess' arrival.

'I will take you across, with the hare-girl. She will bring you back. You must learn the way before you try to bring Tristan. He will not be so easy.'

Experience so far made Isoldé nod sourly, she could well believe it. Memories of another of Tristan's songs came to her. 'Who are you?' she asked again.

'I think you already have a name for me,' the Moon-Lady replied.

'I was thinking of Tristan's song, Olwen of the White Track, would that be you?'

The Moon-Lady smiled. 'The name fits,' she said, 'as you will see.'

The moon rose higher behind her now. The silvery pathway shone ahead of her across the sea to the bank of cloud on the horizon. The Moon-Lady, Olwen, stood beside her.

Isoldé knew she had to step out onto that pathway. It came right to the edge of the cliff, touching the top step where she stood. It seemed solid, she could only faintly see the waves through it, but she couldn't move. Now she wished for Mark, he would have helped her, encouraged her. No good, another part of her mind told her, this you must do on your own.

Beside her Olwen touched her arm. 'You must learn to do this of your own will,' she said. 'It requires work, focus, concentration.'

'Help me ...' Isoldé whispered. 'Help me. I want to learn to cross.'

The pathway changed, became more solid, strewn with white flowers. Isoldé bent, picked one up. 'The white track ...' she muttered. The story, song, told of Olwen, daughter of the giant who was keeper of the world, being courted by the young hero

Culhwch; wherever Olwen walked white flowers grew in her track.

'That's right,' Olwen said. 'That is one of the stories about me. Take the flower, keep it, use it to help you cross.'

Beside them now was the hare-girl. She hopped out onto the path, following the flower track, stopping every now and then to sniff at the white blossoms. Isoldé put her foot on the path.

An owl swooped over her head, landed in the path before her, slivery white with a hint of gold. The heart-shaped face stared up at her. She stood gazing into its eyes. It began to melt, flowing, transforming, becoming the Moon-Lady who, a moment before, had been standing beside Isoldé on the step. She took Isoldé's hand. The touch was cool, almost liquid.

'Like touching feathers,' Isoldé thought. 'Softness that makes you unsure if you're actually touching anything.' Looking down, she could see her own fingers through Olwen's almost transparent ones. The hand tugged at her, pulling her onwards. Isoldé resisted.

'It's all very well for you,' she said. 'You're transparent, made of the same stuff as the path. I'm solid, human. I'm afraid of falling through.'

Olwen laughed. 'If that is what you believe, that is what will happen. Is that what you want?'

'N–no.'

The hand stopped pulling at Isoldé. A sense of warmth began to flow from it into her. 'Better?'

It did feel better, Isoldé felt some courage inside, she stepped forward again. The moonpath held, felt steady under her. She let her weight go into that foot and lifted the other one, stepped forward again. Somehow, she'd been expecting it to sway, like being in a hammock, but it didn't. It felt solid, even though she could still see through it to some extent. She was walking, not floating, as she'd half expected. This was as real as being in the everyday world. She gave a tiny snort-chuckle, magic was real, it was the everyday, it wasn't just something you read about in stories.

'Don't look down, not yet,' Olwen warned her as she began to look about her, excited by the new experience. 'Later, when you're used to it, then you can enjoy looking through it.'

'It still feels a bit weird,' Isoldé said. 'It's OK for you, you're sort of made of the same stuff, you can walk it easily.'

Olwen laughed. 'I don't need to walk it,' she said. 'This is a human path. If I wish to go to the Isle of the Dead my wish alone will take me there. You can't do that, not yet. Nor can most of your species. You need the moonpath.'

Isoldé hadn't ever thought of it like that. Her knowledge was still very much of the fairy story variety, believing the faer folk needed devices to carry them across worlds. Olwen's words gave her to think.

'You must keep walking,' Olwen told her. 'Don't stop. Don't doubt. Energy follows thought and what you believe will happen, will happen. Beware of that, be very careful what you believe.'

There was movement in the shadow at the end of the bridge of light. A form progressed along the way, its edges shivered in the moonlight. As it came closer it shifted into a tall woman with long black hair that floated out around her as if in a breeze. It was the same horse-woman, Rhiannon, Isoldé had met at the Lady's Window. She came to a stop in front of Isoldé, a faint smile playing on her lips.

'Issssolde!' The voice whispered to her. 'Come! You must find your way to the grove. That is where Tristan will be when you come for him.'

'He's not there now?' Isoldé almost paused. It would be too much to see him now.

'No, he's not there. You must find your way, know where you are going. Come!'

With a goddess on each side of her, Isoldé continued along the path. The feelings of joy returned. What she was doing was incredible and yet she completely believed it.

Olwen smiled. 'Yes,' she said. 'You're truly realising that we are real, aren't you?'

Insight struck Isoldé. 'Tristan always knew it, didn't he?'

'And so does Mark,' Olwen answered her. 'And now you do too, don't you?'

'I do so.'

The path ended. Isoldé found herself on white shingle, she could both feel it and hear it crunch as she stepped on it. They walked up a slight rise and onto a path through a meadow. Tall, daisy-like flowers stood up out of the feathery grasses. There were white-stemmed trees ahead. Everything was monochrome. They passed among the trees, still following the path, and shortly came to the grove. It was the same again as the headstone grove up by the cottage, where the well was. Isoldé stopped at the edge.

'This place is between the worlds, isn't it?' she asked her companions. 'It exists in many places at once. If I knew how, I could get here from there, from the grove by the cottage, couldn't I?'

'Yes, you could,' Olwen replied, her eyebrows going up, a slight smile on her lips.

'Gideon said she was a quick study,' Rhiannon added, chuckling. 'This is where you must call Tristan,' she went on. 'You come here, stand here, and call him. He'll come to you. Then you must bring him back across the bridge and get him to sing the song.'

'And you must record it,' Olwen chimed in. 'It must be part of the Ellyon cycle, with the other songs. They all go together.'

'I've sort of got that,' Isoldé said, 'even if I don't altogether know how it works.'

'I don't suppose any human knows that, nor will for a good

while yet,' Rhiannon said. 'Tis enough that they do it, let the songs move them, that's what enchantment is … en-chant-ment, to sing into life. That will work the magic. You don't need to know everything to do it.'

'And knowing comes better by doing than it does by book-learning,' Olwen added. 'Tis in the body then and not all mussed up with too much thinking in the brain.'

'But will Tristan come with me?' Isoldé went back to the reason they were here. She could foresee problems already.

'He will … if you're clever.'

'And quick …'

The two goddesses stood looking at her, a bit old fashioned.

'And what's that supposed to mean?'

'You're right,' Olwen sighed. 'He will want you. Likely you'll want him too. And he'll want to stay here, keep you here with him.'

'I don't want that!' Isoldé exploded. 'I want to be with Mark, in the world. It's not my time to go to the Isles of the Dead.'

'No, it isn't. And anyway, the song is no good here. We know what it says, I am what it does,' Olwen said. 'It must be in the Middleworld.'

'So … how do I get Tristan back across the bridge?'

'With cunning and art,' Rhiannon told her. 'Now, you learn to cross the bridge without us. The hare-girl will help you. You have the art to lure Tristan across the bridge and do all the necessary to record the song, with Mark's help.'

'OK …' Isoldé sighed.

'Gideon is much in your world, he will help you too. And look out for help in unexpected places, Isoldé. Always be aware, notice everything, for everything speaks to you, you need to learn to listen, to hear. And to ask. You're quite good for a human. You do notice and you do learn. But you don't ask enough. Be aware. Every blade of grass speaks to you, child, but you won't hear if you're too busy in your own head to notice.'

At first, Isoldé almost began to bridle at what appeared to be a telling-off, then she stopped, thought about it. It was true. Most people didn't even believe anything not human could communicate with them, didn't even believe non-human creatures did much communicating between themselves, while as for plants and rocks, they were inanimate non-communicating "things" to most people. Uncle Brian had never allowed her to get that bad but she had to admit she could get well wrapped up in herself and forget that other things might have a want or a say.

'I'm sorry,' she said to the two goddesses. 'You're right, I do need to be more aware.' She smiled wryly. 'We're an arrogant species,' she said. 'I'm surprised you put up with us.'

'Humans have their part to play and will be able to do that once they realise they are a part of everything and not the boss of everything.' Rhiannon smiled back to her.

'We had great hopes of the Gaia Principle,' Olwen said. 'And it has made a difference. But modern people know little about how the Sixties were, how people thought then. They think everyone was off their heads on drugs and know nothing about the real experiences many had. And nowadays there is so much dependence on muddled, cheap science that the real stuff rarely gets heard.'

'Head-stuff!' Isoldé snorted. 'Know what you mean. I wasn't there but my uncle and aunt who brought me up are from the Sixties. They know about you, about Gaia.'

'It shows in you,' Olwen told her. 'It's why we can work with you.'

'Now ... you must take yourself home,' Rhiannon said. 'Come, hare-child. You have a job to do.'

The little woodfolk girl came to Rhiannon's skirts and stroked them with a paw, looking up into the goddess' face. Rhiannon crouched down so her eyes were on a level with the hare-girl.

'Take her home,' she said, caressing the silky ears. 'Take Isoldé home. Let her lead when she can but make sure she gets back safely and knows her way.'

'Now … home!' Rhiannon lifted her arms, the sleeves of her dark dress came out like wings. A wind started up in the glade and the silver-stemmed trees all bent together towards Isoldé. She felt herself almost lifted off her feet. The hare-girl clutched at her, Isoldé held her hand. The wind came stronger, blowing them out of the grove and onto the path to the sea.

Together, she and the hare-girl ran hand in hand down the path through the meadow. The grasses immediately to either side were bending and tossing in the wind but Isoldé could see that just a foot or so further out the grasses were still. This wind was intent on herself and the hare-girl only.

They scurried down the path, suddenly the pebbles crunched under their feet, they'd made it to the beach. The wind let up a little, blowing Isoldé's hair and the child's fur but no longer trying to sweep them off their feet. There, just across the shingle, was the beginning of the moonpath.

Isoldé looked up. The moon was still high but it was on its downward arc now, going to set. They must cross the bridge before it did … or there would be no bridge. She took a firm grip on the little paw and hurried across the beach to the end of the moonpath.

The path stood just above the shingle, not actually touching it. Now they were here something gripped Isoldé's stomach, it was difficult to take that first step onto the bridge.

'Must!' the hare-girl told her, pulling at her hand. 'Must! Come! Quick!'

Isoldé shut her eyes and jumped onto the bridge. This time it wobbled slightly.

'Eyes open!' the hare girl told her. 'Must look. Watch. See. No see, no real.'

'Ye gods!' Isoldé muttered. 'Does the damn thing depend on me seeing it?'

No time to bother about that, she followed the hare-girl who was pulling her along the path so fast she was running. They seemed to run forever, time spinning out, almost feeling like slow-motion, there was only running, only this loping rhythm pulsing out on two main notes, other notes harmonising in like cords. She was running a tune, she realised. A tune that spun out of the strands of the bridge.

'I must remember! I must remember!' she told herself.

She was concentrating so hard she never saw they had arrived at the end of the bridge. She went tumbling down the steps to land in a heap, clutching the hare-girl to her.

Mark

The plane landed and Mark was through baggage and out into the main concourse in record time. There was Isoldé, his heart lifted at the sight of her.

Isoldé had got there early, stopped for coffee once she'd found the plane was on time. Now, here he was. It was a weird feeling, part of her lit up at the sight of him. Another part hung heavy, wondering how much to tell him of the crazy adventures she'd had over the past couple of weeks.

He was here, arms outstretched. She went straight into them, hugging him and bursting into tears.

'Hey … hey … what's up?' Mark held her close then gently pulled half away so he could see into her face. 'It's me, OK? What's up, sweetheart?'

Isoldé gulped and swallowed, her sobs slowing down. Mark steered them both towards the coffee, sat her down and got two large Lattes. By the time he came back with them the crying had stopped and she was mopping her face. He gave her the coffee and sat close, his hand lightly holding hers, not asking for any explanations yet.

Isoldé pushed the second soggy tissue into her jacket pocket and took hold of the coffee, sat sipping at it. Gradually her colour came back to normal, she was able to look at him even if her mouth quivered a bit. 'Not sure what came over me,' she said, very quietly. 'I missed you …'

'I missed you too … but I think it's more than that, isn't it? You want to talk about it here?'

She shook her head. How did you begin to talk about all that stuff, especially the Tristan stuff, in a crowded café?

'Shall I drive?' Mark asked.

'Please …' Isoldé squeezed his fingers.

They headed out, got into the truck and Mark took the Dartmoor road. Isoldé gasped but didn't say anything.

'Not this way?' Mark went round the roundabout twice so she could change her mind.

'No … no … it's OK. Let's go the way you want.'

Mark frowned, took the Moretonhampstead exit and continued driving, not talking.

'Tristan had recorded the first seven songs,' she told him. 'I found the CD – well, Embar pointed me at it really, hidden in a cupboard up at the cottage. Well, not hidden exactly but put away.' She plugged her iPod into the radio, it began the Ellyon cycle.

Mark caught his breath, this felt big.

'I've got all the songs sorted,' Isoldé went on. 'The manuscripts, notes, all the heaps of stuff at the cottage,' she said after a moment. 'It's all there. But there's no notes, not even a bar of music for the Moon Song.'

Mark grunted. He wasn't altogether surprised but it was frustrating.

'Why not?' he began. 'Why are there no notes? Especially since he'd recorded all the rest. And left the CD for you to find. Didn't he see anything, no visions? He always saw things, talked with the woodfolk, visited the kieve, spent ages at the cottage. He did all that all the way through the making of the cycle. Why isn't there anything on the last song, the Moon Song?'

'I don't know …' Isoldé began to answer him, then she thought about how Tristan was, not just the time they had made love but the time she'd found him on the edge of the lawn. He'd been doolally, not with it, no help nor use. And she recalled what Gideon had said about Tristan going too soon and how this had affected him.

'Mark,' she began. 'You know Tristan went too early, shouldn't have walked the moonpath then, he should have stayed and finished the song. I've been talking with Gideon, he thinks, says, that going too early did something to him, to Tristan. Sort of scrambled his brains. What if that was going on before he went? Would he have been able to have his visions, talk to the woodfolk? I don't know. It feels like he separated himself from them, from his source, before he went. Else how could he have crossed the moonpath?'

'Hmm! Never thought of that …' he carried on driving for a bit, they were heading onto the moor now. 'So … suicide's not an option?'

'Gideon didn't say that,' Isoldé replied. 'It seems to depend on how knowing you are. If you're just a beginner it's not so important but if you know things, like Tristan, then it can be. Tristan knew about asking but, when it came to deciding about his death he didn't, he just went on and did it without consulting anyone. Gideon said that for Tristan it was more like … I don't know … like glory, like knowing you'd got it right, or thinking you had, and that was right out of kilter.'

'That would make sense. Like I said, Tristan always had his visions and would chat with the Woodfolk all the time, ask them about his work, about what was going on, what was needed. If he took his own decision, without talking to them, about his own death then he went against his own principles. He didn't ask them. I'm sure he didn't.'

'But he was in terrible pain, wasn't he?' Isoldé put in.

'Yes, but that doesn't matter,' Mark replied. 'Well it does but it doesn't make it OK for him not to ask. In fact, he should have asked. He could have taken the whole thing to them, told them how he felt, how the pain was taking his music away or whatever … and I think that's what he felt was happening. If he'd taken it to them they could have helped him.'

'But couldn't they see? Wouldn't they know anyway?'

'Of course they can see but there comes a time on the path when you have to take responsibility for how you are and for what help you get. You have to ask for help before they can give it. When you're a baby, just starting out on the path, Otherworld looks after you. When you get to being a shaman, as Tristan was, then it's up to you when you get help and you have to ask for it. Tristan didn't ask. He thought he knew best and just went his own way.'

'Shi-it!' Isoldé had a wry smile on her face. 'I didn't know how much you knew about all this stuff. That's like my Uncle Brian would say.'

'I didn't live with Tristan all those years and some of it not rub off.' Mark was chuckling. 'I'm not anything like as good as he was and I don't use it all the time like he did but I do know that much, that you have to ask.'

'And Tristan didn't ask …' Isoldé paused. 'I see … that makes sense … he took it all on himself, no sharing, no asking as he always had. So he goes over the moonpath in a state, like a personal state … maybe he gets stuck in that state.' Isoldé stopped, frowning. 'And that sounds like a sort of soul-loss …'

'Which would call for a soul-retrieval …' Mark said.

Second Crossing

Standing on the cliff-edge beside the steps, Isoldé found herself looking down the dark midnight-blue tunnel again. This time she was alone, no woodfolk, no Olwen, no Rhiannon, no Mark, even though he'd tried to insist on coming. She'd let him drive her out here, they'd left the car by Forrabury Church and he'd walked her out across the Stitches to the Lady's Window, then she'd made him stay there at the bottom of the steps to wait for her.

'But I want to come with you,' he'd insisted.

'But I don't want you to,' she had replied. 'You've never done it. I'll have enough trouble with Tristan without you having problems with the moonpath or something. Please, Mark, don't be a nuisance. This is hard enough without you being difficult too.'

It had almost come to a row. He was afraid for her and he wanted to be there, to help her with Tristan. She was afraid that if he was there, with her, but not able to cope, she'd lose the plot. And she was also wondering just what each of them would do when Tristan and Mark actually met again. After all that had happened there was a certain frisson there, an odd feeling. She'd never before been one to fancy more than one man at a time. Now she knew that there was a part of her that wanted both of them, both Mark and Tristan. Eventually Mark had given in, kissed her, sat down on the bottom step and let her go.

She stood at the top of the steps waiting for the moon to rise, for the path to appear. Suddenly it was there. The stone of the steps silvered, joined with the light, which became solid. Before she could think further about anything Isoldé set her foot on the moonpath. There was a slight wobble then it steadied. She began to walk forward without looking back.

'I'm not running away from Mark,' she whispered to herself. 'I'm walking towards the Lost Land, the land of song, of dream, of the dead. I go to fetch Tristan, so that he can sing one more time. And I go to return.'

The way was long, at times it seemed as if she never moved but always she was putting one foot in front of the other, going forward, going nowhere. It was cold, a light wind coming in off the sea, the sky a sharp, crisp indigo, the stars largely occluded by the brilliant light of the full moon, an occasional wisp of cloud blew across the moon's face like a thin black silk veil. It took all Isoldé's willpower to concentrate enough to walk the white track. It felt like being in a dream but it was not, this was reality. The sound of the waves below assured her of that.

Tristan could not come unless she fetched him. She knew that now. When Tristan had come at Caergollo, at the cottage, it had been her own sending that had drawn him to her. She was the power that called. He had lost his power to call along with the soul-part he had abandoned when he chose to die without talking with his muses, with the woodfolk, with Gideon, Rhiannon, everyone who would be affected by his choice to die. She knew she had to call that soul part back.

Was suicide wrong? Her catholic past told her it was a sin, a terrible one that got you excommunicated so you could never go to heaven. Was that right? Did the Old Way agree with that? It didn't feel so, that paternalistic, autocratic way felt all wrong, yet the whole of this trouble had come about because Tristan had, of his own choice, died too soon and without asking for help from any of the magic folk he'd always worked with. Mark had told her how painful it had been to know that he'd never see Tristan again once he'd gone off on the Japanese tour. But Tristan had not talked about it with Gideon or any of the others.

That was the problem.

Isoldé could get a feel of how Tristan must have felt, the effects of the disease closing in on him, restricting his life. Mrs P had described how difficult it was for him to eat, how his eyelids stuck together every morning so it took ages and chemicals to free them up so he could see, how thin he was, how he could keep very little food down, how even writing music became a difficult chore. No, he wouldn't want to live when life became that difficult.

But his life was also part of the life of Caergollo, and of the songs. He'd promised the woodfolk he would write this last cycle, and she now knew just how important that was, but he'd given up, gone, died, before he'd finished it.

Tristan and Isoldé ... the old story came into her mind.

'We three are like that, in a way,' she thought. 'We've got all the right names but we're not quite like the characters in the story. There, Mark was king and I was his wife but I loved Tristan because we'd drunk the wedding cup by accident on the boat over from Ireland. We then spent the rest of our lives trying to fool Mark and be together, and ended up dead with roses growing on each of our graves and twining with each other.'

Isoldé snorted derisively, she wasn't that sort of person now, even if she had been in a past life or something. Now she was quite decisive and wanted to be in control of her own life.

'Which is part of the problem with this caper,' she muttered. 'I'm not in control, I'm having to do things I don't altogether want to do. Things Tristan should have done but gave up on.'

Back to the suicide question again. Could you commit suicide and it not be a sin?

'It depends how far along the path you are,' said a voice in her head.

'Olwen ...?' Isoldé had really hoped she would be there to help but she was still walking the moonpath on her own. There was no more response, she was still alone.

She thought about what the voice had said. So ... if you knew a bit about what you were doing, about the unseen worlds, the magic worlds that lived around you, you had a responsibility to them as well as yourself? Damn! That meant she had too.

A chuckle sounded in her head.

'OK! OK! I've got it!' Isoldé muttered. 'So ... if Tristan had come to you all, said how bad he was feeling, that he couldn't cope, would you have helped? Could he have found a way to die and it all been all right, somehow the song getting finished?'

'That is another world, another lifetime,' came the reply, 'not the one we are all now in. But if he had come to us, told us how he felt, we would have helped.'

'What would you have done?'

'No-one knows now. That time is gone, not here, not in this space-time continuum. We might have been able to support his body, or his mind, or both. We might have been able to find another, like you or even Mark, who could write the song. We don't know now as all that is gone. Those threads, those paths, are not available here. They might have been if he had come to us.'

'But he didn't ...' Isoldé said.

'No ... he didn't,' replied the voice in her head.

'And that's it, isn't it? Once you work with Otherworld, like I am now with you, you can't neglect them or leave them out of your calculations. Tristan should have involved you all, his companions, co-workers, in his need to die, not just gone off and done it as though it didn't have any consequences for you all.'

'That's right,' the voice agreed. 'Once you work consciously with us then everything you do has an effect.'

'What about if you don't know?' Isoldé asked.

'Then we clean up the mess after you, like one does with babies.' The voice was quite acerbic now. 'Most folk don't know, don't work consciously. If they truly are at that stage, unknowing, then there is no deep blame attached. There is a little, everyone has the ability to think if they want to use it rather than run away from it, but if they are still emotionally and spiritually children then the problems Tristan created are not going to happen. For a start, they couldn't be working at such a complex level with us unless they knew what they were doing and did it consciously.'

'What about the bad guys?' Isoldé said. 'Like the black magicians in Dennis Wheatley stories and suchlike?'

'What do you think?'

Isoldé thought for a moment. 'They're conscious,' she said. 'They know what they're doing and they're also selfish, doing it for themselves, their own gains, to control ...' Her answer tailed off. 'Oh ... ah ... umm ... well, I'm a control freak, aren't I?'

Another chuckle sounded in her head.

'You at least know it,' the voice said gently. 'And although you may argue and curse, you know when something needs doing, like now, and you get on with it. Do you think you have the suicide thing more sorted in your head now?' the voice finished.

She did. It was about consciousness ... ha! So what wasn't? It was about asking your friends and colleagues how your actions would affect them. Just like having good relations with your friends in the everyday world. You didn't tread on your friends, you tried not to do things that would mess them up, hurt them, so you behaved as well as that with Otherworld too. Tristan had forgotten that, not consulted anyone but just gone off and committed suicide without finding out if there was another way or how it would affect everything. And that had resulted in him losing a part of his soul, the part that could make the Moon Song, and so not actually even being able to die properly. He was in limbo now, nowhere, going nowhere, unable to go forward or back without help. That was why she was walking the moonpath now, to bring him back to earth so things could be put right and the song brought to birth.

As she realised this, Isoldé found herself coming to the end of the moonpath. She smiled to herself, that too was part of the journey she knew, her own understanding of what had happened, what was happening and her own part in it. She understood now that she could only have reached the end of the moonpath when she reached that understanding in her mind.

'I had to walk until I'd found the answer to my question,' she said.

'Yes, you did,' replied the voice in her head.

At last, and it felt like lifetimes since she had left Mark and begun the journey, Isoldé found herself at the end of the moonpath, standing on the shore of white and black pebbles. They crunched softly underfoot as she crossed the beach to walk the moonlit path between the high waving grasses. The seed-heads shimmered in the light and bright flowers glowed like miniature lanterns. It was the monochrome landscape again of white and silver backed by deep, impenetrable shadow. Suddenly, she began to run, came to an abrupt halt at the edge of the grove. The path opened up into a glade ringed by silver birches. He wasn't there.

She would have to call him. She'd always known that was how it would be but had kept that knowledge shoved to the back of her mind, hoping it wouldn't be like that, that everything would go smoothly, Tristan would be there, waiting for her, willing to come, knowing what he was about.

'Fat chance!' she muttered now. But how could he be? He was missing bits of himself, didn't really know what was going on, what he'd done or anything much about it. Isoldé sighed and walked into the grove.

'How do I call him?' she asked out loud, hoping someone might reply. No-one did.

'Tristan … Tristan …?'

At first nothing happened, then a rustle sounded in the undergrowth opposite and a figure wound its way through the trees towards her. It was Tristan. He emerged to stand looking everywhere but at her. His gangly figure was still clad in the same light slacks, jacket, open shirt and bandana in which he'd appeared at the edge of the lawn at Caergollo. This time he looked far less self-assured than he had then. Eventually he looked at her, saw her and, like that time, waved to her.

This time Isoldé did not wave back but walked across the grove to meet him.

He came towards her. Isoldé halted. 'Which of us is the ghost?' she wondered.

'Isoldé?' Tristan whispered. 'You've come to me?'

'I've come to fetch you home,' she replied. Her voice was dull, monochrome, like the landscape. Now he was actually here she felt none of the fever that had been there last time she had met him in the grove. Just a dull ache in her heart. This was an ending, not a beginning.

He held out his arms, obviously wanting to hold her, kiss her, but she didn't want that, indeed she wondered if she ever would again. Something deep within her stirred at being close to him; it was the soul-part; it knew it was near birthing time and that birthing couldn't happen here or the song would be bound forever in the Land of the Dead.

Tristan's arms dropped and his face fell. 'I …' he began. 'I've wanted you for so very long, since I first met you all those years ago at the master class. I thought … seeing you here … you'd come to be with me.' He stood before her, arms hanging down at his sides, his tall, gangly body looming over her like a schoolboy.

'I know,' she said softly. 'But we have a job to do. Remember?'

'I remember only you.' His voice was husky now, eyes hot, he was remembering their passion.

Abruptly, Isoldé was angry and her frustration got the better of her. How could he be so stupid? The thoughtless suicide, not bothering to ask for help from all of Otherworld, all the folk he'd worked with all his life, had left her … them both, and Mark too … with a difficult job to do. Knowing that though didn't help lessen the frustration she felt at his gormless expression, hot, husky voice and the sex that oozed from him.

'Gods damnit!' she swore to herself, his brain functions had atrophied. Although the passion had been incredible, wonderful, the most stirring thing she had ever experienced, it had completely lost its power over her now. She had a job to do. So did he, if he'd ever wake up to it. She wanted to slap him. Didn't he know the passion had been for a purpose, to engender the song, the song he had died before he had finished writing?

He continued to stand there, looking at her like a lovelorn sheep, as though he had no idea beyond his personal needs of why she was here, why she had made that incredible crossing to find him.

She moved a little away from him. His eyes followed her. 'Tristan, we have to go back. Now. While the moonpath is still there. You have to come with me. We have to birth the song in the everyday world. You have to enchant the moon there, sing her into life. Do you understand at all?'

Tristan stood, staring, his eyes soft and roving all over her.

'Do you understand?' Isoldé repeated.

Tristan took her hand. Isoldé half wanted to pull away but didn't. His touch was electric, it began to turn her on. A pulsing began in the soft flesh between her legs, rippled up through her body, making her want Tristan inside her, pushing, the rhythm of sex ripping through her. She shuddered with it, pulled her hand away as the tide of ecstasy climbed through her body.

'No! That's not what I'm here for!' she cried out, turning away. 'Don't you understand? We have a job to do. The song …'

She was almost pleading with him now. His expression was confused, half sulky, that of a frustrated man who's just been refused. Damn him, Isoldé thought. Why can't he remember? Isoldé found a log to sit on, another one was nearby but not close enough for Tristan to easily touch her. 'Come and sit down.' Isoldé's voice was calmer now, colder, matter of fact.

Tristan came, sat down. He reacted immediately to her voice, like a well-trained dog.

'Tristan, we have to go back over the moonpath …' she waited, watched, did he know what she was saying?

'We have to go back over the moonpath,' she repeated. 'Both

of us. You and me. We have to go back, back to Caergollo.' That got a response, the name, his home, she could see the connections firing. 'Will you come with me? Back to Caergollo?' she said again.

'I'd go with you to hell and back,' Tristan told her.

She gave a half-smile. 'We don't need to go that far,' she replied. 'Caergollo will do fine. Will you come?'

'I'll come with you …' Tristan held out his hand.

Isoldé got up, took his hand to lead him to the meadow path down to the beach. He put an arm around her, swept her into his arms and pressed his lips on hers, his tongue in her mouth.

She pushed at him, turning her face trying to get away from him, the sexual feelings she'd had before were completely gone. 'Let me go!' she said as soon as her mouth was free. 'Leave me alone. This is not the time for any of this.'

He let her go, stood, arms dangling, frowning.

'Tristan! We have to go back to Caergollo. Now! Come with me.'

She took his hand again and led him towards the beach. This time he followed her meekly and there was no electricity in their touch. They crunched across the pebble beach to the water's edge. The moonpath spun its way out across the sea before them.

'Come along.' Isoldé pulled at Tristan's hand but he stood still. 'Come on …' She tried again, with the same response.

'If I go over there, over the bridge, I may never see you again if I come back,' he whispered.

'And you may yet,' she told him, not knowing if it was true. 'But we have to go. You promised the woodfolk, you promised Rhiannon, you promised the Moon her song. And then you left … before you'd done it, before you'd written the song. You have to come back. You have to record it.'

She turned to look at him. His eyes were confused but less than before. He frowned then nodded. 'Yes,' he said, 'I'll come with you.'

'Come on,' she said, pulling at his hand. 'Walk!' she admonished him. 'Just walk.'

Tristan followed her onto the moonpath. They walked together along the shining road. She found herself counting each step as she put one foot in front of the other and gently pulled Tristan along behind her.

It was like being in a tunnel of bright darkness but there was light at the end of it.

8. Soul Retrieval

Not lost, but requiring, pointing to the agony
Of death and birth.
TS Eliot East Coker

Mark

Mark drove the truck up the steep, narrow lane that twisted its way from the road just up the hill from Caergollo's gate to the top where the spring and the kieve were. And Tristan's cottage. It was their back door, or so Tristan had called it. The spring was on a public footpath through the grove of stunted Scots pine that led out onto the moor above, a wild scrub-land where local farmers grazed hardy sheep. The moor was full of birds, especially skylarks. Foxes hunted there, an ancient badger family had made their den at the edge of the woods, probably since the last ice age. Mark had played up there as a boy, pretending to be a great hunter and magic man, remembering the old Rider Haggard tales Tristan had told him as bedtime stories when he'd first come to live at the house. Nightmare tales, many people might think of them, but he loved them, they were the basis for his solitary games.

'Walking between worlds,' he smiled to himself now at the memory.

Isoldé seemed to have caught something of his mood, she put her hand softly on his as he drove. There was a rapport between them, more even than had been before. It was strange how hearing about her tumultuous love-making with Tristan had changed their relationship and for the better. It was far deeper since she had told him, last night. And the fact that she had felt she could, had dared to, had done things he wouldn't have dreamed of. They knew each other in ways most people never seemed to reach, the trust between them was complete.

Having Tristan in the back of what had been his own truck made Mark feel a bit strange. The whole enterprise was strange though. Tristan was dead. The body in the back might feel and seem alive but it wasn't like his own body, nor Isoldé's, Mark knew that. This was a ghost they were carrying, if a very physical seeming one. He wondered what would happen to the body Tristan was wearing once they'd done the soul retrieval. Assuming they could and it worked, he thought wryly. Neither of them had ever done such a thing before and there weren't any worthwhile manuals that he knew of. How the devil would you write such a thing anyway, he asked himself. It wasn't like mending the central heating. Perhaps Isoldé's friend, Darshan, might know but Mark didn't think Darshan had actually been faced with a situation like this, nor did he think the man had really done any soul retrieval himself either.

The hill levelled out and the truck stopped straining and struggling. Mark pulled into the widened turning circle not taking the truck to the grove this time. He could almost see the force-field-like aura at the edge of the sacred space. He parked, climbed out and went to help Tristan but he had already got the back door open and climbed out. He seemed perfectly fit. That was another oddity to Mark, he had expected Tristan still to be sick. He wasn't, of course. The body he now wore was well and healthy, no signs of disease at all, it was like having the young Tristan that Mark had first known back again. No, what was sick now was the mind and the soul, not the body.

Mark helped Isoldé unload the couple of bags they'd brought with them from the back of the truck; she took Tristan's old carpet bag with his magical stuff while he took the blankets, thermos and food. He led the way to the grove, Tristan trailed in the rear. Mark felt his friend was uncertain about this process although he had agreed to it. Whatever, Tristan did come. Mark put a rug down by the head-stone and Tristan went to sit on it. Mark sat on a log to one side, watching Isoldé work.

His mind drifted as he watched her sort through the magic stuff to find the knife and begin to invoke the circle. Tristan's return had been very strange from his perspective. He'd been loath to let Isoldé cross the moonpath on her own to fetch the man back but she'd insisted and it was true he'd never done it himself.

'I'll have my hands full bringing Tristan over,' she'd told him acerbically, 'I don't want you as a problem too.'

Mark hadn't been able to argue with that although his macho self had wanted to. He hadn't ever walked it and, as he saw the moonpath touch the stone step, his stomach fluttered. He might indeed make a fool of himself and be a nuisance to her, she was right. Rather gruffly, he had agreed to stay and watch his end of the path, wait for them, be there when she brought Tristan to middle earth again.

The waiting had been hard and he'd been forever panicking in case a front came up and occluded the moon so the path would disappear. Then, as time seemed to stretch out into forever, and his watch had apparently stuck at ten minutes past midnight, he'd panicked about how long she might have been gone, how long before she returned, whether they were somehow stuck in a time-warp. In fact, he'd panicked about just about everything.

She was right, he'd probably have been a completely useless wreck if he'd gone with her.

When he'd reached a point of complete despair, deciding he would never see her again, he had made out a speck of movement far out along the silver path. The movement had continued, come closer and gradually shown itself to be two figures, Isoldé and Tristan. They had seemed to float rather than be walking along the path, coming closer at an increasing rate until suddenly they were there. Isoldé came first, stepping down the steps, then turning to give Tristan her hand and lead him down onto the earth again. Mark had stood there dumbfounded. What greeting did you give to a ghost?

Tristan, too, was unsure of himself, recognising where he was but moving his feet as though he wasn't certain how solid the ground beneath them was. And staring at Mark. After several moments Isoldé had put their hands together. The immediate sensation had been electric, then it had calmed down and Mark had put his arms around Tristan.

'Welcome, brother,' he'd said.

Tears had coursed down Tristan's face, no words, just silent sobbing and tears. They had walked him back to where they'd left the truck, by the church. That had been a hassle too, Tristan had wanted to go in, see his organ again, in fact he'd been like a child revisiting a loved place all the way across the Stitches and was, still, all the way home in the truck. Once at Caergollo, Embar had rescued them. At sight of the cat Tristan had fallen on his knees and scooped him up, burying his face in the black fur. Embar had led Tristan outside to the summer house, there they'd lain down together and Tristan had slept out the day with Embar purring on guard beside him. That had been a relief, Mark and Isoldé had got something to eat for themselves then some sleep and then made plans of what to do. The previous day Mark had told Mrs P to take the day off, with no explanations other than that he wanted time alone with Isoldé. She had given them a cheeky look and gone, saying she would see them come Friday and hoped the place wouldn't be in too much of a state by then and they did know how to work the dishwasher, didn't they?

Tristan

The head-stone grove by the cottage was such a familiar place for Tristan, that's why they were bringing him there of course, he realised that. The Otherworld version of the grove was where Isoldé had first met him ... his mind lingered there, in that past. Maybe the Otherworld version was the real place and this just a shadow of it, like Roger Zelazny's lands were shadows of the real Amber, his central core world. Tristan realised his mind was wandering all over the shop, he brought it back to Mark and Isoldé. He'd seen how they were together, no real hope for him there, those two loved each other. Mark was collaborating with Isoldé on this soul retrieval they were going to do on him, helping her, not worrying about anything that had happened between her and himself.

'I told him everything,' she had said, watching Tristan's face.

Tristan watched hers, he knew what she said was true. How could Mark not mind? That staggered him. His own memory of the lovemaking between himself and his brother's wife – Tristan's mouth curled sourly at the biblical phrase he'd used – was quite fresh and potent. If Isoldé had gone into details, and she had from the look on her face, then Mark's current non-affectedness was beyond him.

'If our situations were reversed, I would kill you,' Tristan thought as he watched Mark unload stuff from the back of the truck.

His mind flitted again. Still the same truck, still going strong. 'KBO!' he muttered, the sour smile still on his mouth. 'Keep buggering on.' It was Churchill's old phrase from the war years, WWII. When Tristan first heard it years back he'd been taken with it, used it himself, told it to Mark.

'The truck keeps buggering on, and so do I. Buggering on to nowhere is what it feels like,' Tristan told himself in his head. The past time, the few hours since he'd crossed the moonpath, seemed like a limbo, a nothing-place, no time, nothing happening, in-between.

'I suppose that's why they want to try the soul-retrieval,' he mused. 'To take me somewhere, get me going somewhere, not just buggering on here between heaven and hell.'

'I got that right,' he thought. 'I'm going nowhere to Christmas ...' Spike Milligan's old song from the Goons swam through his brain. 'Perhaps I'm as nuts as he was,' Tristan muttered softly.

Tears came to his eyes. Love, human love, was something he could never share, never have for himself, had never had in his last lifetime, not the sort of love and sharing with another human being that Mark and Isoldé obviously had with each other. He'd felt the sense of oneness with the gods he'd worked with, with Rhiannon in particular. He'd recognised it in Mark years back when he'd first told of the organ god, the Pan-like figure he knew, whose back Mark said he rode upon when he was playing the organ really well. He remembered how Mark had first discovered this god while playing the Exeter cathedral organ. That was something Tristan could understand from his own knowing. But this power spinning and weaving between Isoldé and Mark was different and right outside Tristan's ken. It frightened him.

He came back out of his musings. It had been like that all day since she'd brought him back, like riding a great swell, a wave that rose up under him and took him to the shore only to sink away from underneath him and slither back into the mass of the sea, dragging him back with it. So, at times, he was propelled into the world where Isoldé and Mark were, only to be pulled back out of it again, back into the ocean of dreams ... where he lived in what was left of his mind.

Sacred Space

For the pattern is new in every moment
And every moment is a new and shocking
Valuation of all we have been
TS Eliot: East Coker

'Damn it all!' Isoldé swore under her breath. Then she stopped. 'I'm getting to swear an awful lot,' she thought, 'what's going on? I know I swear but this is getting to be every second sentence.'

It was the out-of-control sensation that really got to her. Belfast and her Virgo moon, she decided, were both very strong in her. Belfast had been out of control all her childhood, you learned how to behave, how to look, how to not look, how to respond to each sort of person, all so that you stayed alive one more day. Especially when your mother had been killed because the IRA suspected her of collaboration and your father had run off to New York ostensibly to pull money for guns out of gullible Americans through NorAid. Coming to London, getting her degree there, her good job, her good life, had given her back her control, her power as she saw it. Now, it felt as though she was losing it to a bunch of fairies who had incredible powers over life and death.

She stood still, the sacred knife in her hand. She'd been about to invoke the circle but, looking down, she saw her hands were shaking. This was no way to go on. She'd not invoked a circle since she'd been with Uncle Brian but she could feel all the old knowing welling up again inside her, including the knowing that the mood you were in coloured it and all your workings. Bugger! She must get a grip, stop this fear and get to a sense of herself again.

She went to stand at the centre of the circle. The head-stone was there, Tristan sat beside it, but she took no notice of him. She could feel the glass-coffin-like aura around him that was keeping him separate from her, from the grove, from the whole of Middleworld perhaps. There was a sense of "yes" in her head, the voice that spoke to her more and more often now.

'Who are you?' she asked the voice. 'I know you, hear you, trust you but I don't know who you are. Who are you?'

'I am the Lady,' replied the voice. 'I wondered if you'd ever ask.'

Isoldé blushed at that. Uncle Brian had always told her to ask. So had everything else she'd been in contact with since she'd been with Mark.

'Asking is the best form of protection,' Brian had told her right at the beginning. 'If you ask, if you talk to whoever you meet, then you'll know who it is you're working with and can choose whether to do so or not.'

'But what if they lie to me?' Isoldé had asked back.

'So, you asks three times, girl. Tis what the spell's for and it works. They can lie to you twice but on the third telling it must be true. Tis one of the laws of nature, like gravity. None of us knows why it works, no more'n we do with gravity, but we knows it does. You use it girl.'

'Does it work with people too?' she'd asked.

'Ah ... no, it usually doesn't.' Uncle Brian had shaken his head. 'People have removed themselves from the laws of nature and work mostly with the laws out of their own heads. That's why there's so much trouble in the world. They don't work with everything around them, they work to control everything around them. That's the problem, girl, and one that you can share all too easily. I've been watching you. You're afraid if you're not in control, aren't you?'

Remembering that conversation from twenty-five years and more in the past made her blush again. All that time ago he'd seen her clear, and here she was now still doing it, still grasping at control all the time. And with the same problems the grasping brought ... no control and continual fear, living in her brain and not seeing what was around her, there to help her. She took a couple of deep breaths, and noticed she was gripping the knife very hard. She relaxed her hand, then some inspiration came and she crouched down to sink the knife up to its hilt into the soil at the centre of the circle. It wasn't something she'd ever done, or heard of before but it felt right.

There was a sigh inside her head. 'Is that what you need, Lady?' Isoldé asked.

'Yes …' the voice sounded breathy. 'Yeeees …'

'What now …?' Isoldé asked.

Pictures began to form inside her head now. It was rather like watching a computer screen or a TV. She saw the circle but now there was something like a fountain at its centre, spiralling up from the ground around where she'd inserted the knife-blade into the earth.

'You opened a pathway,' the Lady told her. 'Watch …'

The fountain – it was silvery-white, rather like smoke – twisted its way vertically upwards to about the height of the surrounding trees at the edge of the grove. It seemed to be made of two threads spiralling in opposite directions, reminding her of the double helix of DNA. As the spiral column reached the height of the stunted Scots pine trees around the edge of the grove it curled over and divided itself into four, each of the four pathways going outwards to the edge of the grove in the four directions until it reached the trees themselves. At that point the four branches turned to spin around the grove, two going deosil, the other two going widdershins. It was like a gyroscope of silver smoke, spinning and dancing around the grove, making a dome over the area, quite different from any circle Isoldé had ever thought of before.

'Yes,' said the Lady. 'This is our circle. Only it isn't a circle.'

'It's more of a sphere, made from a spiral,' Isoldé said. 'A three-dimensional spiral.'

'That's right.'

'Is this what we should be doing? Not the usual circle druids and witches do?'

'It would be better,' the Lady replied. 'But we cope with the circle. We always work with whatever is there but if humans can come further into the world, with us, then it makes the working far more effective.'

'This is like the six-armed cross ...' Isoldé whispered, suddenly noticing how the smoke spun slowly round the grove in both directions. 'The vertical column, and it goes in two directions. Then the arms spread out to do the horizontal, and that's in two directions as well.'

'Well done!' There was a chuckle inside her head. 'You noticed.'

'I did so,' Isoldé chuckled back. 'I'm getting there. Although Gideon calls me a quick study I can be as thick as two short planks, the same as everyone else, at times.'

'You'll do,' the Lady told her.

'Is the circle made now?'

'What do you think?' was the Lady's response.

Isoldé was about to reply tartly when she stopped and thought, then stopped thinking and looked, looked around her. What were they here for? What did they need? They'd come here, brought Tristan here, to retrieve a part of his soul that was lost when he crossed untimely to the Isles of the Dead. So what did they need to bring that soul part back?

In the grove were the trees, the soil, plants, water from the spring, the air they breathed. There were little pine-cones in the grass, seeds from last year's harvest. The four elements and powers represented. She went round the grove, finding cones, asking each time before she picked one up if she might do so and if this was the right cone to take. Sometimes she got a yes, sometimes a no, on one of the no's she looked closely and saw that ants were using it, she must not disturb the homes of other creatures. She smiled. When her hands were full of cones she brought them back to the head-stone, put them in a pile.

There was a cup in the carpet bag, she'd seen it before, now she hunted it out of the bottom of the bag, took it over to the spring and asked if she might fill it with water. Getting a yes, she did so and brought that back to the head-stone too.

A roughly flattened piece of clay from the carpet bag came out next, a hand-made dish. Tristan had made it from clay found in the stream by the house and roughly fired it in a sawdust kiln, the pictures of him doing so wound forward in her head like a video-clip. She stood holding it, wondering where to find some soil to go in the dish, which was what it was for, earth to earth ... the words rang through her head from the funeral service. A chill ran over her flesh, was this a funeral they were doing too? She pulled herself back from those thoughts and pushed her focus back to the task in hand.

'One thing at a time,' she muttered. 'One thing at a time ... Now, where do I go for soil, please?'

There was an immediate pull on her from the right. She followed the pull over to a place where one of the pines curled over and down making a small cave-like hideaway under its boughs. Crouching down, Isoldé could see a molehill inside, fresh and sweet-smelling, the lovely scent of damp earth. 'May I?' she asked softly.

She nearly fell over backwards as a black nose followed by a pair of long-clawed paws came out from under the soil-pile and two tiny black eyes stared at her out of the velvety fur. Something happened then. It wasn't like when Embar spoke to her but there was communication there. The thought was terse, abrupt, but the answer was yes. Isoldé remembered from her recent explorations into natural history that moles were solitaries, she chuckled inwardly, this one felt like a gruff old man disturbed at his favourite hobby. She sent a thank-you back from her own mind, saw the black whiskers twitch, then the little creature disappeared underground again. She reached in and took a handful of the soil he'd dug and put it in Tristan's dish.

Fire, water, earth … how was she to do air? Her immediate thought was incense and she was about to ferret in the carpet bag to find some when she stopped. It didn't feel right. What is air, she wondered, apart from a collection of invisible gases and the major means of staying alive. She stayed still, trying not to think, not to reason her way out of the problem – she'd grasped that much from what the Lady had said. Reasoning was great for some things but useless for others, like trying to turn a screw with a hammer, she chuckled at the thought but it was a good analogy. Nothing wrong with either the hammer or the screw, it was just that they didn't work together, wrong tool for the job. What was the right tool for the job she had to do?

'You're definitely getting the hang of this,' the Lady whispered.

'Thanks,' Isoldé replied, 'but not a lot is coming through about how to do air.'

'That's because you're thinking again,' the Lady replied. 'Thinking clogs up the pathways, means we can't get through to you. Too much clutter, like a Victorian mantelpiece.'

'Damn it! I am too,' Isoldé realised, chuckling at the pertinent analogy. She took a breath and sent out the question. 'What do I do for air please?' A rustle in the pine branches and the soft caress of a delicate breeze on her face was the immediate answer. 'How do I hold that for the ceremony?' she asked.

'How do you catch the wind?' came the immediate reply.

How do you catch the wind … in a sail if you're in a boat or a windmill. Something niggled in her brain, pushing and shoving at other thoughts, trying to get itself to the surface. It was when she'd been down to the witchcraft museum on the quay at Caer Bottreaux. Her brow furrowed as she strained for the memory, then she let go the struggle and asked for pictures of the scene. Yes, there it was in one of the cabinets. The label told of how the local witches had been tried and killed, one of their crimes had been catching the wind for sailors and fishermen for a fee and, sometimes, cursing, calling up a storm to drown someone who had upset them. They had sold ropes with knots in them that held the wind.

'How do I catch the wind?' Isoldé asked.

There was rope in the carpet bag, she delved in and came out with it. This was silken rope, beautiful, fine, hand-spun silk. It was a creamy-silver colour, like the spiral fountain that made the sphere when she had put the knife into the earth.

Isoldé took the rope in her hands wondering what to do. The breeze blew about her hands, stroking them, winding round them. Almost unconsciously, Isoldé's hands followed the motions suggested by the wind's caress. She began making a knot and found she was humming, a simple little tune of four notes, going round and round as her hands twisted the rope. The breeze stopped. Looking at the rope, she saw the knot was made, a figure of eight. She laid the rope down beside the fir cones, cup of water and dish of earth.

'Now I have the four elements I need something for the three worlds, don't I?' she said to the grove in general.

Sunlight warmed her, she noticed it especially now although the morning had been full of light since the dawn. The Sun above, the Earth beneath her feet and Middle Earth all around her. How? Yes, they were there but they too must have representatives on the altar she was building.

Sunlight, light … Isoldé dived back into the carpet bag and came out with a crystal prism, held it up to the light. Shading it slightly with one hand she saw the colours of the rainbow reflected onto her skin. Light! Sunlight! Newton's magic glass! She couldn't help but grin. The three colours that the prism split the white sunlight into – red, blue and green – were there too. Were these telling about the three worlds as well? Yes they were, but was it enough?

'Sunlight, light, the three primary colours of white light do tell of the three worlds,' said the lady inside her head, 'but we would like more. The prism is good for the sun, the light. It catches the light as you caught the wind in the rope knot, but we need the others. Keep working.'

It struck Isoldé that most of the witches and Wiccans she'd met through Darshan had a pretty easy time of it. They read books and copied other people's rituals, there was a set of stuff one used, a set of ways of using it, nice and easy, a manual to follow, "traditional" ways of doing things. Just my luck, she thought, not to be able to do it that way. It's much harder when you have to work it all out and ask the powers what they want.

There was a chuckle in her head at that. 'We're working to PhD level here at least!' Isoldé heard the voice say. 'If not research. No rote learning for you!'

That made her laugh again. OK, if that was how it was to be … So, she'd got the light now, with the prism; that was acceptable to the Lady, the powers, wasn't it? There was a mental nod in response. So now I have to find a way of representing the Earth and not just a bit of soil for the ground but a whole darn planet, is that right? Another nod in her head was all the response she got. Ha! Big help.

Isoldé sat down by the pile of stuff that was the altar. Trying to clear her mind, she put her hands on the grass. A whole planet, how would that like to be represented?

Pictures again, like the pictures of the Earth from the old moon shots, the blue globe swirled in white cloud, hanging against a black velvet background. OK … yes … like the pictures of the Earth from the Moon, but she hadn't got any such pictures with her. The globe swam out of focus, refocused, became much smaller and a paler blue. The white swirls were still there but had changed shape. What? Again Isoldé frowned, what was it? What was she being shown? She pulled the bag towards her and rummaged in it again, pulling out a beautiful silk scarf with a hand-painted owl on it, Tristan's rattle-staff decorated with hag-stones, sheep vertebrae, a raven's foot and small skull. There was a little painted box too, containing some lumps of fossilised dinosaur shit, three owl pellets and several glass marbles. Then her hand touched another stone ball, she pulled it out. This was an agate, a blue agate with white swirls flowing round its surface and a pure white colouring at the top and bottom, like ice. There were golden colourings, shapes, under the white swirls, she stared at them closely, they really did look like the continents. Little gold dots were clustered about in both the large blue areas, like islands in the Pacific and Atlantic oceans. It was the Earth in miniature, a little lighter blue than the moon pictures had been.

'Wow!' she breathed aloud. 'That really is cool. I wonder where you found this.

She looked at Tristan but he was still inside the glass coffin aura, he didn't see her and she felt strongly she wasn't supposed to speak with him, not yet.

'Thank you,' she said to the grove, the Earth. 'Was that always in the bag or did you just put it there, shift it there?'

The only answer she got was another chuckle.

'Well, it's beautiful,' Isoldé replied. 'It would be very nice if it's still here after we finish.'

She really felt she was getting a handle on this now. Her asking was making things happen, like when the mole had appeared with the soil she needed. Or maybe enabling them to happen was a better way of putting it, she really must get out of the habit of thinking she controlled things. Perhaps the agate globe had arrived in the carpet bag as a result of her asking the Earth for something to represent her. The thought was both exciting and scary. She had to ask for something for Middle Earth next ... what would that bring?

Nervousness made her fiddle about with the things she already had for the altar, reorganising them, making different patterns and relationships. She knew she was prevaricating, not getting on with it, but the revelations had been coming fast and furious, her mind was whirling, unable to keep up with it all. That was no excuse, she knew. She wouldn't be asked to do anything impossible … at least she hoped not. Would she?

A warmth passed over and through her, comforting. No, she felt, not impossible, but it might well stretch her to her absolute limits.

Another deep breath and she asked again. 'Middle Earth, what am I to use to represent you?'

That was the most direct question she had yet asked and it produced a very quick and direct response. No pictures this time but one of the faer folk themselves was suddenly standing on the grass just in front of her.

'Oh shit!' she breathed.

'I'd really rather not,' the little man replied in a broad Cornish accent, sweeping off his scarlet pointy hat in a bow to her.

She was speechless. He seemed to realise this and carried on.

'I'm a pixie,' he said. 'Not *the* Piskie, of course, but one of the faer folk. I'm quite safe, too,' he added as he watched the expression on her face.

Isoldé knew a little about pixies, and the Piskie, she'd read up about them after the visit to the witchcraft museum. The Piskie was said to be very dangerous and also much larger than the little man standing in front of her. Pixies were like the Little People of her own land, less dangerous according to folk lore but quite tricksy, you had to be on your toes to work with them. She was glad the big one hadn't come in response to her call.

'I'm one of the Ellyon,' the little man went on. 'In your country you call us the Little People. We're the faer folk in whichever of your languages. We hold Middle Earth together.'

Ellyon … the name of Tristan's song cycle. The pixie watched her face, following her thoughts, nodded to show her that she was getting it near enough right. He was dressed in greens and browns with the scarlet hat, and scarlet boots, she now noticed. Her mind gestalted, if she passed him in the woods and he was lying down, curled up, she could easily mistake him for a pile of leaves. The pixie looked at her. I've probably done just that lots of times, she thought, smiling back.

'I asked Middle Earth for something that would represent her …' Isoldé began.

'And you got me …' the pixie answered. 'That's because I can, and I will.'

'Does it matter that you're a person? All the others are things.'

'And you think they're different?'

Isoldé blinked. Things weren't people, were they?

'Everything has soul, has anima,' the little man said, quirking an eyebrow at her. 'I'm an anam chara and so are all the things that came to you, came to help you, when you asked them. How are they different in soul from me? Do you think soul only comes to certain shapes?'

Isoldé swallowed. This was certainly a morning of getting a completely new handle on the world. All the patterns she thought she knew seemed to be coming apart at the seams, making new and shocking valuations of everything she had ever been. She crouched beside the altar pile and began to touch each of the things there, naming them … fir cones and their seed-fire, cup and the water in it, Tristan's dish and the soil in that, the silken rope with its wind knots, the crystal prism that held and divided sunlight, the agate that was the Earth. As she named each one she also thanked it for being there, for holding the energy she needed for the ritual she was going to do for Tristan. She came to the little man last.

'And thank you too … for being here, for the lessons you've given me, for holding Middle Earth together while I work.' She stopped, another idea coming. 'And you, and all of you, please help me to get it right. Help me to restore Tristan's soul-part, make me do the right things, say the right words. Help me make it all come right.'

The pixie came close to her. He had a blade of grass in his right hand and now he struck her cheek with it. It stung. Isoldé managed not to jump.

'You've done well,' he said. 'Learned, learned quickly and as you worked. That's good. We'll work with you because you've asked us. We'll help you because you've asked us. We'll not obstruct you for you are on the work of the Lady, of the Mother.'

'Thank you,' Isoldé replied.

Something was happening in the altar pile. Smoke seemed to be rising from each of the things there, grey and silver, some shot through with red and gold, pink, green, blue. The smoke formed itself into shapes, almost human shapes, shapes she recognised. They were the same as the faer folk she had seen that night here in the grove, when the little demon had first shown her the lines and threads. In fact, the demon was rising now out of the fir cones, all silver smoke sparkling with red and gold.

'You are the spirits that inhabit the things of the Earth,' she said, yet another revelation piling on top of the rest.

'We are indeed, my lover,' they chorused back to her. 'We are indeed.'

They began to dance, circling the grove. They would each dance into the middle, to the head-stone, touch it and then dance back out again. As she watched, Isoldé saw lines forming as they did this, like weaving, a pattern of light-threads forming in the grove, made of all the colours of the rainbow. The threads pulsed, it was a living web.

She saw it then. This was the web, the wyrd the little demon had told her of, this was the web that Nial meant in biodynamics, even if it might not be quite as he thought, this was the web of life, all interconnected. She saw the threads touching herself, the trees in the grove, Mark, Tristan. If she peered hard enough she could see the threads reaching to every blade of grass. She blinked and shook her head. Seen like that it would make you think you couldn't actually move because you were totally caught up in a bundle of threads. She looked down at herself now, in fact she *was* a bundle of threads. Her clothes, her body, her form seemed to have almost disappeared, wavered in and out of existence, but what was strong in this new sight she had suddenly got was the interweaving of the threads. All the new age stuff about all life being interconnected was true, she could actually see it, all the threads interwoven with each other. She watched a blade of grass grow, it was like a natural history film of speeded up slow-motion. As one thread grew so other threads reached out to join with it and the threads it came from extended and grew to become the new grass.

Her mind boggled. She blinked, shook her head and shut her eyes.

'Can't do it anymore!' she gasped. 'How do I turn it off?'

It was gone, immediately, just like that.

'Just ask,' said the pixie.

Isoldé sat in the grass, taking big, long breaths, eyes shut at first, hands hanging onto grass stems, fingernails digging into the earth.

'Whoof! Ooof!' she gasped. 'That was big! Huge!'

Gradually her breathing slowed along with her heartbeat. She dared to open her eyes. Things were back to the normal she was used to, trees, grass, herself, her own body, no threads visible.

'Thanks,' she whispered. Then a thought struck her. 'Eliot was right, you know, TS Eliot the poet. He said *"Humankind cannot bear very much reality"* and he was absolutely right. If everyone could see that they'd go nuts.'

The pixie was sat beside her now. He chuckled. 'Mmm! We know. But there's the problem … as long as human beings think everything is separate they make a total cock-up of everything because they try to work it all as separate things. Something has got to be done about that and that's what Tristan's songs are about and why we need the Moon Song to bring it all together.'

'You aren't proposing that everyone sees what I just saw, are you?'

'No. Well not at first, not until they can. You couldn't have done it, seen it, if you hadn't wanted to, if your soul hadn't known it already, if your Self hadn't wanted to see it.'

Isoldé cocked an eyebrow at him.

'It's self-limiting,' he said. 'You can't see until you can see. That's what things being occult is about. They're hidden, occluded, by the person's own ability to see, until that person is able to see.'

'You mean,' Isoldé said slowly, 'it's like Uncle Andrew in the Narnia book where Narnia is created, sung into life by Aslan. Uncle Andrew has arrived there by accident, is terrified of the lion, of Aslan, as the light comes up and he can see him. He doesn't believe it can possibly be a lion singing so he tells himself, over and over, "Lions only roar … lions only roar" and so convinces himself that the lion is only roaring. He never hears Aslan's song, only roaring and growling. He never gets any of the joy and beauty and blessing the others get … because he has told himself it can't be so.'

The pixie was looking sad. 'Yup,' he said. 'Some of you folk call it mind over matter. You are so strong in your brains that you can convince yourself black is white and you often do, unfortunately. That's why the world is in such a mess. And why we need you and Tristan's songs to help begin the process of getting it balanced out again.'

'So … how do I help the process get started?' Isoldé asked.

'You already have,' the pixie told her. 'You enabled us to show this web here, rebuild it, or rather, reaffirm it, as it already existed or the grove wouldn't exist. Now we have to get Tristan's soul-part back with him, get him to sing and Mark to record it, then get Tristan back where he belongs.'

'Is that truly in the Isles of the Dead?'

'The Isles of the Blest, yes. When you take him back this time he will be blest indeed.'

Tristan

I said to my soul be still, and let the dark come upon you ...
I said to my soul be still, and wait without hope
For hope would be hope for the wrong thing; wait without love
For love would be love of the wrong thing; there is yet faith
But faith and love and hope are all in the waiting.
Wait without thought, for you are not ready for thought;
So the darkness shall be light, and the stillness the dancing.
TS Eliot: East Coker

Tristan had followed Mark and Isoldé to the grove, sat beside them so they were in a circle by the head-stone. Sunlight, dappled by the young leaves, filtered green-gold onto the three of them and onto the little pile of things Isoldé had collected in the middle of their circle. Some he recognised, others he didn't. His hand went out to touch the agate globe then drew back before he reached it. It looked like a miniature Earth. Had that been his? He didn't think so. Where had it come from?

There was a tension, a presence in the air, like a newly strung harp. Tristan peered, looking at the other two more closely, they were powerful, far more than he'd ever before thought Mark could be. It was their love, he realised. And it was Isoldé herself.

'Are you ready?' she asked him.

'As ready as I know how,' Tristan replied. 'What are you going to do?'

'I don't know. Whatever the spirits tell me when I ask,' Isoldé told him.

That sort of rang bells ... asking ... letting the spirits help ... but asking intelligently and asking the right questions.

'How will you know what questions to ask?' Tristan looked at her.

Isoldé smiled at him. 'Somewhere, inside of you, you know the answer to that. I suspect it's part of what we're looking for.

The part of you that knows how to ask has got lost. It's that part the Moon Song needs, that part that she has to show to everyone, through you.'

Tristan looked at Isoldé, for once he didn't desire her, that seemed to have washed out of him. He felt empty inside, sort of cleaned out, perhaps walking back across the moonpath had done that. He felt himself fading into and out of existence in this world he sat in, here and not here. He wondered if he could hang on long enough to do whatever was necessary. His gaze was caught by a movement. Here, in the world again, Isoldé had taken a birch twig bound with hawk-bells out of the old carpet bag he recognised from the cupboard in the cottage.

Of course, she'd found his stuff, he realised. That was some of it in the pile there in the middle between them. Oh yes, he'd seen it before, just now. Memory was difficult. Had they just arrived? Had he been here a little while?

She was going to conjure him with his own paraphernalia. That made him smile. She was right, it would work, he would be caught by his own magic and there would be nothing he could do about it. In fact, he realised, there was nothing he wanted to do about it, he wanted the transformation … transmutation, he corrected himself. It wasn't his form that needed changing, it was his essence that needed moving on, moving out of the rut he'd landed himself in.

He stopped, shook his head, that was a new thought, one he'd not had for … oh … it seemed like ages, not since he'd been in this limbo place after he'd crossed the moonpath. What were they doing? What was Isoldé doing already to change him?

Light Organ

After Isoldé had begun to invoke the sacred space Mark slipped quietly to the edge of the grove. He had no idea what was going to happen but the feeling of power from her was almost overwhelming. It reminded him of playing something huge and wonderful on Exeter's organ, or being inside the crazy land of pipes that was the Liverpool organ when someone was playing that.

He knew he had to get out of her way. He'd been necessary to bring Tristan to the grove but now he absolutely knew he must not be within the sacred space any more. Things were already happening there and they would affect him too if he was inside.

He found himself a perch on a tall stump that sat up like a stool growing out of the ground. It was just the right height, just in the right place. Sat there he was outside the circle but he could watch, be there to help if needed but not be in the way.

His vision flickered. It was like there were lines, like threads, in front of his eyes. He blinked, rubbed them, the threads were still there. He screwed his eyes up and peered through them to see properly.

'Hell!' he swore under his breath. 'I can't see properly, what's going on?'

'That is the wyrd,' said a voice from somewhere. 'The web.'

'Eh …?' Mark peered around him, there was nobody there. 'I am *not* going nuts!' he told himself. 'Not now. No time. Isoldé needs me.'

'No,' the voice agreed with him, 'you're not going nuts. You're seeing what she sees.'

'Eh …?' Mark said again.

There was an exasperated sighing sound in his ear. 'For goodness sake,' said the voice. 'Get a grip! You're seeing what Isoldé is seeing, so you can help if necessary.'

'Who are you?' Mark managed a reasonably intelligent

question at last.

'You know me best when you play the organ,' the voice replied. 'But I'm here all the time. You just don't notice me.'

'Eh ...?' he said for the third time, then realised how daft he must sound, and that he wasn't concentrating on Isoldé, and that he didn't know what was going on. 'Err ... sorry, but is this the time for introductions?'

'Yes, it damn well is!' The voice was definitely cross with him. 'She needs you to help with those threads. We need you to help with them. For goodness sake get it together.'

Mark shook his head, very confused, but he sensed the urgency in the voice, in the atmosphere around him in the grove.

'I don't know what to do,' he said.

'That's why I'm here, to help!'

'Well, please help me then,' Mark too was feeling exasperated now. 'But I can't see properly with all these lines across everything, it's like looking at a TV screen that's gone wrong.'

'Is that better?'

The lines toned down quite a bit, their intensity lowered. Now they were faint but still there. He could see the grove properly.

'Much! So what do I do now?'

'Stretch your fingers out, like you were playing the organ.'

Mark did that. It felt slightly foolish at first then he suddenly felt the threads under his fingers. There was a real sensation there, not like the organ keys, more like a harp on its side, or a dulcimer maybe. If he put a slight pressure on the thread he could feel a response. He looked up. The web was huge, how on earth was he to play that?

'I need the threads to come together more, like a keyboard and the foot-pedals for an organ,' he said, looking round vaguely. It was odd speaking to someone without being able to see them. At least with a phone you had that as a point of focus. 'I wish I could see you,' he added, without much hope.

A column of smoke grew out of a grass tuft directly in front of him, began to take form. Shadowy goat-legs grew downwards, ending in delicate cloven hooves, a brown-skinned torso rose above the legs, hairy-chest, strong shoulders and sinewy arms ending in long-clawed fingers. The head, on top of a longish neck, was bearded and had thick, bushy, black eyebrows over brilliant golden eyes. It was topped with curly black hair out of which grew a pair of spiral, silvery horns. The effect reminded Mark of Mr Tumnus from "The Lion, the Witch and the Wardrobe".

'No!' the creature told him, very firmly, 'I am *not* Mr Tumnus.'

'Err … no,' Mark agreed. 'I think your name might be Pan …?'

'Harrumph!' the satyr-figure snorted. 'That will certainly do better. Now, what was it you wanted? Apart from being able to see me?'

'It would be easier if the threads could come together like an organ keyboard,' Mark said. 'And, as I've got a seat here, I could do some of them as base cords, like organ pedals. Is that possible?'

As he made his request, Mark was watching the threads form up into a fantastic organ console. Some of them even came together as stops. The whole thing seemed to be made of light, strands of light, all the colours of the rainbow.

'That do?' Pan asked him.

'Looks good.' Mark had his hands on the keyboard and his feet on the pedals already. The sensation was electric, and very sensitive. 'Shii-it!' he exclaimed as he got the feel of it. 'This is incredible.'

'Well just get on and play the damn thing.' Pan's voice was acerbic. 'She needs your help. I've been holding time while you got yourself together, can I let it go now? Can you do your stuff?'

'Yup!' Mark felt as high as a kite but also completely competent. He knew he could do it.

Pan stepped back in amongst the trees, out of sight, but Mark distinctly heard him muttering, 'Sheesh! Humans! Who needs them?'

Another voice answered Pan. 'We do,' it said. It sounded like Gideon.

Mark looked up and out into the grove. Isoldé was standing. It was as though she hadn't moved since he'd backed out to the side-lines, as if the whole episode with Pan had taken no time at all. Pan had said he was holding time, that he'd just let it go again. Ha!

Mark's fingers on the threads felt the tingling, the threads wanted to be played … how?

'Let us show you …'

Mark blinked … it was the threads? The threads themselves were talking to him? Sheesh! Well … anything was possible and now was no time to argue or discuss. Get a grip, he told himself, and do the job. His fingers, meanwhile, were doing it, whatever his head thought. His fingers played the threads, pulled and pushed the stops, his feet pressed the pedals, it was like music … but not. He didn't so much hear it as sense it, right through his body, but hearing was there as well.

He saw Isoldé had the calling bells in her hand, Taliesin's silver branch. She was asking the faer folk to show her what to do, to put the right words into her mouth, to help her as he had asked the threads to help him. She began to dance, and to sing. The song followed his fingers … or did it lead them? … as they played the incredible light-organ.

Her dance also seemed to follow the threads. Some of her steps pulled threads away from Tristan where he sat by the head-stone, connecting him to the grass, trees, leaves, plants, to the grove itself. Others she drew towards him, from the things that made up the grove, seeming to bind them within and around him. Isoldé was spinning a web. She was reconnecting him to the greater web that was the grove and, from that, outwards and outwards to the land itself, to the Earth. As he realised this Mark let go of thinking. His hands took over and began to play the threads in time and in tune with her dancing, it was as if he was being played rather than doing the playing himself. And so I am, he thought, Otherworld is playing me ... no ... not just Otherworld, this world too. These are the threads that make up this world. A big grin settled on his face as he realised this, it was wonderful, being a part of the whole so consciously, like orgasm only better. He allowed his hands to take charge.

This sort of sensation happened to a lesser extent when he was really doing well on the ordinary organ in a cathedral performance, not quite the same but so similar. His mind, now with nothing to do except observe, wondered idly if it really was the same, that somehow when he was playing, he connected to the web of the music and the web of the place and the web of the audience.

A chuckle sounded softly at the back of his mind. Of course, it seemed to say, how else can you connect with everything, with the composer, with the instrument, with the listeners?

Soul Part Calling

Isoldé stood up. She had the calling bells, the silver branch of Taliesin, in her hand. She had asked the faer folk to show her what to do, to put the right words into her mouth, the right movements and things into her hands, then she'd let go. Finally, she had let go, trusted enough to allow her body to be shifted by the wyrd, by the pattern of Life itself.

That realisation had at last come through to her. It wasn't a bunch of fairies who moved and shaped and shifted her, it was the web, the wyrd. She was part of it and, if she stopped fighting it, it moved her where it needed her to go, where she, her spirit self, needed to go ... she'd got that message in the last few seconds too.

Each second seemed to be eternally long, stepping in a dance, a long slow dance where each footfall was significant, and she was that dance. The bells in her hand rang softly as she moved, stood up. Their echo spun its way out across the grove, she knew it was making all the threads that the faer folk had woven vibrate and sing. A background part of her could hear them, a part, the foreground part was concentrating on listening and hearing, seeing and doing, not on thinking.

The threads, the weaving had become possible when she sank the knife into the soil and released the energy. It had needed her will, her cooperation, her bloodletting for the earth to enable that to happen. Realisations were crowding in on her again.

'Wait!' she called in her mind. 'I must do the work first. Help me to do the work.'

She was back with the singing bells.

Tristan sat with his back to the head-stone, touching it. The altar pile was before him. He had tried to touch it once but drawn back. Isoldé had felt herself about to stop him but he'd stopped of himself without her interruption. Now he sat quiet. She could sense he had no real idea where he was, who he was even, and certainly not what was going on.

Isoldé's feet began to dance round the head-stone. She began to sing.

Soul, be still, let the dark come upon you.
Wait in darkness, wish for nothing.
No hope, no love, no faith, no thought.
Wait in the darkness of the womb for your birth.

Soul, be still, let the dark come upon you.
In the darkness is nothing, no reason, no thinking.
Like the caterpillar you lie in the chrysalis of being.
Wait in the darkness of the womb for your birth.

Soul, be still, let the dark come upon you.
I am stirring the cauldron, the soup of your being.
In a year and a day the wisdom is coming.
Wait in the darkness of the womb for your birth.

Soul, be still, let the dark come upon you.
In a year and a day the cauldron will burst.
Three drops of wisdom will spring out and burn you.
That day the womb breaks is the day of your birth.

Soul be up dancing in the bright darkness.
The year and a day are all coming to pass.
Thirteen moons have arisen, come full-bellied and pregnant
Now must they die and so give you birth.

Soul, break the prison, like the Mabon arising.
Soul come forth now out of blindness to see.
Soul tear down walls and walk free in the sunlight
That shines from the face of the Moon to the Earth.

Soul, be still, let the stillness be dancing.
So, from the moonshine that darkness is light.
Soul hear the Logos, the words that are wisdom,
That weave us the wyrd of Life on this Earth.

Isoldé's feet trod a spiral path about Tristan and the grove. Her mind was fully on her job as her eyes followed the wyrd-lines she saw in the grass and in the air around her. Her voice carried on humming the simple tune although the words were all done now, all spent, out there, humming along the threads. Her dance went on as though it would never stop.

Cocoon

Mark's attention came back to focus on Tristan. Something was growing, there, in front of the man. A misty-white and formless something, writhing like the smoke from an incense stick. It seemed to come from out of the altar pile. Mark's fingers fell on threads that gave out a minor key, plaintive, unsure, timid. Isoldé danced over to the smoke, crouched beside it, no longer singing. The smoke-thing leaned towards her, licking at her hands, she took it up, holding it loosely but giving it somewhere to be. Then she offered it to Tristan.

Something changed in Tristan. His face had been blank, unknowing, unfocused, throughout the dance. Now the eyes saw, clicked into focus on the smoke in Isoldé's hands, the mouth firmed up, there was expression in his face. Mark recognised the man he had lived with all those years. Tentatively, Tristan put out one hand. The smoke coiled a tentacle towards his finger in response. Smoke and finger met. Tristan's whole body jerked, the smoke flinched too but neither let go.

Isoldé stood up, still holding the smoke, standing over Tristan. He lay with his head back against the stone as she bent over him. She held the smoke in her hands and leaned towards his mouth as he opened it. Again she offered the smoke, then she blew it into his mouth.

It disappeared within him. As the last bit went in he lifted his hand and touched his own lips so the last particles that still clung to the finger entered his mouth. It was done. Isoldé's hands were empty, Tristan's mouth was shut now, his eyes closed, tears coursing down his cheeks.

Mark's fingers drew soft cords from the light-organ. He watched the thread-cords curl around Tristan now, enfolding him in a cocoon. It looked just like the chrysalis a caterpillar wove in order to turn into a butterfly, only this one was man-sized, Tristan-sized. As he watched it began to darken to a soft, gold, buttery colour, losing its transparency so he could no longer see Tristan within it.

Isoldé stood up just as Mark's fingers fell away from the light-organ. They both looked up together, at the same moment, and saw each other properly for the first time since the soul retrieval had begun. She looked exhausted. Mark went to her and she put her arms around his neck, leaned into him. After several minutes she whispered into his shoulder, 'It's done.'

'I know,' he replied.

'Yes ...' She pulled enough away from him so she could see his face. Hers was smiling. 'You were there. You played the threads.' Her lips brushed his cheek. 'I couldn't have done it without you,' she told him.

'What now?' he asked.

'He's becoming butterfly soup,' she said, on a half chuckle. 'Or rather, Tristan soup. He has to remake himself and then be reborn again whole.'

'How long's that going to take?'

'Until the moon rises again, so they tell me,' Isoldé replied. 'I'm going on what the Faer folk and the Powers are telling me. What do they tell you?'

Mark realised he'd forgotten to ask again, blushed. His eyes went slightly out of focus then flicked back. 'Yup, same,' he said. 'I'm not used to this asking thing yet. I nearly screwed up at the beginning, then Pan came and sorted me out.'

'Me too!' Isoldé said ruefully. 'I'm so used to sorting every-thing out for myself that it's weird having helpers, only needing to ask in your head and then finding yourself doing and saying the right things even though you didn't know you knew them.'

'Too right,' Mark agreed. 'It's like when I'm playing the organ, the ordinary organ. I get a similar feel when I'm playing really well, as though I'm being played rather than playing of my own will. When I practice it's usually sort of me-in-charge, then, when I perform I let go and just run with it.'

'Sounds like you're better used to it than me.' Isoldé snuggled against him again.

'But what do we do with this, with the cocoon, the Tristan-soup?' he asked. 'Do we just leave it here? Do we stay with it? What?'

'We could go to the cottage,' Isoldé said practically. 'We brought coffee and sandwiches, we could have those while we think about it ... no, while we ask about it,' she corrected herself, grinning. 'Old habits die very hard,' she finished as she let go of Mark and made to collect Tristan's paraphernalia bag. The altar she left.

The pixie sat beside Tristan now.

'We'll be here,' he told them. 'There'll be nothing to see, not until tomorrow, and there's others waiting to show you things. You're not needed here. Go to the cottage.'

'Come on,' she took Mark's hand, led the way down the path towards the cottage, leaving the chrysalis in the head-stone grove.

9. Moon Song

Gideon

Gideon soared over the moors above Caergollo. Raptor sight gave him a full view of the grove and all that went on there below. He feathered the fingertips of his raven-wings, tilting slightly and banking down closer, then tumbling head over heels with a loud "Cark" just for fun before stalling to rise again over the treetops. Raven was his favourite form for flying, ancient, wild and tricksy ... like himself. He screamed again into the wind as he plummeted down from low cloud height to overfly his prodigies. He looked on Isoldé, and Mark too, as his phenomena, his bright stars and his enfants terrible too. They were good but they were hard to manage, as were all creatures that thought for themselves and asked questions. Asking questions, not taking what he said at face value was important. He wanted their knowing to be in their bones, not rote-learned in their heads and all befogged with thinking, if they questioned him, fought him even, then they would know because they knew intrinsically and not just because he told them. Gullible folk were no use at all.

They'd done well. Tristan was cocooned now, gone back into the spiritual atoms of his being to coalesce again into his full self, to put all the pieces of his soul back together. Gideon had sighed with pleasure as he watched Isoldé find and take the soul-part in its smoky form and blow it back into Tristan. He knew, he'd rummaged about inside her brain and her mind, that she'd never done such a thing before. There were wisps of memory from the druid uncle and the Hindu boyfriend of how shamans did this. Isoldé had caught hold of those memories and woven them with the on-the-job knowing she was pulling from the threads and she'd done it successfully.

And Mark ... well, he'd done great. Gideon hadn't seen the

threads played as a cathedral organ before. He had to chuckle, most folk would take it as a Christian symbol but the organ was just a great musical instrument, full of all the tones and notes, very appropriate for weaving the threads of the universe. Idly, as he soared again, Gideon wondered how this experience would change Mark's organ playing in the everyday world. That it would change there was no doubt. The experience was in Mark now, a part of him, he was not the same person he had been while driving up to the grove, his soul was larger now and more inclusive from doing the work. As he wasn't a dunce he would grow into that larger size, that greater experience, and make it a part of himself. Sailing out across the cliffs now and over the sea, Gideon sighed with pleasure again. Yes, his prodigies were doing very well. It was time now to go down and be with them again, show them some more. The most dangerous part was yet to come and even Gideon didn't know how that would end.

The Kieve

At the cottage above the waterfall, Mark halted at the threshold. 'I can't,' he said. 'Not yet, not now.'

Isoldé stopped beside him, the door half open.

'It was his private place,' Mark told her. 'It would be like walking in on him making love.'

Isoldé saw the tears come. She held him, understanding some of what was going on inside.

'We could go down to the kieve?' she suggested.

Mark nodded, turned back and led the way down the steep steps into the roaring silence of the kieve.

They settled on a log-seat off to one side in the shelter of the cliff, silent for the moment, while the coffee and food brought them back to some feel of normality.

'I'm sorry,' Mark began. 'Just couldn't do it.'

'Not a problem,' Isoldé said. 'I've a feeling we're supposed to be here anyway.'

They sat silent again for a little while.

'Did you see that rhythmic pulse ripple through the cocoon-thing?' Mark asked her. 'Every few seconds the colour would change, darken slightly as it did? What was all that about?'

'Don't know,' she said. 'I think it really is like butterfly-soup though, he has to change, remake himself, in order to assimilate the lost soul-part again.'

'It'll be a day and a night until Tristan wakes, emerges … and then what?' Mark said.

'Then he must sing,' she said. 'And you must record him so the album is complete. It's his voice will do the trick, so the Faer folk tell me. Nobody else will do.'

'And then he has to go back to the Isles of the Blest.'

'Yes … and I have to take him,' Isoldé said.

'Oh ye gods!' Mark turned to her, grabbing her hands. 'I don't want you to go. Or if you have to then I want to go with you.'

'Not possible,' said a voice from above them.

Looking up, they saw a raven perched in the branches of an ash tree above them.

'Gideon?' Isoldé asked.

The raven spread his great wings and floated down to stand beside them. Then the morphing began, it was amazing, like watching a film ... but this wasn't a film, Mark reminded himself, this was real life. Everything happened at once. The shimmering black feathers became brown, weather-tanned skin; the whole creature grew, expanded, lengthened; the claws became feet in soft leather boots; the eyes shifted shape and colour from round black pits to almond-shaped gold with vertical pupils. That was weird. It ensured that Mark knew in his bones that Gideon wasn't human, even if a lot of the time he assumed human form. This was a creature of another world.

All this passed across Mark's brain at the speed of light, yet seemed to take forever. He blinked, he was sat beside the Gideon he knew, hunkered down on his haunches beside them.

'You can't go, Mark.' Gideon said softly. 'You have to hold this end of the bridge.'

He paused, looking away as Mark frowned at him. 'We've not done this before, well not in our living memories. We cannot hold the bridgehead. Wrong sort of stuff, wrong sort of matter. Ours is too close to the matter of the Isles, not like how it is here. Yours is Earth-stuff. Ours is only partly Earth-stuff and only a small part at that, just enough for us to manifest here.'

Mark was frowning still. It almost sounded as if Gideon was talking a sort of physics. Isoldé was eyeing the shifter too.

'Why did Mark have to weave the threads' she asked. 'Why didn't you, or Pan, or whoever, do it?'

Gideon smiled wryly. 'I keep saying it, don't I? You'm a quick study.'

'What?' demanded Mark. 'What are you talking about?'

'I can't weave the threads here, on the everyday Earth,' Gideon said. 'I can weave them in the Isles, in Otherworld, but not here.'

'Tristan knew that too, didn't he?' Isoldé asked.

'Uhuh.' Gideon nodded.

'That's why it was so wrong of him to die before his time, wasn't it?' she went on.

Gideon nodded again.

'If you don't know how you fit with all the worlds, if you aren't yet awake and aware, then when you suicide it doesn't really matter too much, doesn't have too many consequences to things other than yourself. You can get away with it anytime,' Isoldé went on.

Again, Gideon nodded.

'But if you know, know how you fit into even the non-human part of the everyday world, let alone the unseen worlds, then you also have the ability to know how your death will affect all that. And if you know the unseen worlds as well ...' she left the sentence hanging.

'Then you have as much obligation to that as you do to the humans around you that you love, and the place you live, and the creatures who share your life,' Mark continued. He stopped, thought a moment, then started off again. 'I can weave the threads because I'm human. And I know a bit about them. And I know a bit about what all this is and how I fit into it.'

'That's right,' Gideon said. 'So how is the moonpath built?'

Isoldé chuckled in spite of herself, she was feeling both excited and scared. 'It's built of threads,' she said. 'But ... and this is a guess ... I suspect those at this end are made of Earth-stuff and those at the other end, in the Isles, are made of whatever it is over there. Does the stuff sort of change as it gets nearer Earth, further from the Isles?'

Gideon grinned. 'You know, you're a real pleasure to work with.'

He stretched out a claw-like finger and gently stroked the back of her hand. A shudder ran through her, his sensuality very evident. She wondered what Mark thought, she could tell he'd seen, knew. Somehow, it didn't bother her. It had happened, it had been pleasurable for that instant and now it was gone. And it hadn't changed her feelings for Mark one iota. She looked at Mark, he was actually grinning.

'Do I pass?' he asked Gideon.

The shifter burst out laughing. 'With honours, cum laude!' he replied. 'Thank all the gods. It's good to have you to work with.' Gideon held out his hand to Mark, looking him right in the eyes. Mark took the hand, there was a moment's pause, each gripped the other, then they let go.

'Music crosses a lot of boundaries, doesn't it?' Mark spoke to Gideon directly now.

'It does.'

'It's part of the Logos, is that it? Part of "the word", the sound, the note, all that stuff various esoteric babble goes on about?'

'Yes.'

'So … Tristan's singing … my playing … whoever's music … all that is part of how the word, the Logos, gets out into the world, to people who aren't yet aware, consciously aware, of all this stuff. That's part of why people like music so much too, isn't it?'

'It is.' Gideon's face was more serious than either of them had ever seen it before. 'Tristan knew all this … but his physical pain and mental longing were so great his personality took over and he couldn't resist. That's why he walked the moonpath that night and left his old body at the bottom of the cliff. Being in his personality-self made him act like a child and not talk to us. He was afraid we would say no. His mind had gone small, squeezing out all his lifetime experience of us and transforming us into severe parents who wouldn't understand. He ran away, trying to steal a march on us, but all he did was screw himself up. And us too, of course.' Gideon paused a moment, then went on. 'So you're right, Mark, you can weave the threads though music, as could Tristan. And we need you to be very sure you hold the threads of the moonpath so Isoldé can return after she's brought Tristan back to where he should be. Once you've recorded him.'

Gideon stood up. Suddenly, Isoldé was aware of how far the sun had moved. When they had come here it had been early morning. Now, from the way the shadows fell, the sun had moved to late afternoon. She cocked an eyebrow at Gideon.

'Yup,' he said. 'Time can do that. We need to get on. You have a job to do.' He was speaking directly to Mark. 'You know how to do the recording. You've got the stuff you need?'

Mark nodded. 'It's all in the truck. I've got all the portable kit in a bag. Is it time?'

'It's time,' Gideon said.

They followed him back to the grove.

The Singing

The clear pure tones of Tristan's voice spun out across the air. Tristan sat on the head-stone, eyes near shut, a half-smile on his face, hands moving gently on the harp as his body swayed with the rhythm of the song. He had given Isoldé his drum.

'Here, you can play this,' he'd told her, laughing at her astonished face.

'I can not!' she'd replied. 'I'm a beginner, I'm not good enough.'

'You are so,' Tristan had mimicked her Belfast accent which had become very pronounced as she'd tried to refuse the instrument. 'And they think you are.' He pointed down at the group of little folk, all carrying their own drums, who stood clustered about her heels.

Isoldé started, she'd not seen them and nearly dropped the drum as she jumped, then tried not to tread on any of them. There was a wave of laughter as they got smartly out from under her feet.

'Come on, girl, we're wasting time,' Tristan said. 'We need to get this song done tonight and the moon is already rising, coming to hear her song. She must give her approval.'

It was a very different Tristan who had broken his way out of the chrysalis soon after Gideon had brought them back to the grove.

The chrysalis had lain in the grove by the head-stone, a dark gold, fat cigar shape, like some of the early ideas about alien spaceships from black and white films. Embar sat on guard beside it, upright with his tail curled around his paws just as they had left him hours ago, as though he had never moved. The Ellyon too sat around, watching, waiting.

Mark and Isoldé went to sit on the tree trunk close by. As the first star showed in the darkening sky there had been a crack, like a branch breaking, and a fissure had appeared in the chrysalis.

There was a thin, transparent skin inside, they could see hands trying to tear it open, like a chick trying to escape from an egg. Mark moved to help but one of the Ellyon got in his way.

'No!' he said. 'The man must find his own way out. If he cannot birth himself then he's not fit to be reborn.'

Mark sat back, tense. Isoldé took his hand. Hers was cold and shaking slightly, he could feel the tension in her too. Tristan had to make it … or what would happen if he failed?

The struggle continued. At last they saw Tristan biting at the membrane, it was difficult, the skin was stretched tight inside the chrysalis but eventually a tooth made a nick in the skin. He pressed his face against it, working his teeth, getting an eye-tooth into the hole, pulling, tearing, making the hole bigger until he could get his hands into it. The stuff was very tough, it took all his strength to make the rip bigger but he persevered. Gradually it widened so he could get his arm and shoulder through it, he pulled and stretched, got a leg through. The membrane ripped. Tristan fell out of the chrysalis and onto the grass. He was naked.

Isoldé leapt up and went to him, pulling the shawl from her shoulders to cover him. This time the Ellyon didn't stop her. Mark followed, snatching up a blanket and helping her wrap the man.

He was breathing, great shuddering gasps, eyes still closed like a new-born kitten. Embar came close and licked gently at his eyelids. They opened, cat and man stared at each other, then Tristan smiled. He tried to speak but only managed a wheezing, choking cough. Isoldé was there with the water, letting a tiny amount dribble into his mouth. It worked. After a few moments Tristan's breathing eased, he pulled himself to sit up and was able to swallow properly as she held the cup for him. He came back to consciousness.

'Thank you,' he whispered. 'Thank you.'

'No problem,' Isoldé said softly, holding him upright with one arm while she kept the water near his lips.

'No problem at all,' Mark added. 'Welcome back.'

Isoldé was amazed at the difference. Now Tristan's eyes were bright, sharp, focusing on them and everything in the grove. The very feel of his skin was different, tighter, firmer, the muscles strong. She realised that, when they had made love, his body had been relatively weak and flabby in comparison to now. Memory told her this was nearer the Tristan she had known at the master-class, although that one had been well on with the disease and not as fit as now.

To Mark it seemed he was helping to hold the Tristan he had known as a boy so many years ago, before the disastrous North African trip where Tristan's compassion for a dying little boy had given him HIV. His arm tightened round Tristan's shoulders, touching Isoldé as well. Mark felt Tristan sense the caress and move his body in response.

They got him dressed and fed, just last year's wrinkled apples and nuts that the faer folk brought, and water from the spring.

'Fruits of the forest,' the little man said. 'They'm best for y' now. Nothing too much.'

Tristan had nodded, accepted the fruit and eaten slowly. It grew dark, the time of the song had come.

As the clear pure tones of Tristan's voice spun out across the air Mark could see the song-threads weaving. To actually see the threads of sound as well as hearing them was amazing, he had to stay very focused in order to keep watching the levels on the portable recording gear he'd brought with him. He pulled the headphones over his ears so he heard exactly what would go on the recording, hoping it would lessen the impact of seeing the threads of sound. It didn't.

'Please,' he whispered. 'This is quite awesome but can we turn the thread-sight down some? I'm finding it very hard to concentrate.'

The threads faded gently like a rainbow after a storm. 'Thanks! That's better.'

'You only have to ask,' said a voice at his elbow.

Mark jerked, he'd been engrossed in his own thoughts. Looking round, there was Pan, sat cross-legged beside him, cleaning his hooves.

'Sheesh! I wish you wouldn't do that, I almost jumped out of my skin,' Mark said crossly.

'Good for you,' Pan replied, equally acerbic. 'Out of your skin you might be less bound up in your head. You need to get used to reality. Spent all your life, so far, thinking I was some figment of your imagination, that I lived in your head. I don't, I'm real and I'm here. Anyway the inside of your head is cluttered up like a Victorian boudoir!'

'Thanks a bunch!'

Pan laughed. After a moment Mark laughed too.

'You're right,' he said. 'It's just I'm not used to you being visible and audible in the same world as me.'

Pan snorted. 'You'd better get on with the recording,' he said.

Looking across the grove again, Mark saw a shadowy figure growing at the far side of the clearing. Long ears seemed to stand up from the head, huge eyes, liquid brown like a limpid stream, were followed by whiskers, twitching nose and soft brown fur. Long hind legs stood the hare up tall so she could see what was happening. The light began to change, darkening the sky. A pale silvery-gold light began to spread from the bottom of the sky upwards. The full moon rose. The moon-hare stood waiting to enter the grove.

Sister, mother, granny, lover,
Water lady come to me.
Flow the earth-blood in the silver
Lines the dragons make to be.

Tristan repeated the chorus of the song again.

The hare-girl's long, silky ears extended, stiffening, quivering, pointing across the grove towards the singer. He was singing her names. He was, wasn't he? It made her blood quiver, her skin itch under the fur. She looked down at the paw-hands, the claws. She saw the tatters of her dress half-covering her furry nakedness. Her shape was upright, like a human, but her gait was bowed, bent from the long legs bent backwards at the heels of the huge feet so she didn't stand straight. She was beginning to see herself through the words of the song, the singer. It had never happened before.

Oh, she knew herself when she peered into a pool, saw the reflection of her face hanging there in the water. She knew it was her face, she had tried moving her mouth, her whiskers, putting a paw to her nose. The reflection copied her every move. It was like the ghost-part of a soul, lost in the mists of half-being. She had seen plenty of those, most recently the singer's own. But now the woman had brought that part back to him and he was singing. He was singing her song.

Dragon lines that shift the power,
Strands of darkness carry life,
Threads of the toadstool-giver
Carry water to the fife
Of the plants who lie there birthing
In the winter soil of strife.

Toadstool? The hare-girl's brow furrowed, her big eyes stared across the space between them. What did he sing of? Pictures formed in the space, she saw the plant-roots hunting, searching, reaching out for water and food. There was something else there. Silvery threads, seeming to grow out of nowhere and reaching out to the rootlings. There was a bright flash as they connected, rootlings and threads. Right through her body the hare-girl felt the lightning-spark of life. The threads made it possible for the roots to feed, to drink, to live. And they were something to do with her … but she wasn't a toadstool. Was she? No, she could see better now, the silver strands were brought to life by the toadstool-beings. She could see them now, like flickering sparks of light darting across the darkness of underground.

She realised she was underground, in the soil, the winter soil, when all is sleeping up above where the low sun shines for just a few hours every day. Then, all the life is deep within, growing, changing, preparing for the springtime birthing.

The paw-hands reached out to touch the silver threads. As they did another lightning-jolt cracked through her body. Something had gone out of her and, at the same time, something had come into her. She was a part of the process. As she touched, so the light brightened, the lightning life-force felt more potent, the rootlings grew stronger.

'If I touch them it makes the life flow better,' she whispered, beginning to understand. 'They need me.' She looked down at the paw-hands. The skin showed through the fur now, the fingers were longer, they had nails instead of claws. 'I am shifting,' she whispered. 'Shifting … changing … just as Root-mother said.'

Suddenly she stood up on tiptoe, teetered there. 'What?' she thought. 'What?' The sun balanced in front of her eyes, like on a see-saw. It teetered too.

Sun at threshold
Teeter totter
Will she come or will she go?
Life at change-point
Moving forward
See the winter come and go.
Springtime maiden
Stepping lightly

Silver flowers where she treads.
Hoots the owl, the queen of night-time,
Bringing life above the ground.

'What?' she whispered again. 'What is he singing now?'

Springtime? Yes … that was when the sun passed over the threshold. The humans called it equi … equi … something? Equinox! The word bounced into her head as Tristan sang. She knew it now, it meant equal nights. Yes! After that point the nights got shorter, there was more light than dark each day, up until the high point at midsummer. She felt her own innards churning at the thought, thinking about male hares, about how they would chase her, about how she would box them away, making them work and run and fight to claim her. Her teeth bared in excitement.

And in the ground … she could feel and see it now. The shoots pushing up through the earth. Incredible! They were so fragile but they heaved aside the heavy winter soil and thrust themselves up and out into the light, growing, fecund, full of flowering buds.

Her hands … hands now and no longer paws … reached out to touch the newborn shoots. Again, as she did so, sparkles of light sprang in the shoots. Some reached upwards through the baby plant, going on into the air, catching the sunlight, drawing it down into the green leaves, making food for the plant. Other light-sparks went downwards into the roots, connecting with the toadstool-threads, drawing on water and the chemical atoms of food in the soil.

The Moon-hare girl quivered. The plants needed her. She was needed. She was a part of the whole, it couldn't work without her. It was the most glorious feeling she had ever had. No longer was she a spare-part, a useless shifter who couldn't shift properly, something that had to be cared for and looked after by all the others. She was useful. People would come to know her, know her usefulness. Tristan would help.

The sun stood still ...

Judder, judder,
Sudden standstill,
Sun no longer moves in sky.
Will it ever? Will it never?
Is the world about to die?
No! the moon comes, brings reflection,
This has happened oft before.
Sun climbs mountain,
Reaches utmost,
Then it is the time to fall.

Moon is watching, always watching,
Coiling spirals round the Earth.
Magic spirals, carry sunlight,
Pour it down upon new birth.
Birth is death, is leaving somewhere,
Coming somewhere new again.
Death is leaving, death is coming,
To go is only to return.

Moon revolving, always showing
Only one face to the Earth.
Drawing water, upwards, downwards,
Pumping cycles of rebirth.

Tristan sang and sang. The moon-hare-girl listened and listened. He was singing of her, of what she did. He was singing of life and death, the widdershins and deosil of being, coming and going, growing up to die down.

'One must follow the other,' she whispered.

That was wise for her, the sort of thing she thought of the

root-mother saying, not herself. She looked about. There, beside her, was the root-mother, her rose-cabbage face folded into smiles. Beside her again was the blue water-girl, shimmering, and she was smiling too, holding a green shoot in her hand. Yes! Water! That was it, she realised. Water was what the leaves were about. The root-mother held the strands of the michoriza, the toadstool-strands, connecting the roots to the soil and the soil to the roots, making it whole. The water-girl carried the flow up into the budding plant, bringing forth the leaves, making it possible for the plant to feed from the sun.

'We need you,' the root-mother told her.

'We need you,' the water girl agreed.

And there was the beech-girl, all green and gold and lovely, swaying gently in an almost-breeze that was as much sunlight as air.

'We need you,' the beech-girl added her voice to the other two. 'You make the cycles of growth, of death and rebirth possible. Come alive to us. Come alive to the humans. Bring us alive.'

The moon-hare-girl smiled. She reached out hands, hands not paws, and touched each of her sisters. 'I am coming,' she said with confidence now. 'He is singing me alive.'

The fiery red fruiting harvest sister came to sit with them, reached a hand out to touch the moon-hare-girl. Fire spun through her, lighting her up.

Turning, turning, world is turning,
Moon hangs low upon the sky.
Big and bold her belly swollen
In Harvest moon our future lies.

Red and gold, she turns the seeds,
The flowers burst apart at last.
Bright and dark, the seeds hang heavy,
Feasting now is at the heart.

Birds come, hungry, calling, telling.
Moon hangs watching in the sky.
Blood the colour, blood the life-juice,
Blood is given sacrifice.

All the growth the Moon engendered
Comes to fruit now bursting forth.
Earth gives food and life and water
So her creatures live once more.

Moon and Earth, eternal partners
While this cycle ebbs and flows.
As the one lives so the other
This is how the garden grows.

Tristan sang the song. The moon-hare-girl heard, listened, allowed it to flow through her spirit, along the threads of light that made her body and out into the land around her, through the plants, through the soil, into the animals and insects and birds, all the creatures. All was connected, no creature, not even human, was alone, disconnected. All were a part of the whole. And she, the moon, spun the threads, sang the song, helped the dancing that made the web of life.

Lady Moon, we call, we greet thee.
Step the white track for us now.
We will follow, we will help you,
Only come and show us how.

Sister, mother, granny, lover,
Water lady come to me.
Flow the earth-blood in the silver
Lines the dragons make to be.

Dragons come, show the ley lines,
Lines that carry life for all.
We will help you, we will walk them,
Make the trees to grow so tall.
Make the flowers shine so brightly,
Giving perfume, scenting call,
Bringing bees to carry pollen
Carrying life-sparks for us all.

Butterflies and dragons too come,
Birds and insects, life so small,
But so vital,
Without them dead are we all.

Come Moon-Lady,
Teach us, lead us,
Show us how to be on Earth.

Sister, mother, granny, lover,
Water lady come to me.
Flow the earth-blood in the silver
Lines the dragons make to be.

Tristan held the final note forever, allowing it to fade and disappear into the dawn light. The song was over. The sun was rising over the tops of the trees, putting stars and moon to flight. In the circle now, the hare-girl stood, shimmering, hare-girl no longer but the lady of the moon. Gideon stood beside her.

'Not you to make my body this time, but a human man,' she said to him.

Gideon smiled down to her. 'You are lady of the moonpath,' he told her, 'of the white track, of the silver ley lines that connect everything to everything. You are Olwen here on Earth.'

'So I am. And I have a body in this world that makes sense of that, so I can work with the plants and with everything that lives and moves and has its being here on Earth.'

Olwen went over to Tristan. He looked exhausted but triumphant.

'Thank you, master,' she told him. 'The songs can go out now, the Moon Song is here, holding them all together.'

'I'm glad, lady.' Tristan went to take her hand, she gave it to him, he raised it to his lips. 'And I'm sorry that I left before it was all finished.'

Olwen smiled, a rueful, twisted thing. 'We need Isoldé too,' she said. 'Somehow your soul knew this, your body too. Without knowing, you made it possible, imperative even, that she come here, work with us. Not all that looks away is necessarily so.'

'Now, I must go back,' Tristan said.

'Yes … and Isoldé must lead you back. You have not the strength to do it on your own, you have given me all your strength, in the song.'

This was true, Tristan was sagging where he sat on the head-stone, he had put the harp on the grass at his feet, there was no spare energy left in him.

'I'll take him,' Isoldé said, coming up to them. 'I'll take him tonight.'

'I think not,' Olwen said.

They all stared at her.

'Tonight is the eclipse,' she said. 'My face will be covered, it is the night of the blood moon.'

The faces of the humans fell. Gideon smiled again, a harsh thing.

'How long has Tristan got?' Isoldé asked. 'When must he go back by?'

'Before the sun rises again,' Gideon said.

'And I cannot make the path while my face is covered,' Olwen said.

'It's not covered all night,' Mark said. 'Only at the high point.

You will shine again before you set.'
    'And how long will that be?' Isoldé asked.
    'Not long,' said Olwen. 'Not long.'

10. Endings & Beginnings

Blood Moon

The vision shuddered into blood-stained monochrome. Isoldé stood in darkness watching the moon's face gradually disappear as the Earth crept across it. This was not an ordinary full moon. Tonight was the eclipse, the sun's light, which usually lit the moon, cut off by the Earth, the only light that reached her now came through the Earth's atmosphere. The sky was clear, every star was out and brighter than ever. But the moon's face was filled with blood.

How was she to work with no moonpath? Tristan would not be able to return to the Isles, he would have to stay here, remain an uncertain ghost, never to go home. And he couldn't go without her. Now he had written the song, sung it, recorded it, he was an empty shell. Oh yes, he still lived, still loved her, but they were no good to each other in the world of everyday. She knew she needed to take him home, but how?

The Earth-shadow crept forward. Only a tiny sliver of bright silver light showed like a crescent in the sky, like a waning moon. Soon even that would be gone and Isoldé would have no path across the sea. True, she knew it would come back, but could he last that long, or would he become a shrieking wraith with no home in either land? That was her fear. The blood moon drained all will from out of him and, seemingly, out of her too.

She stared out of the window at the growing darkness. There was no point in taking Tristan to the cliff top, not yet. Maybe there never would be. She went back down to the library, Tristan was sat there in the armchair, Embar in his lap. He looked up as she came into the room, watching her face. Seeing no hope in it he dropped his gaze back to stare into the fire. He was a cold ghost, they had lit a fire for him.

I can't use the moonpath, Isoldé thought, there is no

moonpath, not while the moon's face is hidden by the Earth. But I must get him back.

A picture of the head-stone grove formed in her mind. It was there in both worlds, in this world and in Otherworld. She recalled saying this to Rhiannon before, and how Rhiannon had said that she could travel directly from the one to the other ... if she were good enough.

Now was not the time to think about that. She had to be good enough. She had done so much in the past days, was that not enough? She didn't have time to ask anyone and she didn't dare to, they might say no and she couldn't bear that. Tristan here, in the house, in their lives, neither alive nor dead, would drain all the life out of herself and Mark. Mark already looked grey and worn, despite being unfailingly kind both to Tristan and herself, and that was worse than anything. 'Come on,' she said abruptly to Tristan. 'It's time. We must go.'

Tristan put Embar down and stood, looking confused. 'There's no moonpath,' he said.

'There's another way. I can get you home.'

'But can you get back?'

'Yes,' she said confidently although she was far from feeling it. 'I can.'

Embar stared at her. Tristan followed her out of the room. Embar followed him.

'Come on,' Isoldé ordered Tristan out of the truck and pointed him to the path to the grove. 'Go!' He did as she bid him.

Embar leapt out of the back of the truck and stood at Isoldé's feet, glaring up at her.

'I must,' she told him.

'Ask ...' The word formed in her mind like a shout.

'I can't,' she said. 'What if they say no?'

The cat continued to glare for a moment then turned and followed Tristan down the path.

The light in the grove was a red monochrome from the bloody reflection of the eclipsed moon.

Isoldé wondered what she must do to walk between the worlds from one grove to the other. She stood by the head-stone, then crouched beside it. It really was a face, a head. There was the mouth as a mossy crack in the rock. The nose, slightly bulbous, stood out as a bulge of stone. And the eye. The eye was carved, a circle with an equal-armed cross inside it, the astrological symbol for the Earth. The carving was over four thousand years old but those who had done it knew what they were doing. The head itself stood out of the grass as though the rest of the giant figure was still buried in the ground. Perhaps it was, no-one had ever dug here to find out, Tristan had never allowed it and neither would Mark.

Isoldé could feel a presence in the eye, as though it watched her back. 'I want to walk between the worlds,' she told the presence in the head-stone. 'I want to take Tristan back across the worlds to your counterpart in the grove in the Isles of the Dead, the Isles of the Blest, where he belongs. Will you help me?'

From somewhere impossible, a shadow blinked across the eye. A sense of "Yes" came inside Isoldé's head.

'What must I do?'

'Blood,' came the reply.

'My blood?'

'Your blood.' It felt as if there was a chuckle came with the words. 'It is the night of the blood moon after all.'

'All right,' Isoldé agreed, trying not to think about what she might have agreed to.

The chuckle came again.

She delved in the bag she'd brought, what was there she could prick her finger with to draw blood? Her fingers felt something long and thin, she took it out, it was a long needle. 'What do I do?' she asked.

'Draw blood,' came the reply. 'Smear some on Tristan's

forehead and your own, then onto my eye. Then take Tristan's hand and look directly into my eye.'

Isoldé took the needle and stabbed her finger. Blood welled up immediately. She smeared a little on her forehead then stood to do the same for Tristan. She squeezed her finger again and put the bloody tip to the centre of the eye in the stone head. As she finished she felt Embar twine about her legs. She bent at once and rubbed the last of the blood between his eyes, then, taking Tristan's hand she pulled him down beside her looked straight into the stone eye. Embar jumped into her lap and also stared at the stone.

Isoldé felt herself shooting forwards, into the eye, like rushing down a dark tunnel. She could sense the man and the cat were with her but there was no feeling at all, it was as though she didn't have a body, just a knowing, completely bodiless. Suddenly the sensation stopped. She had no idea how long it had gone on for. She felt dizzy and sick as she jolted to an apparent stop to find herself crouched on grass, along with Tristan and Embar, all of them facing the head-stone.

It was different. The blood-red colour of the light was gone, replaced by a white-gold along with monochrome stone and the grass. It had worked. She was in Otherworld and she'd brought Tristan home. She turned to him.

He stood up, pulling her with him. 'Thank you,' he said. 'But you must go. Now. You cannot stay. You must go home.'

Isoldé turned back to the stone, stared into its eye. There was a chuckle in response. 'It only works one way,' the stone-voice said inside her head.

'Oh ...! You didn't tell me that!'

'You didn't ask,' said the stone. 'I only tell you what you ask. If you don't ask it, I don't tell.'

Isoldé sagged. She was a fool. She should have known that, after everything that had happened recently, all she'd learned. She'd behaved like a foolish child ... and got the appropriate response. What was she to do? She must get home.

'The moonpath,' Tristan said. 'Hurry!'

Embar's claw slashed at her trouser leg, he yowled impera-tively.

'OK!' She caught Tristan quickly to her and kissed his cheek, then turned and ran after Embar down the meadow path towards the shingle beach.

The shingle skidded and clattered under her running feet so she nearly slipped. Holding herself together she raced for the shore. The moonpath was there, just. The moon was low on the horizon, about to sink into the sea. Without thinking at all she leapt onto the silver path, not worrying if it was solid, and raced along it following the streaking black cat. It swayed under her feet but she no longer cared. The light was going, the path fading into nothingness. With all her last strength Isoldé leapt for the rocky steps she could just see ahead of her.

Mark

Dawn points, and another day
Prepares for heat and silence. Out at sea the dawn wind
Wrinkles and slides. I am here
Or there, or elsewhere. In my beginning.
TS Eliot: East Coker

Mark sat on the top of the three steps on the headland. The moonpath stretched out in front of him. Looking out across the sea he saw the Lost Land, far away, at the other end of the path. It would be very easy to get up and step onto the path, walk to the cloud land and stay there.

It had been three months now since the night he had recorded Tristan, since the night of the blood moon, since Isoldé had disappeared, run away with Tristan and Embar. It was three months now that he'd been alone.

He had come here every full moon. He had to guard the path, watch the weather, look out for storms which would tear the cloud land apart. So, every full moon, he came to the Lady's Window to sit looking out across the sea with the moon path at his feet. If he did not then Isoldé would never come home.

Dawn was coming up, he could tell by the change in the light. The moon was sinking into the sea at the end of the path, the path itself was fading. It would be another month before it came again. Mark stood up, looked along the path one last time.

There, above the stone steps that were the physical end of the moonpath, hung a figure, it seemed to be suspended there, unable to move. The soft, golden hair flew out behind the beautiful face as though the figure was running at great speed, the arms were outstretched, the long legs stilled in a fantastic leap. There was fear and hope in the blue eyes.

'Isoldé!' Mark stood transfixed.

Next thing he knew was a black fur-ball crashing into him,

knocking both the wind and the paralysis out of him. 'Catch her!' the words shouted across his mind.

He reached up and found Isoldé's hands, pulled, caught her body in his arms. They fell together into the wet dew of morning.

Isoldé

The dancers are all gone under the hill
TS Eliot: East Coker

The vision shuddered into monochrome. Isoldé felt herself shooting across the sea. Everything broke into shards of light, she leapt, then found herself hovering above the cliff edge, her feet not able to touch down on the stone steps.

Mark was there. He stood staring at her as if she were a ghost. She cried out his name but no sound came.

Then she felt his hands pulling her, his arms came around her and they fell together into the grass. Looking up and back she saw the moon set, slipping away below the curve of the Earth. The pathway across the sea was gone.

Much later, in the kieve, their ears battered by the incredible roar of the waters, Isoldé stood with Mark. He had his arm about her waist. 'Done and dusted,' she said.

'Yes.'

'And I made it home.'

'More by luck than judgement, and only by the skin of your teeth.'

She chuckled. 'True enough! But I did so …'

'Aye, you did so …'

In order to arrive there,
To arrive where you are, to get from where you are not,
You must go by a way wherein there is no ecstasy.
In order to arrive at what you do not know
You must go by a way which is the way of ignorance.
In order to possess what you do not possess
You must go by a way of dispossession.
In order to arrive at what you are not

You must go through the way in which you are not.
And what you do not know is the only thing you know
And what you do not own is the only thing you own
And where you are is where you are not.
TS Eliot: East Coker

COSMIC
EGG
BOOKS

If you prefer to spend your nights with Vampires and
Werewolves rather than the mundane then we publish the books
for you. If your preference is for Dragons and Faeries or Angels
and Demons – we should be your first stop. Perhaps your
perfect partner has artificial skin or comes from another planet –
step right this way. Our curiosity shop contains treasures you
will enjoy unearthing. If your passion is Fantasy (including
magical realism and spiritual fantasy), Horror or Science Fiction
(including Steampunk), Cosmic Egg books will
feed your hunger.